THE BRACELET

NUHAD BANNA

ISBN: 978-0-578-63352-7

CONTENTS

To my eldest child, without whom there would have been no book.

To my husband, my muse. Your tears over the story inspired me to proceed.

To my sister and each of my children for their never-ending support, encouragement, and years of patience for every time I talked about the book.

To my editor, your talent brought this book to life.

To my graphic designer, your creativity is second to none.

CHAPTER ONE

LAURA: PRESENT DAY

1964

*L*aura found herself on a horse wearing a strange riding habit. How she'd come to be on a horse, she didn't know. Fear filled her heart as she and her horse raced the wind, the chiffon tail of her head-covering trailing behind her. After a few moments, she again heard the distinct pounding of hooves from behind, threatening to catch up to her. A mysterious rider persistently urged his stallion in pursuit. Laura did not know where she was going but felt an overwhelming desire to push onward. She kicked her horse with her boot spurs and sped up. Her heart beat thunderously fast as danger grew ever closer, encroaching on her heels. Ahead of her she saw him, a knight, frantically waving. He beckoned her forward, reaching his arms wide to enfold her. He called out her name.

Lauraine.

Laura felt confused. Did he call her Lauraine? Why?

A deep longing to reach the man unfurled within her. His face seemed so familiar, yet she did not know him. She called out to him, but her words were lost in the wind. An ancient yearning, an aching call, escaped her lips as she fought to reach him.

"Laura, wake up!" Her mother gently shook her shoulder.

"Mama! What's wrong?" Laura said in a groggy tone. Startled and disoriented, she sat up in her bed, scanning her surroundings to see her familiar, modest looking bedroom rather than a moonlit desert. Disappointment sat heavy in her heart as she thought back on that mysterious man calling her forward, desperate to hold his...Lauraine. She shook herself and studied her room, attempting to dismiss her dream.

Her room was spacious, with wide windows and a nice oval mirror with cabinets and glass tops for her toiletries. The cupboard holding Laura's clothes was made out of brown oak. A desk with a side lamp, covered in books, was placed near the window overlooking the west side of the house under which bushes of gardenias and roses were planted.

"It's time to wake up from your nap." Her mother gave her a concerned look. "You were yelling in your sleep again."

Her heart still thumped in her chest as the fear began to subside. It took a few minutes to calm herself down.

"I am okay. I just keep having this strange recurring dream."

"The dream about that mysterious man?"

Laura nodded. "I've had it many times over the years, but now it is happening more often."

"When did you last have it, that is, before this day?"

"Two days ago, the day Rana came to visit. Maybe I shouldn't have taken this nap." The feeling of apprehension subsided a bit but did not leave her. Her mother sat next to her and seriously pondered the issue. She felt grateful her mother didn't dismiss her dreams as strange flights of fancy.

"Your dreams could be an echo of inner unsettled feelings from the past, or things yet to come. All dreams reflect some form of reality, some unfinished business from our past or present. Perhaps you must assess if there is something within you that must be discovered."

Laura raised an eyebrow. "I have no idea what that means." Her mother smiled. "Never mind. Shake it off, my dear. It is time to get ready for the party. Happy birthday to my darling girl." Juliette kissed her daughter's forehead.

Laura took her mother's palm in her hand and gently put it on her cheek, feeling the battered skin from years of hard work. A hand that worked hard to make things for her. She suddenly looked at the wall where her mother's wedding picture hung and thought how beautiful her mother was. Skinny, dark wavy hair, a delicate heart-shaped mouth, and a pretty smile. At six feet, Juliette was tall for a woman, yet she was graceful and elegant in her movements. The wedding picture brought a smile to Laura's face as she looked at the image of her father standing on an elevated wooden step to reach her mother's height. She was still beautiful except for a thick waist and streaks of white hair appearing here and there. She adored her mother.

She loved hearing her father and mother share the events leading up to their first meeting and eventual courtship.

In his youth, Emile had decided to study in college to become a land surveyor, which he enjoyed very much. He also became proficient in seven languages. After graduation, in 1929 he'd received a job at the Land and Survey Department in Jaffa, the State of Palestine, and became popular among his co-workers due to his humor and friendliness.

At work, he had become close friends with a man named Nicholas Kane. They always went together on camping trips for work or entertainment in Tel Aviv. At one point, Nicholas had invited Emile for dinner at his sister's house. She was married to Mr. E. Monta, who worked at the Secretariat of the British viceroy in Haifa.

During the conversation, Emile had leaned over and confided to Nicholas, "If your sister was not married, I would have asked for her hand. She is very pretty."

"Really, do you want to get married?" Nicholas had asked.

"Yes, I think it is about time. I am not young anymore. I am thirty-eight," Emile answered.

"Well, I have another sister for you, even prettier than Mary."

Nicholas shared with Emile that he had always admired him for his candor, honesty, and kind personality. Thus, Nicholas took Emile to Acre where he met Juliette Kane, a very beautiful woman whose face lit with a smile that stole his heart. Within one visit, he'd known Juliette was his future.

Every week after that visit, he sent a letter to Juliette filled with romantic, passionate declarations of love. He kept asking her to marry him, and after six months of weekly love letters, Juliette agreed to marry Emile Salem. Laura's mother had been twenty-nine years old at the time.

The thought of those love letters always made Laura smile. She wondered if she would ever find a love like that in her own life, and her thoughts immediately went unbidden to that mysterious man in her dreams. She shook it off but couldn't dismiss it because her vision at the seer's cave had validated her nightmare. Had that happened only a few days earlier? It felt like an eternity.

The visit had happened when her lifelong friend, Rana Sadeq, had come for a visit. They'd sat on the veranda chatting, enjoying the evening breeze, a jasmine scent filling the air. A canary bird sitting in a beautiful bronze cage had chirped long, beautiful whistles while her mother had made coffee for them.

"You girls enjoy your visit," her mother had said as she left the coffee set in front of them.

"Thank you, Mother," Laura said.

After her mother left, Laura looked at Rana, noticing a longing in her eyes as Rana stared after her mother.

"What is it?"

Rana gave her a sheepish smile. "I envy the relationship you and your mother have. It seems you can talk to her about anything. My mother..." Rana grabbed her coffee and took a tiny sip. "Well, it's not important."

Laura hesitated to press for more information. Rana had been her best friend since childhood, and they had gone to the same school and were neighbors. However, their upbringings had been different, especially due to their religious beliefs. Even though Laura was Christian and Rana was Muslim, they never once allowed those differences to prevent them from loving and caring for each other, but there were certain topics they simply didn't discuss. Laura wondered if this might be one of them.

After a moment, she decided she really wanted to know. "Rana, you've seemed very troubled lately. If you can't speak with your mother, perhaps you can speak with me."

Rana hesitated then said, "I care for someone, deeply. I am not sure what my parents will think."

"Who?"

"Omar." Rana said it quickly then took a nervous gulp of her coffee.

Laura felt her friend's sadness and nervousness, and she drank as well.

"He asked me to marry him," Rana said, blushing.

"But this is wonderful. Why are you sad?" Laura asked.

From what she understood, Rana would eventually be married to a Muslim, and Omar shared her faith. Omar was also a wonderful young man. However, she realized how Rana's interest in Omar might be a problem for Rana's parents. He was the son of the grocer who worked in a small store two blocks down the hill. Her parents were wealthy, upper class elite, and concerned about social status.

And Rana's brother, Ali…

Once a very kind individual, he had gone to England to study abroad and had returned with so much hatred in his heart she had hardly recognized him. What had once been a healthy belief in the Muslim faith had turned into Muslim radicalism that frightened Laura. From what she could tell, he had adopted some of the more oppressive beliefs concerning women, and she sometimes feared for Rana despite the parents' attempts at reasoning with their son.

She didn't know how he might feel about Rana marrying Omar, but heaven help Rana if he had strong opinions against it.

Rana made a dismissive gesture with her hand and pasted on a brave smile.

"Never mind. We will talk about other things."

Laura took the hint and allowed her friend to change the subject.

They spent the next several minutes talking about silly things, laughing and teasing one another as they finished their coffee.

Looking at her empty cup, with all the designs left behind by the coffee grounds, a tantalizing thought came to Laura's mind as the residue of her recurring nightmare haunted her again.

With a hint of skepticism, she asked, "Rana, do you know how to read coffee grounds?"

Coffee ground readings were a common practice and form of entertainment among the women, young and old, in the city of Amman, Jordan. Visitors could find professional paid seers in the countryside as well.

Laura's Christian upbringing didn't necessarily encourage those types of activities, but black magic performed by very few was not unheard of. Some believed in evil spirits possessing people, and they would go to holy men to undo the evil spirit's control over their children or some relative. Temptation filled her to delve into the supernatural activities that few men and women operated in or even knew about. She had seen on television how one priest had performed exorcisms on people, so she thought maybe it would not hurt to explore the supernatural. If anything went wrong, she could go to the priest!

Thus, the culture was no stranger to superstitions, evil practices, spells, curses, and demon possessions. People fought against black magic with payers, talismans, and charms which were worn under the clothes or placed under pillows.

Laura was desperate to understand these dreams plaguing her. She wanted to know the identity of that man in her dreams.

Rana gave the question some serious thought. "To answer you, no, Laura, I don't know how to read coffee grounds, but there is a very well-known seer. Her name is Mahdiyeh, and she lives half a mile down the road. Do you remember the hillside where a large refugee camp was erected and is now vacant?"

"Yes, I remember very well. Years ago, when I was a child, I used to visit the place with mother, trying to find domestic help," Laura said.

"She lives on that hillside where the refugee camp used to be. Have you heard of her?" Rana asked.

CHAPTER TWO

LAURA: THE PARTY

1964

*L*aura impatiently counted the minutes as the clock ticked closer to her eighteenth birthday party. For that special event, and for her recent high school graduation at the top of her class, her parents had booked the party at the City Hotel Dance Hall. Her parents had been so proud of her, especially when she had stood at the podium a couple of months earlier, presenting her Valedictorian speech, which was very emotional and inspiring. Her party was now a double celebration. She was full of anticipation for the evening's events, admiring herself in the mirror, when her thoughts were interrupted.

"Laura, I am so happy I finished your dress in time. You look beautiful. It will complement your gift perfectly." Juliette gave her daughter an approving smile.

She held out a small, faded, red velvet box. Fascinated by the exterior appearance of the box, Laura gingerly took it from her mother's hand, unlocked the worn clasp, and lifted the lid. She gasped, staring at the wonder of the design and the sparkling sight. Inside the box was a golden bracelet identical to the one in her vision from the cave. The dazzling bracelet had six small flowers, each with five petals of gold. Small diamonds were set around each gold petal, engraved with intricate designs. In the center of each flower rested a ruby. The golden flowers were connected to each other with a delicate gold chain.

"My goodness! Thank you, Mama, this is an extraordinary bracelet. From where did you get it?" Laura noticed the rubies were the same color as her dress. "I will treasure this for as long as I live."

Juliette clasped the bracelet on Laura's wrist. The images of her nightmare flashed in Laura's mind, and she quickly ignored them as she focused on the moment.

"This bracelet is a special one. It has been in my family for generations. Family legend says that a long time ago a knight had this bracelet custom made for the love of his life. This beautiful piece of jewelry was forged from the gold handle of his sword and decorated with her mother's gems. He gave it to her on her eighteenth birthday. Since then, it has been passed on to the eldest daughter of her descendants. Now, I am passing it on to you. You must promise me to protect it, never to sell it, even if it is the last thing you own. You must follow tradition and pass it on to your first daughter."

"Why? What makes this bracelet so special?" Laura immediately felt this bracelet had been crafted just for her, regardless of its many owners. It fit her perfectly, and she loved the way it felt on her wrist.

"It is a link between the past and the present, but the secret of how it is linked has been lost with the passage of time. I was bound by a promise to protect this bracelet as I am asking you to do now."

"Why haven't I seen you wear it before?"

"I wore it once on my eighteenth birthday and kept it hidden until I could pass it on to you at the right time. Simply, it was not convenient to wear it, and it didn't feel right on my wrist."

Feeling the enormous responsibility of having such a valuable treasure, Laura determined to honor the promise her mother asked of her.

"What happens if I do not have a daughter?"

"All of the first born of your ancestors on my side of the family were females. Mother believed this had to do with being the keeper of the bracelet. In the unlikely event you do not have a daughter, the best thing to do would be to entrust it to the next female in the family. Instruct her to pass it on to her daughter. I am glad you like it. I will leave you now to finish getting ready for the party. I love you, my beautiful daughter."

Laura got ready and stepped out of her room. She scurried down the hallway but was brought up short as her eye caught a prominent plaque hanging on the wall. She couldn't help but read its carved message for the millionth time, giggling at its meaning. Her father had earned that plaque at the mere age of fourteen.

He had scrimped and saved to attend the First World Scout Jamboree to be held in England in 1920 for all international members. For her father, it had been the most exciting time of his life. He was to meet Baden Powell, the founder of the World Scouts program.

Emile had sailed from Jaffa to dock first in France with his team of Boy Scouts, representing Palestine. A handsome and well-spoken young man, he had shown enthusiasm for all the scouting goals he'd set.

That year, Emile and all the other Jamboree participants had built the Eiffel Tower with scout sticks. It was a magnificent and successful show, but Emile was already considering other ways to make the event a success. As people came to attend the celebration, Emile had set up a table with a sign reading, "The Holy Land", and he had spread his trinkets, crosses, polished mother of pearl shells, carved with amazingly delicate designs, rosaries, and many other items for visitors to purchase.

He sold every single piece and made enough money to cover the cost of his trip, including pocket money. He had enough left over to bring some money back home. When he'd returned, he brought with him this wooden plaque that read, *An Ass can be a Good Scout on a Fine Day*. It had been signed by Baden Powell. Emile had thought it humorous, and he'd treasured the keepsake all his life.

Laura had to admit, it was a humorous message, delivering sage advice. She smiled again as she hurried down the hall and into the living room, noticing the contrasting lights and shadows throughout the house as the sun began to set. The gorgeous ball of light slowly pulled its rays, sinking behind the horizon, painting the cloudless skies with different shades of crimson. She went outside and headed for the gardens. A cool, gentle breeze swept through the place, ushering in a beautiful evening.

The garden was her father's pride and joy. He had spent hours cultivating the ground, meticulously pruning each tree, bush, and shrub, which he had planted from saplings. A variety of trees lined the fence, including lemon, plumb, tangerine, orange, pomegranate, olive, fig, and berry trees, all pregnant with delicious fruits, especially the ones he grafted. Round flower beds were divided by rows of small white rocks, planted with blooming roses, gardenias, jasmine, carnations, azaleas, pansies, and violets which emitted a sweet scent in the air. She waited on the front porch for her family, cherishing the moment. Laura contemplated her future. Her life lay ahead of her like an open road, and all she needed to do was travel the pathway.

EMILE STOOD JUST INSIDE THE DOORWAY AND WATCHED HIS DAUGHTER for a bit, his deep affection for her like the steady beat of his heart. She was beautiful. Her gorgeous, thick copper hair cascaded in soft, curly layers down the middle of her back. Her hair was pulled back from her face with a ruby-red velvet hairband, crisscrossed with a gold-colored string. Her oval face was suntanned, and her large green eyes shone with happiness under delicate eyebrows. Her perfect nose and heart-shaped mouth completed the soft features of her angelic face. She wore a thin, golden necklace, a gift from him. The bracelet rested perfectly on her wrist.

Laura wore a red dress that matched the ruby gems of the bracelet. The sequin bodice with spaghetti straps hugged her slim figure, and the long dress flowed to the floor, ending with a short train. Her mother had spent hours making the dress, and it looked perfect on her. She wore matching silk sandals with moderate high heels, enhancing her already tall stature. Emile watched as she closed her eyes, breathing in the cool breeze that continued to blow gently.

He knew she could smell the fragrance from the jasmine and roses that filled the air. Emile had worked hard to create a beautiful garden for his family to enjoy. He had wanted nothing more than for his wife and children to grow up in a house filled with love and laughter, but life had not always been so easy for Emile, despite his successes.

When Laura had been a mere seven years old, the building the Salems had lived in had a large space originally designed to be a car garage. Emile had agreed with his relative and owner of the building, Mr. Kamal Issa, to rent the garage and open a grocery store with him as a silent partner, receiving ten percent of the income. That arrangement had lasted for a little while, but Issa, seeing a very poor income from the store in the beginning, had decided to cancel the partnership. He removed his name from the contract and assumed Emile would surely close his doors in the near future. Issa had not wanted his name associated with a failed business. He had no idea that the store would grow and gain a good reputation among the neighboring households. The success of the store made Issa indignant.

As the store had grown, representatives of the bishop of the Greek Catholic abbey located two houses down the hill decided to award a contract to Emile to supply the abbey with meat and all the food provisions they needed. The location of the store had been convenient, right on the main road. The abbey and the needs of the nuns had been the main source of the grocery store's income.

Envy and resentment had filled Issa's heart as the store continued to be successful. His envy made Issa decide to hurt Emile in his business, even though they were related. Issa just couldn't get over the fact that Emile was doing well. It boiled his blood. His pride would not allow his failed prediction about the store to go unpunished. He had to act. Issa had influence over the Bishop of the Church and the abbey, since they were part of the same denomination. He made sure they would not renew the contract with Emile by invoking the old conflict between Catholics and Greek Orthodox denominations of the Christian church.

The business suffered, and Emile could not overcome the betrayal of his relative. Since Emile was a foreigner to the area, he'd known it would be nearly impossible to fight for his store against the likes of Issa. He closed the store and decided to become a surveyor again, applying for and receiving a position in the government's Land and Survey Department. This work had supplemented his pension to make a good life for his growing family.

They had moved out of Issa's building and rented a temporary room until the construction of their own house was finished. Yet Issa was not satisfied. He continued to cause trouble for Emile.

Every day, Emile had walked Laura and her brothers to their school down the hill. He used to wait for them to reach the school, a short distance from the corner of the abbey's gate. When the children waved to him to indicate they had made it to the school entrance, he would then continue to his office, half a mile to the other side of the abbey. Laura always watched her father cross the road, walk to the curb of a side street, and disappear around the corner.

One day, after Emile had dropped off his children, he crossed the street and came upon the deranged Issa, still angry over the loss of his rental income. Doing his best to avoid confrontation, Emile silently passed by him and continued on his way. Issa had taken a small boulder, one he had hidden under his large jacket, waited until Emile turned the corner, followed a few steps, and threw the rock at Emile's back, knocking him out and causing him to tumble down the steep hill.

A military guard stationed to protect the house of a government official had seen what happened and took immediate action, most likely saving Emile's life since the attack and subsequent fall had given Emile a concussion, bruised body, and a few broken ribs. This was the shock of his life. It was the first time he had experienced such personal physical violence. It caused him to worry for the future of his children.

~

"MY BEAUTIFUL YOUNG LADY, HAPPY BIRTHDAY." EMILE PUT HIS ARMS around Laura's shoulders. "You are stunning, my dear." He placed a kiss on her forehead.

Laura gave her father a happy smile, grateful to have him join her in their special place. They regularly spent time walking through the garden, talking and laughing together.

"Thanks, Papa. You always make me feel good. I love you very much. Thank you for all you're doing for me tonight." Laura cherished her father's complements, and in turn, gave him a tight hug and a kiss on his cheek.

She never took for granted his hard work and determination to provide for them, despite the envy and machinations of others from which he suffered silently. She still remembered one incident when her relative had attacked her father when she was just seven years of age. No one, not even her father, knew she had witnessed the attack, but she had felt helpless to do anything. Her only consolation being the military guard who had immediately flown to her father's defense and arrested Issa.

She had continued on her way to school, trembling, but holding her brothers' hands tightly. She'd spent the day sick to her stomach but did not open her mouth to speak, paralyzed into inaction. Being just a child, she knew no one would have listened to her. Adults did not think children worthy of attention, so Laura had learned to keep quiet unless spoken to. No one had asked her what she was upset about, and she had never felt so small and helpless like she had that day.

When the school day had finally ended, she'd hurried home with her brothers, relieved to find her father awake in bed, despite his obvious injuries. She'd never forgotten about this incident because it became the catalyst for her strange dreams. That night, she'd had her first nightmare concerning her pursuer and the mysterious man who called her Lauraine.

THE GRAND ENTRANCE TO THE HOTEL WAS ELABORATELY DECORATED with shining marble tiles and walls. Several green plants, which grew in copper pots, were distributed around the lobby. Beautiful crystal chandeliers dangled from the ceiling.

While Laura's favorite music filled the hall, she moved around the room, graciously greeting and welcoming her guests. A young man caught her attention as he walked towards her along with her friend, Dian Catin. Her heart started beating fast, and she felt the same way she had in her dream. She froze, staring at the man from her nightmare even though she had never met him before.

"Laura, this is my cousin, Roland Catin."

"It is very nice to meet you, Laura." Roland appeared mesmerized by her beauty. He stared at her as if he experienced a sudden pang of recognition.

"Nice to meet you too, Roland."

"He just came back home from Germany for the summer. He is studying to be a pharmacist," boasted Dian.

An electrifying current ran through Laura as she raised her hand to meet his. She blushed at his touch as she caught his hazel eyes shining with a mischievous look. Laura's heart pounded in her chest, beating so fast she was afraid it could be heard by everyone in the hall. Nothing had prepared her for this sudden attraction and recognition for a man she had just met.

ROLAND'S FLASH OF RECOGNITION CAUGHT HIM BY SURPRISE. HE PAUSED, closed his eyes, and opened them in wonder. It was as if her very presence had put him under a spell. He pulled himself together and put on a charming smile, one he hoped she would find attractive. He stepped forward towards Laura and took her hand, and as he held it in both of his, a warmth seeped into his being.

"Happy Birthday, Laura." Roland frowned. He really did feel as if he knew her. "Have we met before?" Roland asked perplexed at the feeling. The attractive blush at her cheeks made him wonder if she felt it too. It was an age-old attraction, a bone-deep familiarity, as though they were soul mates.

"No, I don't think so," Laura mumbled. He thought she smoothed out her expression well, but he had caught that unanticipated feeling of familiar intimacy towards him. Something she could not explain.

He couldn't explain it either.

"May I have the first dance?" Roland kept holding Laura's hand. He knew his smile reached his eyes as quiet desperation filled him, over-whelmed with her beauty, the unfamiliar and inexplicable feeling of precognition. He led her to the dance floor.

Blushing profusely, she kept her hand in his, and she silently moved with him.

Laura's blush in response to his touch covered Roland with an emotion of his own as he escorted her to the dance floor. He was sure of having met her before, but he could not place when or where. He could not form rational thoughts as he held Laura close. The sequins of the bodice felt good on his skin as he pressed his palm to the small of her back. Laura captivated him. Her hair smelled like night jasmine, and her skin was as soft as ivory. He had never felt this way before. He grabbed the moment, holding fast to it with his heart. He did not want this feeling to end.

The sparkling of jewelry on her wrist caught his attention, and a startling memory of a similar bracelet flashed in Roland's mind, disappearing as suddenly as it came.

"This bracelet you are wearing is just fascinating!"

He took Laura's wrist with the bracelet and gently held her hand to his chest. Roland could not explain the misty, wonderful sensation he experienced when holding Laura in his arms.

"It is an heirloom passed on from generation to generation on my mother's side of the family," Laura whispered.

Her logical explanation broke Roland's moment of unearthly, mystical reality. They twirled to the music. Laura's feet barely touched the floor of the dance hall as she lightly followed his lead to perfection. Caught up in a magical cloud, they forgot the people surrounding them.

~

As the music faded and the next song began to play, Laura invited Roland to meet her parents. Laura tried to curb her excitement as they walked towards her parents' table.

"Mama, Papa, this is Roland Catin. He is Dian's cousin."

"Hello, Roland. I wonder if Felix Catin has any relation to you. He was our friend many years ago. I just can't remember you. You must have been too young to hang around older people like us. Take a seat." Emile pulled out a chair, gesturing for him to sit down.

"Yes, he was my father. How wonderful to see you again. I remember you and Mrs. Salem from years back when you used to visit my parents and play cards," Roland said. "I was a child then, but I don't remember you bringing your beautiful daughter with you."

Juliette laughed and said, "No, you wouldn't remember her because visiting friends and playing cards while the children were left in bed is when adults take a turn to have fun!"

Emile said, "I remember your father, Felix, told us a fascinating story about his grandfather, Tanius Catin, and the love of his life, Badiya. A true love story, sacrificing everything for her."

"Oh yes, a touching story. Do you know about it, Laura?" Roland asked.

"No. I have never heard it. Tell me, please."

"While the villagers in the area were busy with a big wedding for the community leader, my great grandfather, Tanius, discreetly asked the love of his life, Badiya, to meet him at the bridge and run away with him. She loved him, too, so she agreed."

"Wasn't that terribly dangerous for them? Her family would have been furious," Laura said in surprise.

"It wasn't something that was allowed, but my great grandfather knew what he wanted." Roland gave her a meaningful look.

She smiled shyly. "Please, tell me more," Laura said while everyone at the table listened, curious as to what had happened.

"WELL, IT IS ACTUALLY A VERY ROMANTIC, ADVENTUROUS, AND WILD story, so maybe I should start from the beginning. The Catin family moved to southern Lebanon after the Crusaders wars of the twelfth century. They stayed for generations, cultivating their lands and making a life for themselves. It was in the year 1880 when Tanius Catin decided to risk it all for the love of his life. He inherited the lands, but Badiya meant more to him. He had watched Badiya everyday as she would go to the well to fill her water jar. She had dark curly hair like a gypsy. Her angelic oval face, bronze in color, melted his heart. My grandmother told us she had a wild gypsy kind of beauty. She was fifteen years old at the time."

Roland became animated as he continued the story.

"*Can I help you carry the jar?*" *Tanius asked the girl.*

"*Oh, no, no, thank you.*" *She put the clay jar on her head and moved her body in a brilliant walk, balancing the jar in perfect step.*

"*I will see you again at the well,*" *Tanius said with confidence.*

"*Don't follow me, or you will suffer at the hands of my brother,*" *Badiya said.*

"*He is my friend, and he trusts me,*" *Tanius said with a smug grin as he walked behind her.*

Badiya smiled but never turned. She had a heavy burden on her head.

"*We need to be careful, Tanius. You are a Christian, and I follow the Druze faith. We do not belong together,*" *Badiya said with concern.*

"*I will find a way for us to be together. It took me a whole year to gain the courage to talk to you alone.*"

LAURA LAUGHED AT HIS GREAT GRANDFATHER'S ENTHUSIASM. "THEN what happened?" she asked.

"Tanius fell in love with the young girl," Roland said. "He knew that this was not permissible. Her family was from a Druze tribe that had farmed the land for his father before him. He could not live without her anymore and could not ask her hand in marriage because her family would have killed her and killed him if they were caught together. He planned their departure. He knew that the only way they could be together was if he kidnapped her. It was his only choice. He knew it would cause her family to be heartbroken, but he loved her, and she loved him.

The night they ran off, he took her to a convent and gave the Mother Superior some of his gold to pay for her expenses. She promised to keep her safe. Tanius returned to the village as if nothing had happened." Roland shook his head as he related this next part. "He quietly sold his land while watching Badiya's family frantically searching for her. Tanius joined the searchers, but after two months, they gave up. One night, my great grandfather was no longer found in the village, either. He rode to the abbey in Tyre to claim his beloved."

"That is a very romantic story," Laura said. "And Badiya had waited all that time for him?"

"Not only had she waited, but according to the Mother Superior, Badiya had fallen in love with the Christian faith and had decided to surrender her life to Jesus," Roland continued.

"Really?" Tanius said. "How wonderful! Now we can get married since she converted. Bring her here. I want to see her."

"The Mother Superior was shocked," Roland said. "She had no idea Tanius had planned to marry her. It took a moment of convincing with a few well-placed threats to get her to bring Badiya to him. He asked her to marry him and she quickly agreed. The nuns prepared provisions for them to take on the road."

"Amazing," Laura said.

"They got married, and he paid the Abbey and the Priest with more of his gold. He let them all think they were going to Turkey on their honeymoon in case anyone decided to follow them, but they actually ended up settling in the City of Jaffa. He bought farmlands and planted orange orchards, fig trees, and sycamore trees. Badiya was sixteen when she gave him his first son, followed by six more." Roland smiled widely.

"Nasib, the eldest of the seven boys, joined his father in farming the land and got married to Zahieh Innab. A big wedding took place, and nine months later, Felix, my father, was born followed by my uncles Tanius and Joseph. These are all my ancestors that I know of."

"Oh, what a romantic love affair. Do you believe in this kind of love, Roland?" Laura asked.

"If someone meets the right person, surely they would give everything to live a happy life with them." Roland winked at Laura.

"What do you do now, Roland?" Emile enquired.

"After high school, I went to Germany and stayed with my older brother who was already there. It really took me some time to decide what to study. I decided to become a pharmacist."

Laura's two younger brothers and sister eyed her and Roland with curiosity. She loved them very much and always felt they were her responsibility. Mark was a quiet child and did not talk much, unlike Michael who was always talkative and full of energy. Nana was a typical younger sister, always wanting to join the boys in whatever they were doing. Laura introduced them to Roland.

After Laura finished the introduction of her family, Roland hastily said, "Laura! I just remembered! I do recall meeting you as a child. You attended our school chapel on Sundays where I served as an altar boy. I was taken by your beauty then, but never in my dreams would I have guessed that I would meet you as this gorgeous lady later in life. I told you, Laura, I felt that I had met you before. The face you have is unforgettable!"

Roland smiled, causing another blush to flush her cheeks. As he put his arm around her shoulders, she couldn't contain the sudden tug at her heart.

"I am sorry. I must have missed noticing you. Well, I was too young then." Laura blushed.

He gave her a warm smile that nearly did her in. If he kept this up, the blush on her cheeks would become permanent.

"Mr. and Mrs. Salem, I am very glad to have seen you again. I hope to see you more from now on."

"Of course, you may come visit. Enjoy the night," Juliette said, "and when you go home, say hello to your mother for me. It has been a long time since I have seen her. I am sorry for the loss of your father. He was a good man."

"I most certainly will. Thank you," Roland said.

For the next several minutes, Roland continued to sit with Laura at her family's table, whispering to her about Europe with its green majestic forests and the large winding rivers on which he went rafting with his friends. He listened as she told him how much she loved traveling, painting, sculpting, and most of all, reading books.

"I hope you don't mind me monopolizing your time," Roland said with a chuckle, a fixated gleam in his eye. "I fully intend to keep you dancing with me all night."

Once dinner was served and the guests enjoyed the meal, everyone chanted the traditional Happy Birthday while Laura cut the cake. Music started up after dinner, filling the hall again. Laura spent some time with her friends around the ballroom, but being separated from Roland for any length of time made her feel restless, and she kept eyeing Roland as he walked with his cousin, stopping and talking to some guests. Roland glanced at her every now and then. From his expression, it was obvious he felt a desire to stay by her side throughout the night. The look of longing in his eyes matched the magnetic pull she felt every time she looked at him. She was drawn to him, and it was a relief to know that he felt the same way.

He kept reaching out for her whenever she had a free moment between talking to her guests. As he was finally catching all of Laura's attention, Roland said, "Will I be seeing you again? I'd love an entire, uninterrupted evening with you."

"I will look forward to it." Laura giggled and blushed as her heart started racing again.

The evening passed very quickly, and the music filled the air. Roland held Laura in his arms as he led her in a waltz. She closed her eyes and saw the face of the man in her dreams. The abrupt realization that the recurring dreams were of Roland calling to her was overwhelming. She opened her eyes wide with bewilderment, and he met her gaze. All at once, a strange sensation engulfed them both, and the feeling of exhilaration added to the almost exploding emotions.

Roland stared at her pretty face, touching her gorgeous copper hair. The last dance was announced, and in a dream-like state, they floated in the air, waltzing to the tune of the Blue Danube amid a sense of elation. A magical moment, a tender touch, the dazzling sparkle emanating from a beautiful bracelet, and the ethereal music transported both of their spirits, allowing them to soar into a different world.

Dazzled, Laura felt Roland tighten his hold on her, bringing her closer to his chest, wrapping his arms around her waist. They glided together in one rhythm, flying in swirls and spiraling through space, to the past, to a different time. To a different place.

CHAPTER THREE

ROLAND AND LAURAINE

1191

The battle outside the eastern wall of Acre had raged, the sound of metal clashing filling the air, the cries and moans of the injured rising above the soldiers' yells of combat. The land had been sprinkled with blood and littered with dead bodies from both sides; Crusaders and Muslims, scattered in the battlefield.

The Templar Knights had driven with full strength, fiercely fighting those who occupied the city. King Richard had captured the entire garrison. They were able to defeat the occupying regiment of the Muslims, forcing them to surrender the City.

The nobles of Acre had joined King Richard in the combat against Saladin. Most of their acquired properties were already taken by the Saracen, and they had to recover what they could. Lords John Salem and Jeffrey Catin had sent their families to Bassa village away from the dangers of a bloody fray.

Many kings and sovereigns, foreign and local, had left their imprints on the City of Acre. The combination of religious movements, Canaanite, Greek, and Roman cultures made it one of the most important cities of that era, combining East and West cultures. It colorfully engraved the city with a distinctive stamp and extraordinary place of art and religion.

Acre's location on the Mediterranean Sea made it an ideal port city. The walls built around it stood strong against many attackers. The Hospitaller Knights of The Order of St. John, who came with the First Crusade, built fortresses and citadels adding to the fortification. Regardless of this, the Muslims were able to reconquer the city in 1187.

After the recapture of Acre, the European kings returned to their own lands and Richard II found himself alone in the arena as the sole leader of the Third Crusade. However, King Conrad of Montferrat, an Italian nobleman, was supposed to be the heir as King of Jerusalem. He was assassinated a few days before his election by a secretive murder cult, the "Hashishin" or "weed sniffers" from which the word "assassin" was derived. It was suspected that King Richard and King Guy had something to do with King Conrad's death, thus gaining the enmity of Duke Leopold and King Philippe of France.

DESPITE THE MANY BATTLES AND ENDLESS UNREST, LAURAINE HAD HER father and her beloved, Roland Catin, throughout the years. Soon after the battle was over, and it was safe, Lauraine Salem had returned home to Acre from Bassa. She and her father, Lord John, had opened their palaces and hospitals to treat the injured. She had always wondered where her knowledge of healing had come from. She was intuitive and talented in the field of healing.

Lauraine was very popular amongst the locals and famous for her healing skills. She searched her father's vast library for a book on specific herbs because earlier that morning, as she had been visiting the market, she was approached by a young woman with a child four years of age. The child had inflamed skin on his legs and arms from itching and scratching. The woman had asked for help, and Lauraine had told the woman to come to the palace the next afternoon to see what she could do.

The palace library held numerous volumes with which she had already become acquainted, educating herself as best she could. She counted herself fortunate, considering most women were not given a formal education. As she continued to search through the shelves, she found the book she needed and pulled it out, but as she did so, thick parchments tumbled to the floor. She picked them up and examined the beautifully handwritten words. She sat upon the sofa, becoming engrossed in what appeared to be a lengthy history of the Middle East. It had experienced terrible wars with so many vying for power, hoping to possess the region.

Lauraine grew sad, thinking about the conflict going on even now. Over six hundred years ago, Muslim Arabs had come from Arabia, a true force to be reckoned with, driven by a faith that was established by the Prophet Mohammad in Mecca, in the Arabian Peninsula. From its inception, Islam had become an ideology aimed at expansion.

From her previous studies, Lauraine knew the Muslim Arabs had conquered the Byzantine and Persian empires in 636 AD. The bloodshed had not stopped there. The Muslim Arabs had even fought battles amongst themselves. Eras were identified by the rulers' names, such as the Abbasids, the Umayyads, the Ayyubids and the Ottomans, taking control and fighting to maintain power.

Lauraine felt utterly exhausted with the never-ending conflict.

Muslims had occupied Jerusalem and the rest of Palestine, including the holy Christian cities of Jerusalem and Bethlehem, in 637 AD when they conquered the Byzantines in Syria. The populations were given three choices: convert to Islam, pay taxes in order to remain Christian, or die. Sometimes they took churches and converted them into mosques.

Pilgrims were not safe, and nomad bandits had raided many villagers who were peaceful and unarmed. However, the Muslim Arabs had subsequently lost to Emperor Constantine in 670 AD. He had used a new weapon known as "Greek Fire" by which Constantine decisively defeated the Muslims, and the victory stopped the Islamic expansion into Europe for almost thirty years.

Throughout the bloody history of the Middle East, Christians had survived and lived with whomever was in power. Calif Abdul Malik ben Marwan had built Al Aqsa Mosque in Jerusalem on the ruins of the Jewish Temple Mount after he had conquered the city in 691 AD. He declared that their Prophet Mohammad had stepped on that special rock location when the Prophet claimed to have ascended to heaven as was recorded in the Prophet's life chronicles. The Mosque became a holy shrine for the Muslims, adding endless conflicts between Jews claiming ownership.

And so it went, Lauraine thought.

Christian pilgrims continued to be attacked. Pope Urban II became involved and wanted to free the Holy Land from Muslim occupiers, thus also assisting the Byzantine Empire against the Muslim Seljuk Turks. The first crusaders had battled for control of the Mediterranean Coast from Antioch in the North to Gaza in the South. Pope Eugene III decided on a Second Crusade in 1147 AD. King Louis of France and Conrad of Germany had led the remnants of the armies towards the Holy Land, fighting several battles on the way before arriving in Jerusalem. However, that crusade was a total failure, with Jerusalem falling and Muslims the victors. Reginald de Chatillon, a French Nobleman, joined the Second Crusade in 1153 when he lost his patrimony in France. He became Prince of Antioch when he married the daughter of King Philip I of France, Princess Constance, who ruled the area as regent of her son from a previous marriage.

Then, in 1161 AD, Reginald attacked the local peasants of the River Euphrates Valley, looting and plundering with such brutality, the wrath of Aleppo Governor fell upon them from the north. Reginald was captured and put in prison for fifteen years. He was released in 1176 for a huge ransom.

Five years ago, Lauraine thought, *Reginald raided a caravan on its way from Egypt to Syria, ignoring the truce between Saladin and the Kingdom of Jerusalem. Such evil men in power, destroying the lives of others.*

He had killed the guards, had stolen the merchandise, and had taken the merchants hostage. King Guy and Reginald had refused to pay back what they had stolen when the enraged Saladin requested compensation through envoys who returned with nothing. The offense caused a huge war between Saladin and King Guy and Reginald. The battle of Hattin was the greatest calamity the Crusaders had suffered, resulting in the eventual loss of Jerusalem to Saladin and the death of Reginald in 1187.

Saladin was shrewd and made truces with the Crusaders, keeping control over Jerusalem and most of Syria and Palestine. Battles continued between the Muslims and Crusaders, breaking truces and agreements on either side, heralding in the Third Crusade, called for and led by King Richard the Lionheart just two years ago.

A crusade my sweet Roland is slowly being drawn into, Lauraine thought, blinking back tears.

King Guy had proclaimed fealty to King Richard the Lionheart and had been victorious with the Siege of Acre for the last two years.

Lauraine thought of how she and her family had come to be in this region. Many nobles who had migrated with the first Crusade of 1096 AD had stayed and established roots in the Holy Land. Their children had inherited ranks and acquired lands throughout the years.

Among them was her beloved's father, Lord Jeffrey Catin. He had decided to remain in the area rather than returning to Scotland with his wife. Roland had stayed with his father, growing up among the knights and nobles of the city. He was trained in chivalry, use of weapons, and was given an education, at which he excelled.

Her father, Lord John Salem, had met a beautiful local girl many years back whose father, George Kane, was a Christian, notable in his village of Bassa. Mary and Lord John Salem were married. Even though her mother had been a strong young girl, Mary had a very difficult childbirth. Lauraine's mother had died of complications.

Every Sunday, Lauraine attended mass at the church built by the Templar Knights. The priest often accompanied Lauraine when she visited her grandfather's village nearby. While he ministered to the villagers, Lauraine would gather the children and tell them stories about The Savior, Jesus Christ. She always felt the presence of God in her life. She sensed the protection and peace that came from the Lord in the midst of turmoil, wars, and battles that took place as she grew up.

Her father and Lord Catin had promised to protect King Richard's back as he traveled south to Jerusalem. He had marched along the coast, taking her sweet Roland with him. Roland was a courageous and brave knight, tall and handsome, but she still feared for his safety.

Lauraine stared down at the parchment in her hand, praying for the safe return of Roland. It had been ages since she had seen him, and the ache she felt at his absence ate away at her peace of mind. She shook herself, stood, and placed the parchment back on the shelf. She had people who needed her skills of healing, and reminiscing on the past could not help the present. She resumed her search for books on herbs.

CHAPTER FOUR

LAURA: PRESENT DAY

1964

*V*isions of a past life with Roland suddenly faded away, replaced with the sounds of music and chatter as Laura blinked a few times and came back to herself. Her eyes immediately went to Roland's, searching for answers, wondering if he had experienced the same thing. Yet his expression of bewilderment told her enough. It was clear that he had experienced something remarkable as they had waltzed across the floor.

"Did you see that?" Roland asked.

"Did you?" she asked.

The sudden pull of reality bewildered them as clapping and whistling ensued. She stood gazing into Roland's eyes, frozen in time. She could not say a word. She was afraid if she spoke, the enchanting moment would be lost forever, as would the strange vision they had both shared. While people continued to clap as the dancing came to an end, she heard the soft whispers of those in attendance. Everyone had noticed that Laura had not danced with anyone else.

And she found she didn't care what they thought. She cared only for Roland and what they had just shared.

ROLAND FROWNED AND HELD LAURA TIGHTER AS HE HAD NOT EXPECTED the magnitude of what had just happened. Who would? Past lives? Visions? It had to be a hallucination. Except...she had seen as well. Hadn't she? He began to doubt himself and his sanity, unable to say a word for fear she might think him crazy. After all, how could he explain what he saw in his mind's eye and still be considered sane? He kept quiet and noticed guests approaching them to wish Laura well and to say goodnight. The last of the guests left, and Roland continued standing beside Laura, reluctant to leave her side.

He leaned forward, and in a gentle voice he said, "It has been an unforgettable night, Laura. Happy Birthday my dear, and until we meet again, I wish you a goodnight."

"Until we do, good night, Roland," she said, capturing him with her eyes, a question in their depths.

Did you really see it too? He wanted to ask. Perhaps she wished to ask the same question.

He wanted to say so much more before he departed, but he still doubted himself and what he had seen. He reluctantly pulled himself away from her and left her standing there, baffled from the events of the evening. It wasn't just the vision that made him feel as if too many things had been left unspoken. It was the knowledge that he had found what had been missing in his life.

He had been missing Laura.

AS LAURA WATCHED HIM LEAVE, SHE STILL COULDN'T COMPREHEND what had happened between them. She knew him...had always known him...the love of her life. The man from her dreams. The one she had seen in her elevated state at the seer's cave. She wanted to run after him, to stop him from leaving. This called for a huge explanation.

Unfortunately, the party was over. Roland had to leave, and everyone else went home.

Laura went to bed in the early hours of the morning. She was tired and happy but baffled and confused. With a tingling sensation, she touched her bracelet fondly. She closed her eyes and tried to sleep with her heart full of new emotions, passion, and wonder. Soon, the same mystical feeling took over, and her memories of the past met her in her dreams.

CHAPTER FIVE

ROLAND: BATTLE OF ARSUF

1191

King Richard moved south along the coast to Jaffa after the Battle of Acre and his victory in taking back the city. He was determined to reach Jerusalem and win the war. He was safe from the seaside as his fleet moved south along with the infantry on land, providing food, munitions, and safe medical care for the wounded.

They were able to defeat the Muslims in the battle of Arsuf just a few months prior, recapturing the port of the City of Jaffa. The City of Jerusalem was almost in the King's sight, and Saladin had finally decided to negotiate.

It was a late summer day when three knights galloped at full speed towards the King's palace. Their leader dismounted quickly, not waiting for his companions as he took the stone steps two at a time, entering the palace's grand foyer. He continued forward and eventually stood in the middle of the hall, removing his helmet and giving it to a page boy who came hastily to serve him.

"Where is Lady Lauraine?" Roland Catin inquired.

"At the beach just beyond the wall where the coves are," responded the page.

Roland turned on his heal, returned to his horse, and galloped towards the beach. He smiled to himself as he remembered a time when Lauraine was barely two years old, trotting after him wherever he went. He could not believe how beautiful she had become over the years.

Roland was six years older than Lauraine, and he was very protective of her.

Raised together, a bond had grown between them, strengthening with time. It had turned into a deep love as their teenage years had approached.

While Roland had started his military training at an early age, Lauraine had joined in the training at age eleven. Her education had been highly unusual for a young girl with all manner of fencing and defensive skills included. She had spent hours sparring with Roland, learning from him and what he had been taught in his own training. They used to go riding towards the coastal range of Carmel, visiting Saint Elijah's shrine on top of the mountain and hunting rabbits and deer.

On one of their ventures, Roland had quietly followed a deer, asking Lauraine to stay behind him. He was very much concentrating on the kill, and he did not realize he had lost Lauraine. The deer had unexpectedly stood still with his perfect antlers raised, facing Roland with an intense stare. Roland had stopped and taken a direct shot with his arrow, toppling the deer to the ground.

"I got it. Look!" he had shouted.

He turned to talk to Lauraine, but she had disappeared. Roland had panicked, calling her name over and over, scouring the forest for her. She had just vanished. He had traced his footsteps back to where the horses were standing tethered to a tree. He'd ridden through the trees until he reached Elijah's cave, a place he and Lauraine enjoyed exploring. His hope had been she had wandered over there. To his horror, he saw Lauraine laying down on a rock, unconscious, with a group of women dancing around her, singing the pagan deity Baal song.

A feeling of rage filled him as he had attacked the women. They scrambled around and ran away while Roland untied Lauraine. She had still been unconscious when he lifted her up and took her outside, whistling for his horse. He took the canteen of water and sprinkled her face, calling her name and caressing her cheek, begging her to open her eyes. It took a little while before Lauraine finally responded. In that moment, as her eyes opened and she focused on him, he knew with absolute certainty that he loved her and never wished to be apart from her.

"You really scared me this time, my love," Roland had whispered in her ear as he sat on the ground, holding her to his chest. "What happened to you?" He kissed her face with tender passion. The fear of losing her still gripped his heart.

"I was standing still, watching you track that deer, when a young girl came from behind me and asked if I was lost. I said, 'No, I am waiting for my friend to finish his deer hunt.' She asked me if I needed water, and I said yes since I was thirsty. She carried a jar of water on her head. She put it down, took a scoop, and gave it to me. I drank and that is all I can remember."

Roland's anger had been kindled upon hearing the kidnapping attempt. She would have been sacrificed to a pagan god had he not found her in time. The thought sent a wave of nausea through him.

"I promise I will be here next time to hunt them. I don't usually hurt women, but they cannot attack and sacrifice innocents. They are lucky I was more worried about you. I thought these pagans had already moved to the east towards the big river. If I had thought this area wasn't safe, I never would have brought you with me. Come, let's go home. Amazingly, they did not take the horses."

"You saved my life, Roland! Thank you for protecting me," Lauraine said with adoration.

"Always, my dearest." He had stopped speaking at that point, afraid his emotions might get the best of him. He had brought her home safely that night, watching over her as always.

He continued to watch over her throughout the years while fulfilling his duty to his father and his king. Roland had grown up to be a handsome knight and an asset to his father in enforcing the protection of the city. By protecting the city, he sought to protect his Lauraine as well.

~

It was late in the afternoon as Lauraine sat upon the soft sands of the beach outside the walls of Acre. She was making a necklace from the seashells she had collected earlier, pensively examining a big conch shell and wondering at its beauty, she put the shell on her ear and closed her eyes as the sound of the sea hummed from the shell. She did not hear the hooves of the approaching horse speeding along the sands of the seashore.

"Lauraine!" Roland yelled as he jumped off his horse.

Lauraine's heart nearly beat right out of her chest, recognizing the low timbre of that voice.

"Roland?"

At the sudden surprise of his arrival, she stood and ran into his arms. He lifted her in the air as he always did every time he came back from his campaigns.

"Roland, oh, my dear Roland, when did you come back?" Lauraine asked as he lowered her and held her against his chest.

"About fifteen minutes ago, enough time to ask where you were." He tilted her chin and kissed her with all the longing in his heart.

"Happy Birthday, my love." Roland held her tenderly. "The entire household is preparing a birthday celebration for you tonight. I am very happy I was able to reach home in time."

Roland looked around, seeming a bit anxious as he said, "We need to return to the castle. I must report to my father and yours concerning the treaty with Saladin."

Lauraine's heart squeezed at this. She wanted no more of these Crusades. Roland lifted Lauraine and put her on the horse, positioning himself in front of her. She leaned over and rested her head on the back of his shoulder, placing her arms around his waist for support. They rode the short distance towards the citadel inside the city wall.

~

LAURAINE RETIRED TO HER CHAMBERS TO PREPARE FOR THE EVENING'S festivities as the two other knights joined Roland. They hastened towards the conference rooms where his father spent most of his time, and without waiting for the page at the door to announce them, Roland and his companions entered the room.

"Roland, welcome home, my son." Jeffrey Catin stood and moved towards his son with open arms.

"It's good to see you, Father." Roland returned his father's embrace. "Lord Salem, greetings to you, sir." Roland bowed in respect.

"Hello, Roland, what made you return in such haste?" Lord Salem asked.

"I have a message from King Richard. His Majesty received alarming news about his brother's intrigues in England and Normandy. Even though Jerusalem is very close, more armies have joined Saladin, and His Majesty decided not to move forward. We did not reach Jerusalem. A truce for three years is being negotiated under which the Christians will keep the coast towns and receive free and safe access to the Holy Sepulcher. He is on his way here. He will be sailing back to England within a couple of weeks. I hope the truce will last," Roland said.

"When do you expect His Majesty's arrival?" Lord Jeffrey asked.

"The royal entourage will be here within the coming few days," Roland answered. His thoughts turned to his sweet Lauraine. He feared he might have to leave her again and wished the war and unrest would subside. He wanted nothing more than to live his life in peace with his beloved.

After more speculation on current affairs, Roland excused himself to prepare for the festivities.

AFTER ROLAND LEFT, LORD JEFFRY CATIN TURNED TO HIS FRIEND.

"What do you think, John? Now that Roland is here and the King is coming, won't it be a great occasion to have Roland and Lauraine wed in His Majesty's presence?" Lord Catin asked.

"It would be a great honor. It is a good time to do so. Roland and Lauraine have been looking forward to this decision for quite a while." Lord Salem smiled. "It will be a great union between our two families."

"I am sorry Helen won't come to attend the wedding. She is recuperating from a long illness," Lord Catin said pensively.

Lord Salem placed a comforting hand on his shoulder. "I understand how you feel, my friend. I also wish that Mary was still with us to see her beautiful daughter getting married," Lord Salem said with a husky voice. "Your wife's health is important. It is best she recuperates." He clapped his hands together, giving Lord Catin a happy smile. "That's settled, then. Let us go and celebrate Lauraine's birthday. She must think we have forgotten all about her."

PREPARATIONS FOR LAURAINE'S EIGHTEENTH BIRTHDAY WERE ALMOST finished, and the party was about to start. Roland went to his chambers followed by his page. He was tired from riding all day and needed to rest, but he could not waste any time. He disrobed quickly and immediately plunged into the warm water prepared for him. He closed his eyes and tried to relax for a few moments, but thoughts of Lauraine and the possibility of separation due to these unending conflicts made his heart grow heavy. He washed and dressed in his white silk shirt with ruffles on the sleeves. He put on black pants, boots, and a royal blue sash which he placed around his waist. Lastly, he put on his belt and sword and hastily left the room.

He began to descend the stairs when he remembered the most important item he had brought back with him. Roland banged his head with his palm and ran back to the room, grabbing a small, red velvet box and putting it in his pocket. He turned and headed for the stairs, ready for the festivities to begin in the great hall.

PEOPLE HAD ALREADY GATHERED AROUND IN GROUPS CHATTING AND gossiping about politics, their king, and the latest news from the region when Lauraine descended the stairs.

The ladies were in their best frocks and ready for the celebration. Everyone was in a happy, cheerful mood as Lauraine entered the room. She glowed in her beautiful, emerald green dress. A delicate gold tiara crowned her long, red, curly hair. Her green eyes shone with excitement, searching the room for Roland. She noticed he was with their fathers and most likely discussing the king's business. She hoped they might focus on something more joyful for just one evening.

She approached them with a smile, and the moment Roland turned to see her she knew she had succeeded in banishing all unpleasant thoughts of war from his mind. He looked mesmerized by the sight of her. She inwardly laughed at the ease with which her appearance pleased him. In truth, she did not imagine herself a great beauty, but she knew Roland would always see her as such. Lauraine curtsied, and Roland held her hand, kissing it gently.

"What was it that the three of you were discussing so seriously?" She used a mocking tone of disapproval.

The men answered in unison, "Your wedding!"

Lauraine blushed as they all laughed in merriment.

Lord Catin said, "Roland couldn't have picked a more beautiful bride than you my gorgeous, graceful, intelligent girl. Happy Birthday, my dear."

"Thank you, sir." Lauraine curtsied, taking Roland's outstretched hand. "And what did you determine as far as wedding plans go?" She awaited their answer with bated breath, having anticipated this moment for as long as she could remember.

"King Richard is coming next week, my love." Roland placed an arm around her. "We will have the wedding then. There could be no greater honor than having our king in attendance."

Lauraine blinked back the tears, hardly daring to believe they would be wed so soon. It was more than she could have hoped for.

"You'll still have me?" he asked, giving her a mischievous smile.

She pretended to consider her options, watching as his smile grew wider. "I suppose you'll do. Although, there is a certain guardsman I've had my eye on for quite some time."

She barely got the words out before he pulled her to himself and gave her a stern look, but his eyes held laughter in them.

"Then I shall take this moment to convince you that I am the only man you shall ever need. Shall we dance?"

She nodded in delight as their fathers chuckled at their playful banter.

Couples joined them and the music filled the air. For the next few hours, Lauraine knew nothing but the sight of her sweet Roland and the wonderful sensation of being held in his arms.

At about midnight, Roland waltzed Lauraine towards the arched door and out onto the porch. He stood gazing at her.

"I did not forget your present." Roland smiled. "I hope you will like it." He reached in his pocket and pulled out a small, red velvet box and gave it to her.

Lauraine was stunned, mesmerized by the beauty of the bracelet placed on a white satin lining. It had six flowers, each with five petals of gold. Small diamonds were set around each gold petal, engraved with intricate designs. In the center of each flower rested a ruby. The golden flowers were connected to each other with a delicate gold chain.

"I do not have any words to express my feelings except to say thank you. This bracelet is beautiful. I love it and I will treasure it all of my life. Where did you find it?" Lauraine lifted it out of the box, and Roland helped her clasp it on her wrist. He tilted her chin and kissed her lips tenderly.

"I am very happy you love it. I had it custom made for you, my dear. I hope you won't be angry with me. Do you remember the dagger with rubies and diamonds that your mother left for me? Your father was to give it to me on my twentieth birthday."

"Of course." Lauraine's eyes widened in surprise. "Oh, Roland, you don't mean—"

"Yes, my love." His smile warmed her heart. "I never used it, and I thought the jewels were magnificent, so I took them and the gold handle of the sword-the one which my father gave to me when I joined the regiment-and had this delicate thing made."

"But those were your precious items, Roland."

"Nothing is more precious to me than you. It would please me greatly for you to wear this, a token of my eternal love for you."

"I accept it with all my heart, Roland. Thank you."

She didn't realize she had been crying until he lifted his hand and wiped away her tears. "Come, let us dance once more with this token of my love shining for all to see."

Lauraine closed her eyes and floated in Roland's arms as he held her tightly, waltzing around the hall. A sensation of elation and happiness covered them, with a feeling of ecstasy, a bond of love formed for all eternity.

HERALDS WERE SENT AROUND THE COUNTRY ANNOUNCING THE WEDDING date of Roland and Lauraine, inviting people to the celebrations.

On the day the king arrived, the people of Acre hailed him as he entered the gate with his knights. The soldiers camped outside the city, waiting for the order to go sailing back home. They were enjoying a time of peace.

Lord Catin, Lord Salem, and Roland received the King's entourage and accompanied him to his quarters.

"Lord Catin, I am so grateful for your assistance and support." King Richard sat at the dinner table with the nobles and Templar Knights. "It was a crucial moment, Lord Salem, when you supplied us with those regiments. They turned the whole situation in our favor and helped end the war." King Richard's praise was gratifying, but Roland noticed his pensive and troubled gaze.

"It is my honor and duty, your Majesty," Lord Catin said. "We wish you the best, my King, and we are here for you."

Roland had an idea of what troubled the king. Betrayal by his brother was surely on his mind, but he could not find a way to subtly bring up the subject. Instead, he changed the subject to cheer the king.

"I have a small request to ask of Your Majesty."

Richard raised his head in question.

He turned his eyes to his father, finding it more appropriate that he address the king concerning their request.

His father smiled and turned to the king. "Roland and Lauraine's wedding is in three days, this coming Sunday." Lord Catin said. "We would be honored if Your Majesty would preside over the wedding and give them your blessings."

The King stood with a smile, as did everyone present, and said, "We drink tonight to the health of the young couple. May the Lord bless their days to come. I am happy to be able to see them married before we leave." The King smiled and drank his cup all the way down. "I must also say that young Roland is an exceptional man. He is a brave warrior and was of great help to us."

Everyone cheered and enjoyed the festivities.

THE PREPARATIONS FOR THE WEDDING WERE ON-GOING, THE WHOLE palace was in a hustle and bustle. Some guests had already arrived with their children the day before and filled up the hallways.

The families from her mother's side arrived. Lauraine's grandfather, George Kane, whom she adored, was first to step down from the carriage. Lauraine eagerly greeted him, running into his open arms.

"My pretty little girl. I hear of your escapades often, helping here and there, healing the sick and taking care of people and little animals alike."

"How fortunate you heard good things. It would appear I've skill-fully hidden all the bad." She kissed him on the cheek.

George Kane chuckled as he swiftly returned the affection. Lords Salem and Catin welcomed the old man.

"She reminds me so much of her mother," he said with a sad smile.

"They are alike in every way," Lord Salem agreed.

"Grandpa, you must see my garden. It bloomed exactly as you told me it would, and I followed every instruction you gave me. It is really beautiful." Lauraine's eyes shone with pride.

"I am sure it must be wonderful. Let me rest for a little while, and I promise before dinner we will enjoy your garden on this beautiful summer day." George winked and accompanied her inside with Lord Salem and the rest of the nobles.

"We must pay homage to King Richard," George said as Lord Salem led him to where the King sat. He bowed deeply to King Richard who accepted his reverence with grace. "I understand you made a truce with Saladin, Your Majesty. I hope he will honor the agreement. Thank you for all you have done."

Lauraine felt proud to stand by her grandfather as he addressed their king.

"Thank you," King Richard said. "Peace is preferable to what we have seen thus far. We will learn how to live with the Muslim people as long as they respect the laws and promises made."

"Will Saladin keep his word?" Lord Catin asked.

"I am sure he will keep his word, this time," King Richard said.

Lauraine certainly hoped so. The lives of many, including Roland's, would be influenced by Saladin's decisions.

THE DAY OF THE WEDDING CAME. THE HERALDS ANNOUNCED THE entrance of the King, and everyone in the spacious hall bowed down. The ladies knelt until he passed. Roland entered and took his place in front of the King. As the tune of the wedding march played, a vision entered the hall.

Lauraine looked angelic in her long white dress. The high neck was adorned with pearls. The long sleeves ended with sets of pearls, and the whole dress cascaded along her slim figure in a silky wave. Her veil was held in place by a tiara, sparkling with diamonds and small green emeralds. The train spread behind her as she stepped slowly forward. She held a bouquet of red roses in her delicate hands. Roland could hardly contain his emotion at the sight of her.

Her father came forward, and she took his arm, allowing him to lead her to where Roland stood waiting for her.

After the formalities of the wedding took place, and the King announced them husband and wife, Roland kissed his bride, and everyone moved to the tables assigned to them. The bride and groom took their places at the King's table.

With plenty of dancing and drinking, the celebrations continued long after the newlyweds took their leave.

TWO DAYS LATER, KING RICHARD THE LIONHEART SAILED WITH LORD Catin back to England in October of 1192, leaving Roland to help Lord Salem attend to business. Lord Catin owned farmland to the east of Acre, a half day's travel, and the farmers worked the land. His properties were adjacent to Bassa village, and he usually visited the tenants twice a month to see to their needs.

Lauraine's grandfather lived in Bassa, and the land was fruitful and produced plenty. Many times before, during the wars, the village had been attacked, and farms were ravaged. However, the villagers were able to defend themselves as much as they could. They frequently gave food and shelter to pilgrims and injured people who were attacked by bandits.

The Kingdom of Jerusalem was now relatively secure, with its new capital at Acre. The second incarnation of the Kingdom of Jerusalem would endure for another century.

CHAPTER SIX

LAURA: TRAGEDY

1964

*L*aura woke up the next day and sat in her bed. She recalled what had happened the previous night at the party, but she could not say anything to anyone lest they think her crazy. Her heart filled with fear. She tried to remember every detail of her previous life with Roland, including this most recent vision of their planned wedding and the years of history they had shared.

She now knew the secret of the bracelet, and the reason for the continuous nightmare that had plagued her for so long. Yet now she had to wonder why it still felt like a nightmare when her beloved Roland was in it, beckoning her to him. With sudden inspiration, she understood the message. An impending sense of doom always filled her in the dream, and no matter how often she had the dream, she had never ever reached her beloved Roland.

Until now. It wasn't a mere dream. It was a lifetime of memories, and she feared there may have been no happy ending.

"Rana is here to see you, and it is about time for you to get out of bed," her mother said as she stuck her head into the room. Laura realized the lateness of the morning and jumped out of bed.

"Rana, please come in," she called as she moved to her dresser.

Rana entered the room with a big smile on her face. "Party too much last night? Perhaps you had sweet dreams of a certain someone named Roland?"

Laura rolled her eyes, worried her friend would see she had guessed correctly. "And how would you know about Roland when you weren't allowed to attend the party?"

"Your mother is a delightful informant."

Laura laughed. "Roland is a very handsome young man," she said in a measured tone.

"You should run off with him, elope somewhere exotic and have a real adventure." Rana threw herself on the bed and sighed dramatically.

Laura laughed at her antics, but she worried that Rana wasn't necessarily joking. Despite her friend's Muslim religion, she knew Rana found the traditions very restricting, and Rana rebelled against many of them in her heart. Although they didn't discuss their faiths openly with one another, they still shared secrets like any teenager, talking about their hopes and dreams, and Laura knew Rana's dreams did not involve a traditional Islamic life.

She worried for her welfare because of this.

"My dear Rana, I wish you were able to come to my party last night." Laura hugged her friend. "You would have had such a wonderful time. I have so much to tell you. First, look what my mother gave me." Laura raised her arm to show Rana the bracelet.

Rana widened her almond shaped eyes in awe. "Oh, what a beautiful bracelet." She pulled Laura's arm closer and inspected the delicate jewelry.

"Thank you," Laura said impishly.

"I want details. Tell me everything about Roland." Rana leveled her with an expectant look, and Laura finally gave in to her friends demands.

"He is very handsome. He is twenty-four years old, is going to college in Berlin, Germany, and I am going to see him on Sunday." Laura could not contain her excitement.

"There's more," Rana said, giving her a measured look. "What aren't you telling me?"

"Maybe one day I will tell you the strange experience I had last night, and you might be able to explain it to me. There really isn't time to go into it now, and if I don't explain it thoroughly, you will think I am delusional."

"I watched you levitate above a table in a seer's cave a few days ago. I doubt anything will surprise me at this point," she said wryly. "How about your parents? Will they let you go out with him?"

"Well, we discovered that his parents knew my parents very well. They might not let me go out with him alone. I am amazed that I've never met him before considering our parents' history with each other. They actually live two streets over from here."

"You are so lucky to have your parents' approval."

Laura knew that look. More difficulties at home. "Now tell me what is happening with you and Omar."

Rana blushed and said, "Omar's father and two of his uncles are coming tomorrow night to visit with my parents."

"This is wonderful!" Laura felt so relieved for Rana. "You are going to be engaged. Congratulations, my friend." Laura gave her a fierce hug.

When she pulled back, it was to see a frown on her friend's face. "What is it?"

"Frankly, I am worried that my father will not accept him, or my brother Ali might cause some problems."

"Why should he? Omar comes from a good family, and I thought Ali and Omar were close friends, right?" She hoped the social differences between their classes would not pull them apart. "I will pray for you and wish you good luck."

"My parents' social status is very important to them, and I think they might not approve because he is a grocer's son," Rana guessed. "No matter who we marry, you must promise me we will remain close always."

Laura knew that growing apart was a real possibility since they did not share the same faith. Muslims and Christians were friendly with each other, but adults typically could not be close. Whomever they married would play a large role in how their friendship would continue.

"I promise."

Time passed as they chatted about more frivolous subjects, and then Rana left later in the evening. Laura spent the next hour helping her mother in the kitchen preparing dinner. Soon, everything was ready and the table was set. Her brothers and sister came rushing in, claiming they were famished, and they started nibbling on the salads.

The phone rang, distracting Laura from her task. She grabbed the telephone, and her heart flipped as she considered the idea that it might be Roland calling her. Instead of hearing his low voice, she heard the formal tones of a man identifying himself as an official from the police department.

"I regret to inform you that your father was seriously injured in an accident."

"I'm sorry? He's been hurt? How?" Panic crawled up Laura's throat.

"He was accidentally hit by a car. Witnesses called an ambulance, and he was taken to the General Hospital in critical condition. Please inform your family and arrive at the hospital as quickly as you can."

"Nooooooooooooo," Laura screamed. Her knees buckled under her, the telephone falling from her hand. Her mother heard the scream and came running from the kitchen.

"What happened? What is it?" Juliette looked frazzled as she reached Laura's side and grabbed the phone.

"Hello?" she said. "What is..." She listened to the speaker as Laura sat there looking at her mother, knowing she couldn't save her from this heartache. She felt the whole world shift beneath her.

Her mother put the phone down and stood silently for a moment. Then she made another phone call.

"Mother, what are you doing?"

Juliette sobbed as she said, "I'm calling a taxi. We must get to your father as soon as possible." She looked at her daughter, her expression distorted with anguish. Her mother embraced Laura, explaining to her siblings what had transpired, and the family comforted each other as they waited for the taxi to arrive. Her father had serious injuries, but he was still alive. She tried to reassure herself. Yet Laura feared the worst.

~

THE PAST WAS ALL LAURA'S MOTHER COULD THINK ABOUT AS SHE watched the machines monitor her husband's vitals.

She and her husband had been through so much together, and even before she had met Emile, her life had never been easy. Sitting at the side of his bed, she thought back on earlier memories, one horrible event in particular.

The silence on the night of March 23, 1948, was shattered with the sound of explosions in the distance.

That night, Juliette and Emile had held a dinner for some Jordanian army officers in their large suburban home.

During the visit, the captain had suddenly dropped his silverware, stood up, and said, "Now that we have shared bread and salt, it is my duty and honor that I should warn you. Tomorrow at dawn, this City of Ramla will fall to the enemy. We are evacuating in two hours. I will send you a truck, and you must take only what is necessary of your belongings and leave immediately. Go across the River Jordan."

Staring in disbelief at the man, Juliette had clutched her seven-month-old baby girl in her arms, the reality hitting her hard that all was lost, all was gone.

Juliette and Emile were not the only ones to be displaced. The exodus of one million immigrants had flooded the territory and disgruntled the Jordanians. Juliette had started to support her family after arriving at their new home. As a midwife, she earned her license and continued to deliver babies. For two years, Emile could not find a job in the small town of Zerqa, while waiting for their promised return to Palestine by politicians. Eventually the family moved, by then with three children, to the capital of Jordan, where Emile's brothers were living after the immigration.

Juliette sold the last of her jewelry to buy a piece of land. Emile and Juliette were able to build a nice house on top of a hill overlooking a valley.

Falling from riches to rags, she had walked for miles on end to her daily house calls to save on bus fare. The years of struggle had permanently affected Juliette. It had changed her. She'd become bitter to some extent. Immigration to the desert land had made her long for her green meadows of Palestine, for the city of Acre on the Mediterranean shores with its huge wall and ancient castles, a beautiful place where she had lived in her youth.

She stared at her husband, feeling that same pain of loss and displacement at the thought of him dying, something that now seemed inevitable.

CHAPTER SEVEN

ROLAND AND LAURAINE: ATTACK

1194

*L*auraine's confidence stemmed from taking responsibility for the household at a very young age. Over the years, she had learned how to be strong. She often wondered if she would have been a different person had her mother lived after giving birth to her. She had heard stories of her mother's strength and determination, and she wanted to follow in her footsteps. She hosted her father's social affairs. She participated in horse riding competitions, fencing, and then learned about plants and herbs from her grandfather.

Many farmers continued to seek her advice concerning their crop problems as she researched botany books written by agricultural scholars of her time. She helped as much as she could. She wanted her father to be free from common concerns so he could give his full attention to political and military affairs. Having Roland by her side made her feel complete. She was warm and gentle yet firm and assertive. Often, she took the lead when needed and was able to solve various problems. Everyone who had the opportunity to work with

Lauraine loved her for her kindness and respected and recognized the strength in her.

"Come, beautiful Lady, I want to read your fortune," an old woman said, stopping Lauraine on her way to her grandfather's house during one of her visits to the village. There was a small community of gypsies living in the area. They moved a lot, but in the end, they always came back to Bassa village to settle for the winter.

"Thank you, Fatima. You know I do not believe in fortune telling. You have been trying to read my future for many years now." Lauraine smiled and gave her a coin.

"No, Lady, no. This time I cannot accept the coin. Please, let me read your fortune."

Curiosity overcame Lauraine as the old woman insisted more than usual.

"Okay, Fatima, when I come in the afternoon to read for the children, I will visit you first."

"You will not regret it," Fatima promised.

As the sun set that day, Lauraine entered the gypsy's tent where she sat on the ground facing a low table. A crystal ball sat atop the table.

"This time I am calling my niece to show you a different way of reading. I am sure you will see something unusual." She went outside and called a girl of about ten years old. The girl sat on the ground in between the two women. Lauraine watched the woman put a drop of oil on the girl's thumbnail, and she started chanting an incantation.

> *"Dahbour, cantour, devil's curse go away,*
> *Keep the track clear, and be held at bay.*
> *But may the angels come and fill the night*
> *Stars that shine with the dazzling light."*

She kept her eyes closed, invoking the powers with prayers Lauraine couldn't understand.

"Now, my lady, look at the nail and watch the little girl describe what she sees," the old woman said. The little girl started humming a tune, and then suddenly she stopped. Fatima said, "You will be happy for a while. Look with me and see. You are in a huge hall. Magical shimmering lights drop from crystals that sparkle and hang down from the ceiling. You are in a long, ruby dress. Your knight will lead your way. Back and forth, you will travel in forests, across the seas in a carriage flying in the air. You will see wars, battles, and triumphs. You will see a wooden box with people talking and moving in it. You will be in one of them. Now go in peace, my lady, and meet your destiny."

The girl closed her eyes and did not move. Lauraine watched the scene with her jaw open, surprised at the utter nonsense she had heard but terrified at the stream of pictures she had seen moving through the nail.

Feeling bewildered, Lauraine left the tent. She sat down with the children of the village, staring at the horizon. With her beautiful voice she sang to them, and the children joined her in the Lord's prayer, but she couldn't shake the chills that crept within her bones.

ONE DAY, LAURAINE CAME TO HER FATHER AND SAID, "IT IS TIME TO GO and visit grandfather and see to the villagers. Somehow, I feel an urgency to do so. This time Roland and I will go together."

"It has been a month since my last visit," her father said. "Indeed, it is time to go. Take Dr. Louis with you. There might be medical needs for him to attend to. There have been reports of illness amongst the farmers."

"We will leave tomorrow, early in the morning, and be back around dusk."

"Be careful along the road. It is not completely safe," warned Lord Salem.

"Do not worry. Two other knights and the physician are accompanying us. I love you, father. Have I told you lately that you are the best father in the world?"

Lord John smiled while Lauraine winked at him and left to prepare medicines and herbs to take with her on the trip.

Roland and Lauraine traveled with the other riders, and eventually they approached the village. They were horrified at the sight they came upon.

Nomad clans known as Bedouins moved from the deserts of Arabia to Syria. They never settled for long in one area but kept moving from place to place, going after food for their sheep. They also traded with villagers. Sometimes, rival clans would raid each other and steal their sheep and women. Their lifestyle was raiding, and it appeared a massive raid had happened here.

The land was treadled. Cottages burned and people ran aimlessly, not knowing where to hide or where to go. Many were on the ground dead, and children cried next to their dead mothers, clinging to their mother's clothing. In the distance, a wave of sand could be seen, kicked up by the departing marauders.

"My Lady! Thank God you are here," her grandfather's page said with relief. "I was on my way to see your father for help. We were raided by black turbaned bandits. They stole everything in stock, burned the barns, and killed the men of the village."

"Did you see my grandfather?" Lauraine yelled. Without waiting for an answer, she rode towards the house, while Roland and his companions dismounted. The physician immediately started to examine the injured. Those who had either escaped the raid, or who were fortunate enough to be able to help, moved the dead bodies, wrapped them in sheets, and placed them in the church. It was a terrible day.

George Kane was eighty years old. Generations before him owned the land, and the Kane family continued to live there. He and his family lived on the same land. He had raised his children there. The farmers were happy to serve them because George was very kind and compassionate, looking after their needs.

"Grandpa, Grandpa!" Lauraine called at the top of her voice, terrified and worried, as she climbed the front stairs. Already sick to her stomach, she entered the house to see the interior ransacked. Everything the bandits could not take with them had been broken and destroyed.

Lauraine found her grandfather, dejected, sitting in his rocking chair in the middle of the living room with tears running down his cheeks and a look of shock covering his face.

"Grandfather, I am here. Thank God, you are not hurt. Look at me. It is your Lauraine." She knelt down and held his hands. "You're safe, papa, nothing else matters."

"Lauraine, my child!" He touched her cheek and said, "I am sorry, they were too many. I couldn't stop this rampage."

Her grandfather's housekeeper came running in.

"Maggie, are your children safe?" Lauraine hugged her.

"Yes, my Lady, but my husband was injured."

"Roland is following me, and the physician is tending to the wounded," Lauraine said.

Roland rushed inside the room. Upon seeing George sitting with Lauraine, he said, "Thank God, you are not hurt."

"I am all right," George whispered.

Once the injured were tended to, Roland sent word to Lord Salem, telling him about what had happened and that they would be delayed. The recovery efforts would require additional aide, and he requested some of the monks to come help with the wounded and bury the dead.

Along with the medical supplies she had brought with her, Lauraine found more medicines and herbs that the bandits had not discovered. In a short period of time, the house was turned into a hospital. The injured were lined up in the hallway. The children who lost their parents were housed upstairs in the guest rooms.

It took the rest of the day and most of the night to finish helping the remaining patients.

CHAPTER EIGHT

LAURA: SHATTERED DREAMS

1964

*L*aura stood beside the coffin, staring at her father with tears running down her cheeks. He had been full of life just a couple of days earlier, but now he laid in silence, eyes closed and ashen-faced. She kept staring at her father's face, noticing a bandage on his forehead and cotton in his nose.

Oh, he cannot take a breath this way, she thought. *How could he leave like this?*

She felt he had betrayed her, though she knew it was not his fault.

The silence in the house was deafening. No one made a sound.

"You promised. You said everything would be all right, and all I had to do was just pass the entrance exam for college!"

She bent down to kiss his crossed hands and felt the ice-cold of his skin attack her hot face, wet with tears.

Hands pulled her away from him. Instinctively she resisted these hands. She thrashed and screamed, "Leave me alone. Stop it. I want to kiss him goodbye. Please, let me say goodbye!"

Laura was shattered as she thought about her father in the coffin, begging them to leave her alone. They did not listen. Relatives had to take him to church for final rights. They needed to put him in the ground.

"No, no, please wait, don't take him yet!" Laura begged as her cousins and brothers took the coffin away.

She did not understand why the men took him to church without her. Did it have to do with the culture? Not even her mother was allowed to go with them, although her mother had not seemed mentally present for several days. She and her mother were not allowed to go to the cemetery to see where he was buried. Only the men did that, and Laura felt her heart torn to pieces.

The men returned after the burial and sat in silence. She looked around, filled with anguish. Friends and family tried to console her as she kept sobbing. She wanted everybody to go away. She did not want to see anyone as the horror of what had happened began to sink in. Without her father she was alone. Yes, she had her mother, brothers, and sister, but now she felt a heavy burden passed on to her. She was going to have to be the head of the family. Her mother's frail condition would not handle the grueling life of a midwife again.

She thought about her father, knowing that no one had loved her like he had. He simply loved her.

Emile Salem had left the world at the moment when he was supposed to enjoy his life with his wife and children after years of struggle. He was kind and loved by everyone who knew him. He had a sense of humor that made everyone enjoy his company. His brothers loved him, and his nieces and nephews had depended on him when their father had died. He had always been generous and warmhearted. His many quirks had been so endearing to Laura. He had loved pigeons, rabbits, and chickens, for which he'd made a special coop and spent his afternoons taking care of them, feeding them and catering to their needs.

Many a night he had taken a white bedsheet and placed it on the wall in the corner of the living room, using cartons cut into the shapes of cartoon characters for whatever story he wanted to tell. He had lit candles behind the sheets, creating moving shadows. He had created the character of "Joker Iwaz", an old man who had entertained his children for hours on end. His heart had been happy to hear their merry laughter as the marionettes jumped and danced in the candlelight.

Oh, papa, Laura thought. *What will we do without you?*

JULIETTE WAS OVERWHELMED WITH SADNESS AND WORRY AS ANXIETY took over. What was she going to do? She looked at each of her husband's family members and didn't hold much hope.

"Now you have to be careful with your expenses, Auntie," her husband's nephew, Roger, said to Juliette. He was a successful businessman. "All that I am saying is that the children are still in school, and when they finish high school they can help," Roger said.

"With the Lord's help, my children will go to college and finish their education," Juliette firmly stated.

"If you have the impetus and resources, do it if you can." Roger bid them farewell and left.

Her eldest brother-in-law, Karim, and his son sat there listening as if the subject did not concern them at all. Deep in her heart, she knew that none of them would be there for her once the day ended, despite all the love and support her husband had given them over the years. Juliette silently stifled her rage.

Her own family members were far away in different countries beyond her reach. The disaster was too much to bear. She could not wait to shut the door after the last person left. She slumped to the floor in exhaustion and sobbed. Her children gathered around her to give and receive comfort.

"I do not know what I am going to do. We have to take care of ourselves. No one will be there for us. My health is not good enough to start working again." Tears kept running down her face.

Laura said, "I was devastated when dad's sister said to me 'dogs will feast and gobble you up.' What a miserable woman. I was filled with anger and rage, and my grief doubled. The rich aunt. Instead of holding me in her arms to comfort me, and telling me not to be afraid, she filled my heart with worry and fear."

Laura gazed at her mother, trying to give her some hope. It scared her to see her mother in such a state.

"I am young, but I can help. I do not want you to worry about anything. This house's design makes it possible to split it in two apartments. We will lease a section out. I will immediately start learning to be a secretary, but you need to be strong for us, Mother. You must get father's pension. Tomorrow, you have to go to his office and see to the paperwork. It is going to take six months for training as a secretary. My dreams of college are gone now, but with God's help, I promise you, we will not need anyone, and my brothers and sister will go to college and finish their education. I promise." Laura felt the challenge was hers to take on; the burden hers to bear.

Laura wiped her tears. Michael came to her side and knelt down. "When I graduate from high school, I will help you."

"No, I vow you will go to college. All that I require from both of you are good grades and good behavior." Laura touched her brother's face determined to give them hope and make them feel safe.

She went to her room, closed the door, and threw herself on the bed. Fear of the future and sadness gave her a sense of desperation. A day ago, she had gleamed with happiness and excitement. This day was dark, desolate, and unending. She shut her eyes as her tears rolled down her cheeks again. Her dreams were shattered.

"Just why did you leave me?" Laura said in anguish as she closed her eyes.

"I never left you. I will always look after you, and I will always be there, my lovely daughter."

Laura opened her eyes to see who was talking to her. No one was in the room.

"Dad? Are you talking to me? Where are you? I have to see you." She laughed at herself. How could she think he was here? "You are dead, and you are not here." Laura closed her eyes again, her heart beating at a rapid rate.

"I am here for you. I will ease your spirit and lift you up. Open your eyes." She felt her father's presence strongly. She saw him near the window, and it eased her fears and worries. Even in death, her father would not abandon her.

"You can always talk to me, Laura. I will always watch over you. Just remember the strength of your grandmother, Regina, and how she fought hard to save my brother and the rest of the family."

"When I need you father, I will call for you. I will always love you." She thanked her father in her heart.

"I love you all. Sleep now, my sweet daughter. All will be well." Emile faded away.

Exhausted, Laura drifted off to sleep.

CHAPTER NINE

OMAR AND RANA

1964

The evening clouds were gathering quickly, covering the setting sun and forming a front pregnant with rain. Omar Abbas sat thinking about the first time he had ever noticed Rana, Ali's sister, as anything other than a friend.

It had been a cold winter day in December 1964. Omar had returned home from college for the winter break. He was studying medicine at the National University in the town of Jobeiha, Jordan, where he was realizing his dream of being a healer. As he rang the bell for the bus to stop, suddenly the sky lit up with long streaks of lightning, followed by peals of thunder. The rain started pouring down heavily as he stepped off the bus and opened his umbrella.

Omar nearly fell when he felt two hands grab his shoulders from behind and push forward. He angrily turned around to see the offender, but his anger quickly melted away as he recognized a beautiful flushed face. Her gorgeous dark eyes returned his gaze. Her long brown hair blew in the wind, quickly getting soaked with rain. It made his heart throb so hard it felt as if it might jump out of his chest. He instinctively held the umbrella over her as she began to apologize in embarrassment.

"I am terribly sorry. I tripped stepping down off the bus."

"Rana, are you okay? Did you hurt yourself?" Concern softened his tone.

"Yes! I mean, no! I mean, I'm fine," Rana said shyly as her smile widened hesitantly.

"Here, you can use my umbrella," Omar offered.

"No, thank you. I am fine. I have to go. Goodbye." Rana smiled again.

"Please wait! Take the umbrella!" Omar insisted. Rana looked at him over her shoulder, waved, and started running towards her house which, after all, was just two houses down the street from the bus stop.

That night, Omar tossed and turned in his bed as Rana's rain-soaked face kept crossing his restless mind. He tried to close his eyes tight, but her smile remained there in front of him.

Omar could not sleep.

He had known Rana all his life. She had been his next-door neighbor since they were children. They never played together because girls were not allowed to play with boys. She had always played hopscotch and jump rope with her friend, Laura Salem.

Rana lived with her father, mother, and her brother Ali, who was Omar's best friend in the neighborhood. Omar Abbas and Ali Sadeq had been inseparable before he had left to study abroad. They had gone to the same school for boys and spent most of their time hanging outside, playing soccer, or going to the movies with their mutual friend, Michael Salem.

Rana had never joined the boys in their games or conversations, except for the common friendly courtesy of the culture.

Omar had always viewed Rana as the "little kid next-door" and his best friend's sister. He was bound by honor and tradition to never look at Rana disrespectfully and to treat her like she was his own sister. Until the night she ran into him getting off the bus, Omar had never thought of Rana romantically.

What on earth was I thinking? I should stop feeling like that immediately! She's like my little sister!

For several nights he could not sleep. It was a little after midnight when he got out of his bed and looked outside the window towards his neighbor's house.

The seven hills of the city of Amman, the capital of the Hashemite Kingdom of Jordan, were in deep slumber as snow now quietly fell from the dark sky. It had already covered the streets, the roofs of the houses, and the cars that were parked near the sidewalks. Omar stood staring, not at the snow or the streets covered with the white shining flakes, but at the shadow behind the curtains of the second-floor window of the house next door. He had never before gazed at her window, high above the concrete fence that surrounded their house. It was there all the time, but there had been no reason for him to do so until now.

He knew in his heart that Rana could not sleep either, and he hoped she was thinking about him. Her shadow paced the room for a few moments, when suddenly she pulled away the curtain and looked right at him. She turned around, looking over her shoulder as if to make certain she was alone, and then she quickly waved at him. She shut the curtains so fast, he had no time to wave back.

Omar was stunned. His heart leaped in his chest as he realized that she was, indeed, thinking of him as well. Rana was so close to him yet unreachable and far away. A wide smile spread across his face. He jumped into his bed, covered himself with the warm blanket, closed his eyes, and drifted off to sleep, dreaming of a beautiful face with long brown hair and huge, enchanting black eyes twinkling at him.

ALTHOUGH SHE WAS EIGHTEEN, RANA DASHED OUTSIDE WITH HER woolen red hat, scarf, coat, gloves, and boots, joining Laura and Michael in the street and throwing snowballs with the joy of a small child. They laughed at each other, enjoying the wonder of fresh snow on the ground, hanging on to the joys of childhood as long as possible. It was a time when children in the neighborhoods interacted with carefree abandon, and Omar was already there. Rana started building a snowman, and some of the children came to help. Soon, the snowman was smiling. Rana pulled off her hat and scarf and put it on the snowman.

"Here, use these buttons for eyes." Omar's own eyes twinkled with happiness.

Rana saw her friend Laura give her a knowing, amused look, but she ignored it as she took Omar's offering with a shy smile.

"Thank you," Rana said without looking at him. Her heart beat very fast, and she felt a tingling sensation drawing her to Omar like a magnet. Rana took the buttons from his hand, and as their fingers touched, she noticed Omar's eyes gleam, as if an electric shock had hit him right down his spine. It had definitely done something electrifying to her.

He stared at Rana's gentle face, appearing to wage an internal war. She wondered if he was resisting this magnetic pull of desire as much as she. Rana wanted him to reach out and touch her cheeks or run his fingers through her hair. The spell was broken by an outraged, angry yell from the entrance of her house.

"Rana, come back inside right now!" her brother screamed.

She turned to see a sibling she hardly recognized. It had been that way ever since Ali had returned from England. The loving younger brother she had always adored had been replaced by someone withdrawn, bitter, and distant. He rushed outside and pulled Rana's arm, dragging her fiercely to the front door and pushing her inside the house.

She couldn't believe it. Her younger brother had changed so much.

"You have no business talking to the boys. You are not a child anymore. No sister of mine will expose herself to men," Ali yelled louder.

Outraged, Rana fought back. "How could you humiliate me like that? Who do you think you are?" Rana yelled, trying to get through to him.

Ali's face twisted with rage as he slapped Rana's face brutally.

Her face snapped to the side, and she heard a ringing in her ears. She touched her burning cheek and swallowed back the tears. With a quivering voice she said, "Who gave you the right to..." Rana was stopped in the middle of her sentence with another slap to her other cheek.

"Shut up, or else!" He raised his hand to slap her again, but this time his hand was held back by their father.

"As long as I am still alive, you will never, ever raise a hand against your sister, or I will break it! Even when you have a wife and daughter, I will never let you strike or demean them."

Ahmad Sadeq faced his son with consternation as Rana tried to move past the shock of what her brother had done. Never in their lives had he ever raised a hand to her.

"If your sister needs correction, it is mine and your mother's responsibility to correct her. Not yours, Ali," Ahmad said in a controlled low voice through gritted teeth. "Not to mention the fact that she is your older sister by a year."

"But father, she was playing with the boys outside," Ali retorted in disgust while attempting to use a respectful tone.

"Was she alone outside with the boys or were all the girls, even mothers, outside playing in the snow?"

"This is ridiculous," Rana said. "There were plenty of girls out there, including Laura, and it's not as if I spoke to any strange boys. The only boy I spoke to was Omar!" She stared at Ali, hoping that somehow her reasoning would get through to him. "He is your best friend! He gave us the buttons to put on the snowman. What is wrong with that?" Rana felt indignant and utterly betrayed. She yelled her defense as tears ran down her now burning cheeks, stinging where the finger marks lingered.

Her father lifted her chin, looking at her face in consternation. "You have bruised her, Ali. You had no right to do so."

Ali spluttered his defense as if grasping for more reasons to justify his actions. "Well...you need to cover your hair when you are outside. That is what honorable girls do. Besides..."

Ahmad interrupted his son with a firm voice. "Do you think your mother is dishonorable, Ali? She doesn't cover her hair. Would you become abusive with her as well? It seems the time has come to discuss certain matters. Ali, go to your room, now."

Ali stiffened his shoulders as he walked away.

"You will never force me to cover my hair," Rana yelled defiantly after him. She ran to her room and spent the rest of the morning crying in her bed.

AHMAD DECIDED TO GO TO HIS SON IMMEDIATELY. THIS BEHAVIOR would not stand. He could hardly recognize the son he had raised. As Ahmad entered his son's room, he saw Ali sitting on his bed with a book in his hand, looking as if he hadn't just lost himself in a fit of rage a few moments earlier. It truly disturbed Ahmad.

"What is happening to you, Ali? Where did this anger and fanaticism come from?" Ahmad was puzzled. "You of all people should know better when it comes to the treatment of our precious females in the family."

"Father, you sent me, of all places, to London, the city of the *kuffar*, the infidels, to learn about true Islam, the Shari'a Law, and what our religion truly teaches. Well I have learned. You do not follow the true teaching of Islam! What I learned in a few months in the Grand Mosque of London was more than what you've taught me in a lifetime! There are imams here in our mosques who are corrupt and do not teach the true Islam. They are afraid to teach the truth as it is written, but in London where there is freedom of religion, the imams can teach the truth of Islam without any fear!" Ali argued, breathing heavily.

"Do you hear yourself, Ali?" his father asked with astonishment. "I sent you there for a well-rounded education. I sent you there for a better appreciation of our religious beliefs and an opportunity to

74

study and learn from great leaders. I did not send you to London only to have you fall in with the fanatical factions of Islam. It is abhorrent. If you repeat what you have said in this city you may be able to appreciate what the word 'freedom' means once you are placed behind bars," Ahmad said fiercely.

"Following the teachings of our religion has nothing to do with the false freedom imposed on us by the west. The sheikh in London stressed to us that if our nation of Islam does not go back to the roots, to the Caliphate system of rule, there will be no return to the Glory of Islam. It was in our history where Muslims conquered and spread the word of Allah to the whole known world. Only because of weaklings and enemies of Islam, who associated themselves with the western world and their way of life, did we fall into this status of a third-world nation. Our women need to cover themselves! Father, I do not understand you. All your life you taught us to be good Muslims. All these years we have gone to the Mosque and heard the sheikh preaching modesty in women and correcting them when they broke the Shari'a Law. I know you have never followed any of the rules! I learned in London that women must cover themselves in order to avoid causing men to fall into sin by seeing their hair, wrists, and ankles! Surah Al Nisa 4, verse 34 commands men to make sure that women are righteous and obedient. Now..."

"Do you think men are animals and they follow only their sexual desires? Saying that a woman should cover herself from head to toe for you to avoid sin is the lowest of insults to my dignity and yours! Don't you have self-control? Are you not man enough or moral enough to make the right decisions no matter what a woman wears? A true man does not blame a woman for his own sinful behavior. You, my son, are not going to lecture me about what is right and what is wrong," Ahmad said, angered and shocked at what his son was saying. "Ali, you stop right now. Religion is not by appearance and showmanship of pious and religious prayers. Religion is in the heart and soul of men. How many times did you deserve to be punished by beatings, according to the Quran standards, yet I never raised a hand to you? I knew it was wrong. I corrected you with logic and loving kindness.

Perhaps I should have beaten you as prescribed! Is that what you would have wanted? For if those laws you claim to uphold apply to your sister then they must certainly apply to you, as well."

He hoped that would get through to Ali, but the stubbornness and the flaming anger kindled in his son's eyes had Ahmed worried. He tried again. "Allah calls for mercy in his book, not what other men, filled with complexes from their early childhood, interpreted the religion to say, forcing it on people. And that is what this fanaticism is, a corrupt interpretation. You should read and understand the holy book for yourself, not just memorize the words without using common sense. You can't take everything you read in the Quran literally. You must be wise and consider what is humane, especially in these modern times."

"I have read the Holy Book, unfortunately, I never saw you doing so," Ali replied. "However, I am not going to argue with you."

Ahmed ground his teeth in frustration as his son bent his head low in a show of respect for his father. Yet Ahmed sensed the anger and frustration filling his son's heart. He would have to correct this somehow.

Yet as he left his son, he realized that Ali was correct to some extent. He never studied the Quran anymore as he knew he could not adhere to some of the interpretations and teachings that went against his conscience and against science, and what he heard the imams teach further alienated him from the religion. He never voiced his doubts or questions for fear of retribution, but he felt that the teachings were outdated and illogical. He had chosen to be a Muslim in name only, as many people did, and expected his children to do the same.

He left his son with a heavy heart, worried about this fanaticism. He wanted more for the females in his family, and he wouldn't allow his son to impose such oppressive customs upon them. He had given his family everything he had never had growing up. He wanted a better life for them. He had struggled to get scholarships and eventually earned an engineering degree. He had worked hard to accumulate wealth and provide a decent life for his two children and his wife,

Alia, who was a Professor of Chemistry at the National University. He sat in his rocking chair and closed his eyes, exhausted after the heated exchange.

This incident with his son took him back, years back, when his family was forced to flee their country.

"My dear brother, you have to understand that there are so many things that were done one thousand years ago that do not, and should not, apply today. Also, I am free to apply the scripture and do what I want as it pertains to my family without interference. The smoke of war rumors fills the air, and all that we are concerned about is covering women's heads? To do so is to miss the mark entirely. To be caught up in practices that neither edify nor improve anyone's life."

Ahmad remembered these words as he had listened to his father admonish his uncle about interfering in the women's way of dressing. It was when some women in cities of that time did not cover their heads. The next day, all hell broke loose in the country of Palestine. It had happened in the year 1948, and people had filled the streets, running away from tanks and bombs. The people left in buses, cars, and by foot across the Jordan River.

Ahmad thought back to that time, to how dangerous everything was for women, and shook his head. He prayed that his son would not pursue the path he was on as he knew it would only lead to death and destruction. All the while, he wondered how just a few months in England could have had the power to change him so drastically in such a detrimental way.

CHAPTER TEN

ALI: ENGLAND

1964

A Few Months Earlier

The enormous pine trees stood high and mighty with their thick, dark branches, hugging each other tightly, as though they would die if someone separated them. The mysterious forest was silent and eerie, hiding its secrets like riddles that could never be solved. The bushes along the edge of the forest twisted, as if in agony. The horses that pulled the carriage trotted along the path, winding their way through the forest like a snake. The path seemed endless as the sun set and darkness quickly took over the area.

Judy, a classmate Ali had met three weeks ago, had invited him to a party her family was having in honor of her uncle, Lord Kirk. He had reached his 90th birthday, and family and friends were gathering to celebrate. Ali was very excited. Judy was a pretty girl, and he knew that her father was a successful businessman. He owned a couple of factories that made hand tools.

Ali sat inside the coach admiring the beauty of the land. The rolling hills and meadows boasted all shades of green with forests scattered in clusters throughout. It was different from the city where the streets were always crowded, noise of traffic and the smell of exhaust filled the air. In the countryside it was quiet and peaceful.

He only had to say to the driver that he needed to visit Lord Kirk's residence, as Judy had told him, and the driver knew exactly where to go. The family was very well known so the driver did not need any further instruction. He watched the moonbeams seeping through the forest trees. A strange feeling came over him as civilization was left behind. A sense of going back in time filled him. The horses started galloping up a hill, where the forest continued until they reached a clearing, and in the distance stood a majestic castle on top of the hill. As they approached the foot of the hill, which the castle sat upon, Ali's jaw fell open at the sight before him.

The castle was perched high on a cliff, facing the raging sea. Gray stones glittered in the moonlight, tarots peaking in the sky. As Ali approached the castle, he thought he was making a mistake. At home, many castles had been built a long time ago, but now they were in ruins, nothing had really stood the test of time like this castle.

He stared in awe at the high walls. As he stepped out of the carriage, he saw a knight, riding from the west side of the castle, bursting across the drawbridge on a white horse, draped with a colorful sash and holding his helmet and his sword. The knight appeared arrogant, full of pride in his red, blue, and yellow armor. The knight stopped at the high gate and stood at attention. Ali shook his head, wondering if this was real or if it was his imagination playing tricks on him.

Judy had told him it would be a special day, but never in his wildest dreams had he expected the sight before him. It was like a scene from a movie; not from this day and age. Ali's driver steered the horses over the drawbridge where the knight stood. Ali stared at him as he passed by. Once past the gate, the carriage rolled through the gardens, planted with flowers resting in their beds, emitting an exhilarating fragrance that filled the air.

Ali stepped out of the carriage and looked up the ornate staircase before him. A footman guided the carriage driver to the stables. There were thirty wide steps. On either side of the staircase stood two huge lions carved in white marble. The steps were lit with torches which led the way to an enormous oak wood gate. Judy waited at the top of the steps, smiling at Ali, her long blonde hair blowing with the night breeze around her face.

"Hello, Ali, welcome." Judy started to go down the stairs to meet Ali.

"Hello, Judy. This place is magnificent. Do you really live here?" Ali asked in wonder.

"No, Ali, my uncle does." Judy opened her arms and hugged Ali, who was taken aback. He returned her hug reluctantly. He had never been in such close proximity to the opposite sex. It simply wasn't done in his culture.

"Come, follow me. I will give you a tour before I show you your quarters." Judy took Ali's hand and pulled him behind her.

The huge gate opened with a squeal, shattering the silence of the night. They entered a large hall that was dark, except for a blue beam of light that flickered from one corner near the spiral stairway which was positioned in the middle of the room.

Ali shook his head in puzzlement. "Why is there no one here?"

"The party is tomorrow, and this part of the castle is uninhabited. This is the part of the castle where visitors come to learn about the history of the area and the culture. It's like a museum."

"Oh, I am sorry, I misunderstood." Ali began to wonder if Judy had intentionally invited him a night early to spend time alone together. Before going to university, he had heard that European girls were forward with men, but he had not experienced this yet. He was beginning to feel more confident about her intentions.

"There is no need to be sorry. I expected you to spend the weekend here. There will be a hunting party tomorrow morning. When everybody is back, we will be having jousting games in the afternoon, and then the big dance tomorrow night," Judy explained.

"But I've never..." Ali muttered.

"Ali, do not worry, believe me. I will not leave your side," Judy reassured him. "Just follow me now and enjoy the tour."

Beams of light coming from candelabras lit the second floor. These candles sat on marble stands in the corners of the hallways, casting shadows on closed doors.

Judy opened a door. Crystal chandeliers lit the room with a bright light seeping through the door to the other hallway. It was a dining room with a very large, round table covered with a beautifully embroidered tablecloth. The table could seat twenty people easily. The embroidery around the edges presented a colorful variety of blooming flowers; lovebirds kissed and snuggled among the leaves. The table was set with the most exotic types of foods, fruits, and drinks. Crystal glasses were filled with mouthwatering liquids, waiting for tender lips to sip whatever drink one chose.

"We will be dining here in about an hour." Judy looked to be enjoying the expression of bewilderment on Ali's face.

He smiled, reveling in the joy that she obviously felt at sharing this beauty, culture and history with him. Her family home was something of a tourist attraction, and she was clearly very proud of it. He thought it considerate of her to share this with him, knowing he was from the desert lands and had never seen anything quite like it.

In one corner of the room, a violin, drum, guitar, and saxophone sat upon stands, waiting for the party as if they had never been used before. The portraits hanging on the walls told stories of times when banquets were enjoyed by the beautiful women and handsome men portrayed in them.

The velvet turquoise drapes that covered the arched windows carried the same designs of flowers and birds embroidered on the tablecloth. The floor was tiled with marble, shining and reflecting the chandeliers' light.

"Amazing!" That was all Ali could utter. She beamed up at him, and something in his chest tightened at her lovely smile.

Ali followed Judy up the winding stairs which led to another larger hallway with a corridor to the right. Here the sense of ancient history overwhelmed him. Old paintings hung on the walls; trophies, swords, spears, and knight suits were displayed along the corridor. The only light came from torches lining the old brick walls.

Ali moved in silence behind Judy along the twisting corridors until they reached a spacious hall. The large hall was illuminated with modern chandelier lights hanging from the ceiling. It was pentagon in shape with arched windows around the perimeter. Couches, richly covered with embroidered cloth, were scattered around the spacious room.

Judy opened a nearby door and said, "Here we are, Ali. These are your quarters."

To his amazement, Ali stood in a huge room with a bed covered in royal blue velvet sheets. A chest of drawers stood near the bed. There were side lamps positioned on cabinets carved with all kinds of shapes, and Persian carpets covered the floor, giving the room a warm feeling. Blue velvet drapes covered the walls.

"There are men's clothes in the closets. Choose what fits. Tonight is casual, so no need to be dressed up in formal clothing," Judy said, smiling with delight at his reaction.

Ali wondered how many other men Judy had brought here before. Why else would there be men's clothes in various sizes hanging in the closet?

"Thank you, Judy, this is just wonderful." Ali looked around. "I would like to accompany you to the dinner table."

She nodded with a smile. "I would love that. I'll meet you here in forty-five minutes if that is okay."

Judy left Ali to prepare himself for dinner. Ali moved slowly to one of the doors and opened it. It was a bathroom equipped with every necessity, even running water. This did not match the old castle style, however, it was a relief to have it available.

Ali drew a bath and soaked in the hot water and bubbles. He rested his head on the edge and closed his eyes. Thoughts of Judy flooded his mind. He was nervous about how he could approach her romantically, but he felt more confident with each moment.

Ali opened his eyes when the water went cold. He stepped out and wrapped himself with towels already set on a stool. He looked at his watch and thought Judy would come any minute. He quickly dressed and was ready when she knocked on his door.

Although it was contrary to his religious upbringing, Ali decided to follow the lead of the host and did not object when his glass was filled with wine. Judy's father stood up and raised a toast to Lord Kirk, wishing him many happy returns of the day. He turned to Ali and welcomed him, and they all started eating, talking, and laughing.

"My boy, how old are you?" Lord Kirk asked Ali.

"I am seventeen, sir."

"Ah, what a wonderful age to be! Young, full of hope, and looking forward to adventure."

A question here, an answer there, and the evening seemed to pass quickly. After dinner, each person left to attend to their interests.

"Come, my children, come sit with me on the balcony," Lord Kirk said to Judy and Ali.

Judy gave her arm to Lord Kirk as they walked outside. The moon shone brightly in the sky with the stars twinkling like diamonds all around. There were rocking chairs along the length of the balcony that circled the wall of the castle. It faced the sea. The waves rushed along, crashing into the shore, leaving white foam on the rocks far below. Lord Kirk sat down on the rocking chair. Ali stood watching the sea.

"What are you studying, my boy."

"I am studying engineering of natural resources. My country needs new systems to manage natural resources, especially stormwater management."

"That's good, that's good. Education is the key." Lord Kirk leaned against the headrest. "Let me tell you, many years ago, when I was eighteen years old, I joined Her Royal Majesty's Army. I was sent with General Allenby in 1917, and we entered Jerusalem triumphantly. The legend said that the Turks would never have left Jerusalem until the Man of God came. When they heard his name as Allenby, they heard it as "Al Nabi" (the prophet) as it was written in the Arabic language. They thought he was the man, the prophet whom they should not fight, as their legend said, and fled, scattered all over the country!"

Lord Kirk laughed heartily. "We established the police force there and started rebuilding roads and opening schools. Missionaries came to help, and it was an awesome time in history. My best years of life were spent in Jordan and Palestine. I served under Glubb Pasha. He was a British officer assigned to King Abdullah the First. He established the present Jordanian Army. King Abdullah gave me the title Bek. Both countries were harsh. There were bandits between the two countries, killing, robbing, or taking taxation from traders and travelers. I was one of the lucky officers to negotiate with the chiefs of the Bedouins in the desert, to establish safe routes for travelers."

Ali considered this information with a blank expression. "I remember studying the events in my history classes at school." He tried to suppress the anger that always surged within him when the subject of Palestine was opened in any conversation.

Lord Kirk continued in his reminiscing. "People were very generous and kind. They were very friendly. I made many friends during that time who were very influential, including the Great Mufti of Jerusalem, Haj Amin Al Husseini, and his nephew, Abdul Qader, who was killed in Al Qastal battle while fighting the Jews. I understand that Yasser Arafat is also one of the great Mufti's nephews. These were very chaotic times."

"Uncle," Judy said, giving him a warning look.

Lord Kirk looked at Ali and sighed. "I apologize, Ali. I do not want to bore you with all these events."

"You are not boring me at all, sir. It is very interesting to hear it firsthand from someone who actually lived it, but you never mentioned Lord Balfour's promise in 1917 that gave my country to the Jews." Ali's excitement started to rise, as the subject was becoming very serious. "Did it ever occur to you, Lord Kirk, what was going to happen with the British Policy in the Middle East?"

"Dear Ali, you have to understand that the return of the Jewish people to Palestine was an eminent event. It is their destiny, and England had no choice but to appease the Jewish people. England was indebted to Wiseman for his invention of the gas mask that helped the British Army in World War I against the Germans. We also incurred a substantial financial debt to the Rothschilds. They had to give the Jewish people hope to go to their Promised Land as stated in the Bible. Despite Belfour's promise, or any other promise, it had to happen as it was a heavenly promise."

"My Lord, how would you react if foreigners came here and said this land was promised to them by God, then they took your home, leaving your people destitute, leaving you homeless?" Ali asked in what he hoped was a calm voice, but he saw the distressed look on Judy's face.

"Of course, neither I nor anyone else will allow an inch to go to anybody, but I see your point. Unfortunately, this has already happened, and years have already passed. Israel is a State that no government will allow to disappear. It is a matter of fact. We are living in different times. Should you put the Jewish people in a desperate position to be overcome by over a billion Muslims, then you can only expect the worst with the new modern technologies and arms, not only to the Middle East, but also to the rest of the world."

Ali's anger at this point turned to rage, but he did his best to hide it. He muttered to himself, "So let it be."

"What did you say? I did not hear you," Lord Kirk asked.

"Nothing, nothing," Ali said.

"My son, also remember that the British government realized their wrongdoing. Men, even men in power, make mistakes. They tried to reestablish the mandate, but the League of Nations did come out with the White Book solution to divide Palestine between the two nations. King Abdullah accepted it, but the rest of the Arabs refused even the thought of having an Israeli state. Eventually, King Abdullah was considered a traitor and was assassinated in 1951 by..." Lord Kirk tried to remember the name of the assassin.

"His name is Mustafa Isho. With all due respect, my Lord. It is getting late." Ali realized the futility of the discussion and wished to end it before he said something he might regret. "Thank you, and Happy Birthday."

"Yes, goodnight. I hope you will enjoy your stay."

Judy seemed to be attuned to Ali's distress as they walked towards Ali's quarters. Judy tried to distract him.

"Would you like to listen to some music before you retire?" she suggested.

"It is getting late. I think I will retire now." Ali approached Judy.

"All right. It is better to get some rest. Tomorrow will be a busy day." Judy stood awkwardly before him, and Ali knew his agitation was apparent. He tried to give her a reassuring smile.

"Goodnight, Ali. I will meet you tomorrow at the drawbridge at 8:30. Unless you think you'll get lost!" Judy teased, attempting to lighten the mood. "I can come get you, if you prefer."

"No, I will find my way. Thank you." Judy gave Ali a hug and left.

It was late and Ali felt very tired. He took off his clothes and laid down on the bed, wondering what the secret was behind the greatness of a nation like Britain, despite their blasphemy. Was it their history from which they learned how to govern? Their democracy? Their industry? Their freedom?

He thought of home at that moment. Scenes from his childhood of muddy refugee camps with children playing, dressed in rags, flittered through his thoughts. The hills were now crowded with stone buildings. Some with two-story apartment buildings, some with three, and little, if any, land for gardening. They were built as if in a hurry to accommodate the influx of people that had overwhelmed the country in the great forced migration from Palestine across the River Jordan in 1948.

These people don't understand the hardship of my people, Ali thought. *They don't care what happened to the Palestinians. They only care for the Jews. Stupid old man, he will be punished in hell soon enough.*

THE NEXT DAY, NUMEROUS CARRIAGES PULLED BY DECORATED HORSES arrived. Ali watched as they came across the drawbridge. He stared in wide-eyed wonder at the caravan that seemed endless, and he was mesmerized by the glittering reflection of the sun against the gold and silver rims of the carriages. Once across the drawbridge, the carriages disappeared, one-by-one, behind the huge oak wood gate.

Ali waited at the edge of the drawbridge for Judy, but with all the new people arriving, there was a lot of chaos, and he did not find her in the crowd. As he scanned the mass of people, Judy suddenly appeared, elevated above the crowd as she rode a black stallion. She wore a golden dress, Victorian style, her blond hair pulled up.

"A big surprise, right?" she said as she approached him. Judy laughed at the astonished look on his face.

"I do not know if this is real or if I am in a dream." He looked at her with some frustration. "I did not expect this. I only wore the formal suit you asked me to rent. I am going to look out of place."

"Do not worry. It is a masquerade party. I just wanted to surprise you. You look fine. Help me down off the horse." Ali approached her and lifted her off the horse, placing her on her feet. The feel of her waist beneath his hands made him feel as if his knees were going to buckle under him. The intensity of these different emotions made him stand still, holding her waist between his hands. He did it for his own support.

The games and jousting continued all morning, and colorful ribbons and trophies were distributed at the end of each game session. Ali laughed and enjoyed every moment. He was living a medieval ages event in real life. He was transported through time and cheered the winners, even when he did not know them. Judy sat beside him, and her uncle sat next to her on a podium built especially for such an occasion.

The morning session came to an end, and Judy said, "Ali, let us go to the food tables. The cooks have prepared a nice lunch, and there are some cold drinks too."

Ali and Judy sat on a nearby picnic table eating and talking. She was laughing at Ali's intense excitement at what he had already experienced.

After they finished eating, she said, "I want to take you to the West Gardens." She grabbed his hand and walked with him.

Ali's feelings for Judy grew every minute he spent with her. He had never experienced a feminine touch before, as in his culture, an open relationship between a man and a woman was prohibited. In his mind, any flirtation was considered a Western sexual invitation, and only marriage should heal the frustrations of the youth. He was taught that the open declaration of emotions, depicted in the movies, was a weakness that should not be displayed. However, he was totally smitten by the time they finished the garden tour. In the middle of the garden, he turned to Judy, held her, and kissed her suddenly.

Judy, surprised by his action, pushed him back and became angry.

"What are you doing, Ali? We are friends. We just got to know each other!"

"You held my hand! Come now, Judy, you have been flirting with me since I arrived. You've practically thrown yourself at me, and now you are angry because I acted on your invitation to enjoy your body?"

She looked at him in shock. "Just because I was being nice to you, it does not mean I am going to have sex with you." She angrily spat the words.

Ali was humiliated by her rejection. He looked at her and said, "I am sorry if I offended you. Excuse me. I will leave immediately."

Judy looked immediately contrite. "Ali, wait. This was a misunderstanding."

But Ali wasn't listening, too confused by her actions coupled with his culture and upbringing. To be rejected after such overt flirtations was unbearable. This was the danger of Western culture.

He turned towards the stables and saw the man who had driven him there taking care of the horses. The driver saw the angry face of Ali, did not say a word, and got the horses and the carriage ready.

Ali went back to London.

"To the second and third Muslim generations in this country, I say, do not be deceived by fake freedoms offered to the people by the so-called Western Democracy. Things might look attractive, but they will lead to hell. They might be living in a heavenly world. Islam offers us a much better life now on Earth and in eternity in heaven. Our women should be warned. They should always wear the traditional Islamic dress. They shall never wear or act like the British women. Our young men are professors in Western universities. They are students and even members of the military in these countries. We have people who are ready to sacrifice their lives for our common and holy cause."

Ali nodded in agreement. Judy's Western upbringing had caused him pain. The British had done nothing but cause the Muslims pain.

"Brethren, there will be no World War because the present silent war will put us at the top of the world. We will be in charge, Allah willing. Our blessed leaders decided the time is now to start our struggle and protect our values, unless we take the battle to their neighborhoods, they will fight us even more viciously in our home-lands through their devilish tools like TV, movies, and alcohol. They will deceive our young men and push our young women to rebel against our faith. They are trying to ruin our values, values we inher-ited and have protected for thousands of years. Brethren, the infidels started this second struggle almost one hundred years ago. They pretended to be our friends to help us, and instead, they have humili-ated us through their new imperialism. They are the ones who are trying to ruin our traditions and eventually our faith. They are the ones who implanted Israel in our midst. They first tried to defeat us one thousand years ago. They failed and were defeated by brave men like Saladin and others."

Ali gazed around him, proud to be surrounded by men who believed in the truth.

"Through our unity, we can achieve miracles if we have powerful and advanced weaponry. We have men who are ready to give their lives for the victory of our faith. As I said already, it is decided that the time is now. Our beloved sheikh is successfully putting his plan into action. We have secret training sites for all who are interested in the Jihad (a fight against the enemies of Islam) for the sake of Allah's final war. We brought the Byzantines to their knees, and this generation of infidels will be brought down to their knees too. Eventually, they will see the truth and follow our faith. Had their predecessors not falsified their own holy books, as Allah truthfully told us in Al Maida 5, verse 16, they would have known then the truth and followed the right path centuries ago."

Ali felt incensed. These were the teachings his own father had failed to follow. He would not repeat his father's mistakes. He would bring reform to his family and his enemies would suffer.

"Allah is truthful and has warned us that the believers in His Holy Book should not befriend or take as helpers neither Christians nor Jews. This is in Al Maida 5, verse 51. However, take this from me personally and consider them as your enemies. Brethren, Allah does not lie. Once we start inflicting casualties in the tens of thousands, they will know which is the true and only faith."

The sermon of the Imam at the mosque lasted for almost an hour-and-a-half, urging the young men for Jihad. This sermon touched the wound in his heart and the pain from his injured pride two nights before. Ali had come to the mosque for comfort, and he listened with fervor to what the Imam said.

He continued to attend these sermons and became friends with some of the other Arab students from different countries. Soon, his wounded pride and painful rejection was transformed into seeds of hatred and anger. Those seeds blossomed in Ali's heart, driving out love, reason, tolerance, and compassion. His plans changed accordingly, as he imagined discrimination in every move by the British people around him. According to his sick mind, he developed a revulsion to everything beautiful and wonderful in England.

He failed his midterm tests and decided to return home.

CHAPTER ELEVEN

ROLAND AND LAURAINE: STORMY SEAS

1194

*L*ord Catin sailed with King Richard II and his knights to France with favorable winds in the Mediterranean Sea. The journey started out well, but eventually the skies turned black, the wind blew hard, and the waves rose high, crashing against the ship. The storm raged and the captain lost control of the ship, sending them off their course. Fortunately, the captain was able to maneuver the ship expertly through the rough seas.

The crew officer tried to calm the King's anxiety. "Your Majesty, we lost direction in this weather. We just pray to remain safe until the wind calms down. The ship is strong and will hold. Our Captain is very experienced with these conditions."

"All right. We will ride out the storm and wait for the weather to calm down." The King sat with Lord Catin, discussing what to do next.

All over Europe, people gossiped about King Philippe of France denying King Richard entry to France. It was a troublesome situation for King Richard.

A couple of days passed, and when the storm finally settled down, the travelers had to disembark at Corfu Island, Greece. They then sailed through the Adriatic Sea, but another storm overtook the ship, and this time they were shipwrecked, forcing the King, Lord Catin, and his footmen to march forward through dangerous lands. It was not possible to cross the Alps, so they went to Austria to speak with his brother, the Duke of Brunswick.

Disguised as the Knights of Templar, they arrived at a tavern in the village of Erdberg. The spacious and busy tavern, which was attached to an inn, was a refuge for travelers.

"Do you think we can stay here for a couple of days?" King Richard enquired.

"No, Your Majesty, we have to move on. I saw some suspicious looking men whispering and looking at us," Lord Catin warned. "Even though most of your men went in different directions, we still have a few more than we should."

"I must rest, Lord Catin. I am tired and not feeling very well." The King frowned and looked discreetly at the three men sitting in the corner of the hall near the entrance. One of the men stood up and left, while the others continued eating and drinking.

"They look harmless. Ignore them," the King said. "We will spend the night here." He sent one of the footmen to make arrangements with the innkeeper.

Unfortunately, the two men continued to watch them, and Lord Catin feared they were already suspicious of royalty dining among them. King Richard did not succeed in blending in, especially with his men surrounding him as he gave orders. He was a knight whose authority seemed obvious.

The next day at dawn, soldiers forced open Lord Catin's door. With a sinking heart, he realized he had been right. He wished the king had taken heed of his words. He and King Richard the Lionheart were captured with little resistance from the footmen. In their nightgowns, they were shackled, put on horses, and taken prisoner.

IT WAS ANNOUNCED IN AN EARLIER COMMUNIQUE THAT KING RICHARD'S ship had not been allowed to dock in France. It was said that King Philip helped Richard's brother to revolt. News that Richard's ship was lost at sea spread all over the continent.

Angry at King Richard for killing his cousin, King Conrad, in the Holy Land, Duke Leopold V held Richard and Catin in Durnstein Castle located in Wachau Valley, Austria, for fourteen months. Holding a crusader as a prisoner was against the law, and the Pope excommunicated the Duke.

Duke Leopold handed the prisoners to the Holy Roman Emperor Henry VI of Germany. Henry needed money to raise an army to keep control over the southern part of Italy. He found this as an opportune situation. He continued to hold Richard in Trifels Castle. He requested a ransom from the King of France to release him. At this declaration, the Pope excommunicated the Emperor as he did the Duke. The prisoners were not released but were treated decently.

"I THOUGHT KING RICHARD MADE A TRUCE WITH THE SARACEN. THESE raids cannot go on. We have to do something to protect the people." Roland paced the room with anger. "Lord Salem, why don't we send an envoy to Saladin? Maybe he can control his people."

"Three years have already passed since Lord Catin and the King have left. In Richard's lengthy absence, others are emboldened to break the laws. Unfortunately, our problem is due to some descendants of the nobles who settled here from the first and second Crusades," Lord Salem said. "They do raid the caravans for vengeance. This weakens our position in negotiations. We have to talk to Stephen Longchamp of England--since he was in charge in the crusades--to take action against those who break the agreements, otherwise, no one is safe."

A knight entered the room and said, "Lord Salem, a message for you."

Lord Salem took the missive and broke the seal, reading the message. Roland waited impatiently, his concern growing as his father-in-law's face drained of color.

He turned to Roland and said, "King Richard and your father are missing."

"What? How can they be missing?" Roland was shocked at the news.

"The message says his ship faced a storm, and he had to go incognito via land. However, he was captured by Duke Leopold of Austria." Lord Salem continued reading in disbelief. "Leopold handed over King Richard to Henry VI who is asking for a ransom to release him."

"Now I understand why father did not contact us all these years. I must leave immediately to France and help find my father and the King. Ransom negotiations are notoriously slow, yet I cannot believe they have been held prisoner this long with no resolution," Roland said. His thoughts turned to Lauraine. He hated to leave her. The separation would be unbearable, but there was no other choice. He had to help his father and his king.

"It seems you must intercede on their behalf, Roland. Take Louis with you. His family is large in France and powerful. He has many contacts in Europe. He will be a good asset. In the meantime, I am going to send some soldiers to establish a garrison. We must defend the villagers during this time of unrest."

Roland nodded in agreement. "I also suggest sending an emissary to the Saracen, requesting he control his people. These raids should not be happening."

"You'll not do anything without me," said a strong, determined voice.

Roland turned around in surprise. He felt some amusement that his beautiful Lauraine had managed to hear everything.

"My darling, you can't travel with me or be present at these negotiations. It isn't safe."

"There is a ship sailing next week from Haifa to France. I will go with you to Haifa Port and stay with Aunt Catherine Kane for a while until you come back, love," Lauraine said. "It will make the separation a little more bearable."

Roland considered it for a moment and then nodded. "We will send a message to advise her of our arrival."

Lauraine threw her arms around her husband, grateful he would consider this.

"We must leave at once, my love." He smoothed a hand across her hair and lifted her chin, giving her a soft kiss. "Make haste with preparations."

LAURAINE SAID GOODBYE TO HER FATHER, HUGGING HIM TIGHTLY. SHE mounted her horse and moved with her husband and a cavalry of six men and her maid. They rode nonstop toward the port and soon arrived in Haifa. Her aunt Catherine awaited them outside her abode, a beautiful structure overlooking the Mediterranean Sea. Catherine graciously welcomed Roland and Lauraine as the horsemen took their horses to the stables.

They sat around the table for dinner, exchanging news and concerns of what the future would bring.

Roland and Lauraine spent two days together before his ship sailed for France. They spent time at the market and gathered provisions Roland would need for his journey. During that time, neither Lauraine nor Roland could shake an ominous feeling concerning the future.

The moment of goodbyes came upon them, and Roland held his wife tightly and kissed her.

He did not want to let go.

"Goodbye, my darling, until we meet again." Roland kissed her once more and left with his page.

"Goodbye, until we do, my love," Lauraine whispered after him and wiped her tears.

TWO MONTHS PASSED BEFORE ANY NEWS CAME FROM ROLAND. LAURAINE was relieved to receive the good news that brought joy to her heart. Roland was safe in France, but he was denied an audience with King Phillipe.

After being captured by Duke Leopold, King Richard had been moved to different castles to prevent his rescue. The last placement was in Ochsenfurt. The ransom was arranged by queen mother Eleanor of Aquitaine. She sent her emissaries to negotiate the amount.

Negotiations had been underway for more than a year prior to Roland's arrival. He was able to push the negotiations forward. An agreement was reached to pay 100,000 marks, an amount twice the budget of England.

Roland, through family contacts and friends, was able to arrange a meeting with Queen Eleanor's emissaries, Abbots Boxley and Robertsbridge. Roland and Louis were able to raise the balance of the ransom for Lord Catin as well.

Lauraine felt greatly relieved and hoped Roland would be home soon.

"LOUIS, ARE YOUR MEN READY?" ROLAND WAS EAGER TO ARRIVE IN Ochsenfurt. He wanted to see for himself that King Richard and his father were well.

"Yes, sir, they are ready with horses," Louis answered.

Roland and his companions rode hard, covering as many miles as they could before it became dark. He decided to camp near the river and have some rest. He hid his satchel before he went to sleep. Louis and one of his men hunted for rabbits. They made a fire and cooked the meal. They drank wine and went to sleep.

It was early dawn when Roland was awakened suddenly to a noise outside his tent. Alerted to danger, he whispered to Louis to wake up. They held their swords and slowly moved towards the entrance. Roland peeked outside and gave a signal to Louis, and with a yell, they jumped the two bandits who crept towards their tent.

The cacophony of swords clashing awoke the rest of their men who joined the fray with cursing and yelling. Two other men materialized from behind the trees.

"Hey, you bastards, what do you want? Crazy, drunken thieves," Roland taunted them.

"Your money," the thief answered, attacking Roland.

The fighting continued at a frenzied pace as Roland brought to bear his many years of training and skill.

He arttully ducked and attacked with agility, bravery, and technique. The attackers were ignorant of his fighting style and abilities. Twirling his sword in his enemy's face confused the attacker, making the attacker's sword fly in the air. Before the thief knew what was happening, he found himself stabbed in the heart. He was dead in moments.

Roland dodged the other attacker while his men kept the last of them busy. It did not take long for Roland to kill the other thief as he parried and trapped the man.

The fight had not lasted long. The two remaining bandits fled on their horses and disappeared into the forest, leaving their dead leader--along with two of his companions--behind. Roland and his entourage packed up camp, deciding it unsafe to remain in the area. They did not want to spend another night in the forest. They rode the rest of the distance until they reached the inn on the edge of the forest. He was supposed to meet the Queen's emissaries there and continue with them toward Ochsenfurt. It was dinner time when they went to the dining hall and found the emissaries waiting.

"Lord Catin, we are extremely happy to see you safe and sound," Gerard Bouillon, one of the emissaries said.

"Thank you. I have the ransom ready, and I am very anxious to reach the castle." Roland showed the emissaries the money bag.

"Be careful. We are not in a safe place. Keep the money hidden until we arrive at the Castle."

The next morning, they all rode their horses to King Richard and Lord Jeffrey Catin's location.

IT WAS THE YEAR 1194 WHEN KING RICHARD AND LORD CATIN WERE released unharmed. Roland was finally able to see his father, giving him a relieved hug.

"Roland, my son. I never thought I would see you again. And to think you have once again come to our rescue."

King Richard smiled and gave Roland a bear hug.

"Your Majesty, I am pleased to see you are safe and sound," Roland said.

"We are going back to Acre, right father?" Roland said.

"Yes, and tomorrow is not soon enough," added Jeffrey.

"Are you going back to England, Your Majesty?" Jeffrey questioned.

"No, my dear friend. England is too humid, dark, and foggy for me. I have arranged for Arthur to take the throne. It is better this way."

King Richard turned once again before he left and said, "Goodbye, my friend. May your life be full of the Lord's blessings, and you, Roland, take care of your beautiful wife. Goodbye."

"Let us go home," Lord Catin said as they mounted their horses and rode towards the harbor where arrangements were made to sail to Haifa.

King Richard never returned to England. He died in Europe with no record of when or where his death occurred.

LAURAINE PACED ALONG THE PEER OF HAIFA PORT WHILE WAITING FOR her husband and father-in-law to disembark. As they came down the ladder, Lauraine ran into the open arms of her husband, who lifted her up in the air, then put her down and started kissing her eyes, cheeks, and face. She returned his affections.

She turned to her father-in-law, hugged him, and said, "I am very happy to see you safe and sound."

Catherine hosted dinner that night, and the family spent a peaceful time together. The next day, Lord Catin and Louis rode home to Acre ahead of Roland and Lauraine to give them some much deserved time to themselves.

A WEEK LATER, ROLAND DECIDED IT WAS TIME HE AND LAURAINE returned home. Lauraine never traveled short distances in a carriage. She always rode her horse, enjoying the wind against her face. They galloped north, racing each other at times, cantering and chatting as Roland told her all that had happened with King Richard, and she shared news concerning the unrest at home.

When they were just a few miles from the gates of Acre, Lauraine felt her horse limping. She stopped and dismounted. Roland climbed down to look at the horse's hoof when men suddenly descended upon them.

The yells of "Allah Akbar" filled the air. In his position, holding the horse's hoof, Roland was caught by surprise, unable to pull his sword fast enough before the attackers jumped him. Roland tried to wield his sword, remembering the attack on the villages due to these types of bandits. Lauraine's screams and struggles pierced his heart. Anger and vengeance welled up inside him, but there were too many of them. The bandits overcame him, beating him badly and leaving him for dead.

From the corner of his bloodied eye, he watched as the bandits took his beloved from him. He slowly sank into unconsciousness.

CHAPTER TWELVE

LAURA: FAREWELL

1964

*L*aura woke early the next day. She stretched in bed, and for a moment, the remnants of her dream called to her. Roland's cries for Lauraine had haunted her sleep, only this time their separation had not been caused by distance, but by bandits. She still didn't understand these visions she kept having. She blinked her tired eyes, and suddenly the agony of what had happened the day before came rushing back. She took some deep breaths and tried to calm her fears.

"Geez! Did I really see Dad? I better not say anything, or my family will surely think I am crazy. Thank you for the visit, Father. I love you, too. Rest in peace. Goodbye."

Memories reeled in her mind's eye as she lay in bed.

Laura's earliest memory was descending a dark staircase into a basement, but it was of a new house they had recently moved into in the City of Amman. She had been three-and-a-half-years old at the time. Her father had moved them there just two years after they were driven out of Palestine. They moved to Amman where his other brothers were already established and doing well.

Laura had not understood at the time why their grandmother, who had come to live with them, kept crying. No one had found it necessary to explain to her the events that had led to her grandmother's emotional condition. She later learned that her grandmother was grieving the loss of land and identity, as so many other Palestinians had.

Eventually, the time had come for Laura to attend a school. She did not like being away from her family. Her mother, however, needed time to establish herself as a licensed gynecologist/midwife in order to earn a living and help her husband as they started their new life in Amman. Juliette was her own boss in a time when women typically did not work outside of the home.

Her cousin's family had lived down the street. It was the only place she had been allowed to visit by herself since she was seven years old. Laura, her cousins, and another girl in the neighborhood had spent time playing hopscotch together. Many peddlers would pass by selling cloth. Merchants selling cleaners for copper and iron pots or wool mattress reparations would also pass by.

One day, a man carrying a box on his back had stopped at the corner where Laura lived and started singing a ballad, calling for children to come and watch the magic box. Many children ran, paid the fees, and stood in line. After they were done, all were excited, discussing what they had seen. Laura hadn't had any money, but she noticed that other kids who did not have money had paid with a loaf of bread.

Laura ran to her house, grabbed a loaf of bread from the kitchen, and hurriedly gave the man the loaf. She sat on a stool to discover what was inside. The box was made out of light wood with four, eight-inch circles serving as windows. The windows were covered with glass. She cupped her hands around her eyes to block out the sunlight. Then she stared inside the window and discovered two magnifying mirrors reflecting the stream of moving pictures.

He sang the ballad of *Ali Baba and the Forty Thieves* while he turned a crank that pulled a painted sheet from a roll of paper. He worked the spool from the left side of the box to the spool on the right side. Scenes showed beautiful green forests, blue rivers, and mountains with the thieves going towards their hiding places carrying their loot. Laura was fascinated and did not want the show to ever end. It was a local, primitive version of a Cinema for children. Laura's love for movies and theatre was engraved in her heart forever, a memory she would cherish for the rest of her life.

While Laura's father had been healing from injuries he had sustained at the hands of Issa, her mother fell in the kitchen and broke her hand. It took six months to heal. She hated it when something happened to her mother. Laura always thought that it was her duty and responsibility to take care of everyone, but her grandmother was there and that helped. Sometimes, Laura felt as though she did not exist to her grandmother. Laura did not even receive a gift from her grandmother when she came to visit. Gifts were for the boys only. She loved the boys.

Summer was Laura's favorite time of the year because her parents would take the family to Lebanon where the beautiful Cedar trees covered the mountains that overlooked the seashores of Beirut on the Mediterranean. They first had to pass through Syria, north of Jordan, a country that was overcome with political turmoil after the king was killed. Coups and counter coups kept Syria unstable and dangerous with a few months of stability every now and then.

"Go pack your bags. We are going to Beirut. My sister Mary moved back home from Africa and we are going to see her."

"Mother, is it safe to travel through Syria?" Laura was a little worried. *"I heard at school that the military in Syria keeps fighting, and civil unrest is everywhere."*

"Do not worry. Rumors of war and unrest thrive in this area." Juliette finished packing.

Early the next morning they had arrived at the Syrian border crossing and entered the Syrian customs area. The border between the two countries had been jammed with cars waiting to move forward, but the borders from both sides were closed, and no one knew when they would reopen. They could not go back because the Jordanian borders were closed, and they had to wait in the rented car with their driver until the border reopened. They were told there was a coup d'etat in the capital City of Damascus, and until further instructions were received from the Syrian military, everything had to come to a halt.

It took eight hours of waiting in the scorching heat of the desert sun before permission was finally granted for the hundreds of cars that were stranded at the border to enter Syria. They travelled through Syria without incident and crossed to Lebanon safely. They spent a month with their relatives and had a wonderful time in the mountains and on the beaches. Eventually, the time came for them to return home to Jordan.

Laura remembered that the driver of their taxi had crossed the Syrian border from the Lebanese side and arrived into Damascus that day. Without warning, a sound like firecrackers had broken out around the car. Everyone in the car had screamed as bullets had zipped by the taxi. It was daylight but flashes of artillery from machine guns filled the street. The sound was deafening. The driver kept dodging bullets and yelling at the passengers to duck down. They did as he said. The terror that had filled Laura, and everyone in the car, was unimaginable. They kept praying to God for their safety. The driver sped to the highway. It was another coup.

Young men had fallen in the streets, either dead or injured, no one knew. Laura prayed, "Dear Lord, dear Jesus, help us." They all prayed the Lord's prayer in unison in a loud voice.

That day was July 28, 1962, when a Syrian coup had been planned but was discovered and suppressed by the government. They had passed through Syria untouched. It was a miracle. Laura knew that her prayers had been answered and her faith increased.

Laura's mind reviewed these many memories as she lay in bed. Some were wonderful and some were fearful, but in the end, she could always hear the voice of her father filling every moment.

ON THE THIRD DAY AFTER HER FATHER'S DEATH, LAURA PICKED A BIG bunch of roses from the garden, and the family went to visit her father's grave. Mark and Michael were supposed to know where Emile was buried. Upon arrival at the cemetery, her brothers tried to find the grave, and as they became disoriented, they quickly claimed a grave close by.

"You told me there was no cross or any kind of marker on Dad's grave. This grave has one. Are you sure this is right?" Laura said with tears running down her cheeks.

"Yes, we are sure," Michael said. Laura spread the roses while Juliette sat on the elevated stone of a neighboring grave.

"Why did you leave me? What am I going to do without you?" her mother lamented in a loud voice.

The relatives of the deceased individual suddenly showed up, claiming the grave her family now stood before. Laura was stunned. The relatives became wide-eyed, surprised to see children and a wife, whom they had never met before, crying over their loved one's grave.

Laura roared with laughter at the absurdity of the situation, and everyone looked at her as though she was crazy. Indeed, Laura felt like she was losing her mind with grief. She and her family went home humiliated and dejected. Anger and resentment filled Laura's heart at her cousins' neglect in marking her father's grave until they were able to build the headstone. Their refusal to escort them to the correct grave location was cruel. The location of her father's grave was now lost forever.

Laura's nights were restless. When she would finally fall asleep, dreams of Roland gave her comfort. Despite her longing for Roland, Laura finally awoke one morning to a very grim reality.

"Well, that relationship can't start. I now have many long years of caring for my family ahead of me. I cannot allow anything to distract me. Anything else, including the desires of my heart, will have to wait."

It was as if her decision summoned him to her. By the time she had finished arranging her father's papers that afternoon, Roland showed up for a visit. It was the first time she had seen him since her birthday party. So much had happened in such a short week.

After the customary pleasantries he said, "Laura, we need to talk."

Laura hung her head low so he would not see the anguish and sadness in her eyes.

"No, Roland, I am so sorry. I believe I know what you wish to discuss, but there is nothing to talk about. With my father's death, I fear that fate has decided we are not meant to be together at this time. I like you very much, but I must focus on finding a job to take care of my family. I cannot start a relationship and risk beginning a family when I must support my mother and siblings. I will not be with anyone before my sister finishes college. This will take a very long time. She is just nine years old. You should move on with your life."

She turned to show him out, but Roland took her hand. She noticed the determination in his eyes but felt even more disheartened. He had to accept this reality.

~

ROLAND'S HEART SEIZED AT THE THOUGHT OF LAURA CUTTING HIM OUT of her life, but he also knew that no matter how much time might pass, she would be the only one for him. Even without those visions they had shared, one evening with Laura was all it had taken for him to see his future in her eyes. He would respect her wishes, but he would not move on. Waiting for his beloved Laura to eventually be ready would be worth it.

"If I can help with anything, please do not hesitate to tell me. I am very sorry for what has happened to your father. I know it is devastating. I am sure you know I am saying this from experience."

"Thank you, Roland, I know you are no stranger to this pain," Laura said

Roland hesitated but he continued. "Something happened at the dance."

Laura cut him short and said, "Nothing happened at the dance. I do not want to talk about it."

Taken aback, Roland gently squeezed her hand and said, "One day, we must talk about it. However, I am leaving again for Germany to finish my Master's degree. I believe you are strong, Laura. You will be able to overcome these difficult times. I will see you when I return. Goodbye, until we meet again."

LAURA KNEW THAT LOOK IN HIS EYE. HE WASN'T GOING TO MOVE ON. HE would waste his life waiting for her. She had to do something to discourage him.

"I do not want you to write to me!" Laura's tears ran down her cheeks, and her words crushed her heart, but they had to be said.

Roland gave her a heartsick look but nodded his head with respect and quickly walked out the door.

"Goodbye, my dear, until we do," Laura said in a whisper. A feeling of déjà vu hit her in a rush as a memory of the same sentence flooded her mind.

CHAPTER THIRTEEN

ROLAND AND LAURAINE: BANDITS

1194

*R*oland's wounds were severe.

"Look, look! It is young Lord Catin!" the leader of a group of knights yelled. They were returning to Acre after their replacements arrived in the village. They picked him up and rushed to the city, taking him to the Hospitaller fortress. The physicians immediately started examining him and took care of his wounds. Roland was near death.

Lord Salem was beyond himself, full of anguish and worry. He immediately took a regiment to trace the bandits that had kidnapped his daughter. Lord Catin stayed with his unconscious son. He blamed himself for not staying behind.

By the time they reached the location where Lauraine had been kidnapped, there was no trace of the bandits or Lauraine to be found. They tried to locate the tracks of the bandits, but with no luck. However, something in the bushes had escaped the bandits' attention. It was Lauraine's sack in which she had placed her personal belongings, among them was the small box with the bracelet in it. Lord Salem took the sack and returned home with a heavy heart. He cried to God for the safety of his daughter and for Roland's recovery.

The bandits sped north through the hills towards the Golan Heights where their clan had settled on the plateau for a time.

The plateau measured 690 square miles. To the west was Palestine, to the east was Syria, the Sea of Galilee to the north, and Jordan to the south. The Golan Heights were an important source of water, especially in the higher elevations. They became covered with snow during winter which helped sustain rivers and springs during dry seasons. The majestic Mount Hermon with its white crown stood above everything. Some considered it part of the plateau that fed the River Jordan. To the south, the Yarmouk Valley marked the border between Syria and Jordan. A crater lake in the plateau was fed by surface runoff and springs from underground.

Lauraine's kidnappers rode nonstop during the night until they reached their Bedouin tents where their clan resided. They immediately took her to the women's tent, woke them up, and asked them to keep an eye on her. Lauraine listened as they forbade the women to speak to her. She was exhausted, hungry, and in pain. The moment her captor threw her on the mattress, she closed her eyes and tried to go to sleep, thinking there was nothing she could do at the moment with her hands and feet tied.

To escape her situation, she would need all her faculties clear, working, and get all the rest she could manage.

By the time Sheikh Othman ben Hammad awoke, the seven bandits came to his tent and said they had a surprise for him. One of the men went to the women's tent to get Lauraine. When he saw she was sleeping, he kicked her. She startled awake and began yelling at him in Arabic as she was also fluent in many other languages. The man was caught by surprise and released her feet, at which time she kicked his face, breaking his nose.

The man dragged her to the leader's tent. She entered a spacious room, lined with all the comforts needed from pillows to decorated wool carpets on the floor. Mattresses were arranged around the tent with colorful silk sheets covering them. Small brass tabletops engraved with intricate designs were distributed around the tent and carried hot coffee kettles ready to be served.

As the sheikh caught her angry green eyes, she noticed his intrigue. He smiled, then he frowned. The seven bandits stood in front of the sheikh, bowing their heads. He said in a very calm voice, "What a surprise! Who is the one who treated this woman with such stupidity?"

"We all did, Master. She was like a tiger. We thought you might be pleased," one of the bandits said.

Lauraine felt her blood boil.

"Did you not understand that a woman with such beauty should be treated gently? Fools! You stupid fools! You risk your lives to bring me something of value, and then you destroy that value with your ignorance!"

In Othman's rage, he called for his servant to remove the men. "Take these fools and give each one twenty lashes." He shouted, "You were supposed to watch and report what our enemy Hashim is doing and what his plans are, not to raid or kidnap anyone. Those were my orders, you stupid donkeys!" Sheikh Othman continued with his tirade.

Lauraine stood quietly and observed the sheikh with a shrewd eye. If he could be reasoned with, she would be able to get out of this situation and return home.

"Where is Zaid? Bring him here immediately." Othman's anger turned into rage. Zaid entered the tent with humiliation etched across his face.

"Where were you when those fools and donkeys of men brought the lady here?"

"Master, I was riding ahead of them trying to reach ben Zifa's camp."

"You shouldn't have left your men alone. I am angry now and will…"

"Master, I will make it up to you. I promise," Zaid interrupted confidently.

Will you make it up to me? Lauraine thought. *I would like to go home.*

"Maryam, take the lady and give her a decent wash and the best clothing. Bring her back to eat with us," the sheikh said.

Lauraine wanted to fight, to resist the sheikh, but she knew she must bide her time and behave if she wanted to gain his favor and return home. She demurely followed Maryam out of the tent, even though her every instinct told her she must fight her way out of there.

Patience. I must be patient.

AS THE BEAUTIFUL LADY LEFT HIS TENT, THE SHEIKH TURNED TO THE man at his right-hand and said, "What do you suggest, ransom? She surely looks like she comes from a rich family. The other option is to sell her to the Turks for their Harem."

"Brother, I suggest you sell her to the Turks. This way, her family will not come after us if someone talks." The sheikh's brother thought for a moment and then added, "But why would you bother with one woman? The money she will bring is not worth the risk. In addition, she is not a virgin. She has a wedding ring on her finger."

Sheikh Othman said, "True, but her beauty is very rare. Her red hair, white silky skin, and big green eyes will compensate for the lack of virginity."

"Make sure no one touches her. She needs to feel safe so she will not try to escape," Othman said. The sheikh thought she was a foreigner.

He looked up suddenly, startled to see Maryam had returned with the lady in question.

~

LAURAINE SEETHED WITH RAGE AS SHE LISTENED TO WHAT THEY HAD planned for her. She needed to control herself to negotiate her own freedom when the time was right. Fortunately, they had no idea she could understand them.

She watched as the woman, Maryam, waited for permission to speak. Maryam still held the rope that tied Lauraine's hands together, but Lauraine could not fault her. Women in these situations had to follow men's orders.

"Why are you still here, Maryam? What do you want?" the sheikh's brother asked.

"Shall I keep her tied up, Master?" Maryam asked.

Lauraine's heart warmed for Maryam. She didn't have to do this. Pleading for her comfort was a risk.

"Take the rope off her hands but keep watching her. As usual, you know what to do. Otherwise, you also know what happens if she runs away," Sheikh Othman said.

"Khaled, brother, there is something about this woman that is bothering me. As if I have seen her face before. I just cannot remember where or when." Sheikh Othman frowned and kept trying to remember.

Lauraine remained silent as he continued to scrutinize her. She thought of Maryam and what she had learned in the few minutes she had been walking to and from the tents. Maryam was considered a slave but was in charge of the sheikh's women and their children. These women cooked and served the food, took care of the households, and all of their master's desires.

From what Lauraine could tell, Maryam was the strongest and the smartest. The sheikh and his brother seemed to depend on her to keep the peace among the women.

The sheikh finally gave up on whatever thoughts troubled him and gave them a dismissive wave.

As Maryam pulled Lauraine out of the tent, Lauraine whispered,

"Maryam, take off the rope as the sheikh commanded. I promise you I will not run away."

Maryam appeared astonished that Lauraine spoke not only the Arabic language but also the Bedouin dialect. She untied her. As they walked to Maryam's quarters, Lauraine continued the conversation, sensing this woman was different from the other slaves. She hoped she might find an ally in her.

"How come you speak our language?" Maryam asked her.

"I was born in Acre. My mother's family is from Bassa village. We respect the land and its inhabitants. We negotiated many deals and traded for food and cattle among many clans," Lauraine told her.

"What is your name?" Maryam asked.

"Lauraine Salem Catin," she replied.

Maryam's face went white. "Oh my God, I cannot believe this. The sheikh will be very angry when he finds out. He knows your grandfather, George Kane. What a disaster." She appeared terrified.

"Are you married?" Maryam asked with wide eyes.

"Yes, to Roland Catin."

Maryam shook her head, her expression chagrined. "Now I am sure you will never go home. They will never ask for a ransom. They fear Lord Catin and his knights."

"Why?"

"The sheikh sent soldiers to fight with Saladin. When Saladin lost the war in Acre, the clan retreated from the planes to the Golan Heights and went eastward. Many men did not come back, and the stories told about the Lion King and your husband Roland made the sheikh decide he would never again come near Acre."

"The more you tell me, the better my chances of convincing Sheikh Othman to release me will be. I will promise to put in a good word for him with my family. Just do not say anything about me, and I promise you, we will leave this camp alive."

"He might sell you to avoid facing your grandfather. Sheikh Othman gave him his word not to raid his villages as your grandfather saved his life. It was said that Othman, as a young boy, was injured when another clan attacked his father's camp. He was left for dead."

"That is what these thieves did to my husband." Tears threatened to drench her face, but she was determined to be strong. "Maryam, do not worry. I feel I can trust you. I am planning to negotiate for my freedom. Now that I think back, I believe I remember my grandfather meeting with Sheikh Othman in our village."

"I like you, Lady Catin. I am sure you are a fighter. You are still close to your home. Do not give me any trouble. All right?" Maryam cautioned. "We are leaving this campsite, moving towards Damascus next week. You have to do what you need to do," Maryam said.

"I won't cause any trouble for you, Maryam. Do you want to leave here?" Lauraine was now getting excited, forming a plan in her mind to barter for her freedom.

"I have nobody and nowhere to go. All my family was killed in the northern part of Syria. I was bought by Sheikh Othman in Damascus five years ago."

"If I am successful and obtain my freedom, I will petition the sheikh for you to come with me." Lauraine began to regain her confidence. Having an ally in a camp like this thwarted other slave plans to hurt her due to jealousy. They went into the tent.

Maryam helped her wash and brush her cascading hair. She gave Lauraine a long green silk dress, embroidered with golden threads. It had a modest décolletage and long sleeves with decorative ruffles. A trail of green tulle adorned a small hat, creating a veil to cover her face. Many of the other women slaves pretended to need something near the tent just to glance at Lauraine and assess the situation.

"Maryam, will you come with me and be my help once I leave this place?" Lauraine asked.

Maryam studied her for a moment. "You know your eyes remind me of my sister's. She was killed a long time ago, but when I look at you, I see her."

"Does that mean you'll go with me?" Lauraine prayed she would agree. She wanted Maryam out of this awful place.

"My heart is here. Zaid ben Gassan is my one and only. I care for him deeply. Also, I don't know if Sheikh Othman will agree to that. You seem to be kind, yet strong, and you did not beg or cry in front of them. You are educated, which is rare among the women of this area."

Lauraine finished dressing and was ready to go to the sheikh's tent to petition for herself and Maryam. She couldn't help but notice the hope in Maryam's gaze even though her new friend hadn't committed to leaving with her. If she had it her way, she'd convince the sheikh concerning the necessity of a personal escort back to her home and have Zaid go with them. Whether she would be convincing enough, only time would tell.

CHAPTER FOURTEEN

OMAR: SHOCK

1964

*O*mar had been dismayed at the behavior of his friend. To embarrass Rana like that when she had simply been building a snowman with the others was an overreaction. Ali had access to the best education money could buy, yet he had returned less enlightened than when he had left. He behaved like some of the jihadi fighters Omar had seen attempting to recruit young men for holy war missions. He was deeply disturbed by his change in attitude, personality, and even his appearance. He had grown a thick black beard, and his expression was cold and unfeeling with occasional moments of fanatic zeal gleaming from his eyes.

Ali's last letter had arrived over a month ago in which Ali seemed to be enjoying his time and doing fine in school. He had written about a girlfriend and her rich history and influential family. Omar had been so happy for him. He thought that the wealth of Ali's family would help him rise above the third world status of the Middle East, yet Ali had returned seemingly influenced by something or someone working against the progress of civilization.

Omar's family, although middle class, was progressive in their thinking and always looked to the advances of the West as the future. His father owned a grocery store, and they lived a decent life. It was true that they did not have the luxury of a car or expensive clothing, but they had the necessities of life and a happy family.

Omar's initial fury at Ali for striking Rana subsided as he contemplated the events of the morning. He knew it was lawful for men to chastise women in their family, but he had never expected his friend to ever do it. He turned to go home, stepping on the wet slush that remained on the sidewalk. He was in deep thought, considering whether to confront Ali or leave him alone for now. He was at the entrance of his house when he heard Ali come back outside.

"Omar, wait a minute," Ali called coming towards him.

"Ali, it is good to see you," Omar said, choosing to avoid confrontation until he had the courage to face his lifelong friend.

"You as well," Ali answered.

"I'm surprised you returned from England so soon. I assumed you would be there for much longer. Why have you not been over to visit me since you returned?" Omar put an arm around Ali's shoulder. "I missed you, my friend."

"I needed some time to myself. I am not going back to England," Ali said.

"Let's go inside my house. It is getting colder out here," Omar said. "You must have a lot to tell me." Omar and his friend entered the house.

"Mother, look who is here!" Omar said.

"Ali, my child, welcome, my son, welcome. It is good to see you. I missed you very much." Salma approached Ali with her arms open as her usual welcome to all of her son's friends. When Ali backed away, Salmah frowned. Ali took her hand and kissed it, as was the more formal custom when young people greeted their elders, instead of the usual hug.

"It is good to see you too. Um Omar," Ali said. Casual friends, in the culture, would call mothers "my aunt" as if all of the mothers were sisters. It became formal when one called a mother "Um Omar" or "mother of Omar" because it would not be proper to call any married women with their given first name.

"How is Abu Omar?" Ali kept using the formal address for the older people. Invoking the name of the first born of a man by calling him "Abu Omar", or the father of Omar, as using these very common expressions showed respect.

"He is well. Thank you for asking." Salma recognized the shift of formality in Ali and it triggered a change in her as well. "I am going to prepare for you a nice hot cup of tea with cinnamon, brewed the way you like. It is good for this weather and will warm you up. Omar, take your friend to the guest room."

Omar looked at his mother in bewilderment. Usually, Ali sat with them in the kitchen, never in the guest room when Salmah was there. She looked at Omar with a heavy expression, and he realized she had picked up on Ali's strange behavior. The familiarity between Ali and his mother was gone. It was all formalities now. Salmah and Omar knew all too well what Ali's looks and responses to her meant. He saw that his mother's heart broke for him that night.

Ali sat on the couch near the window. It was a warm house, even though there was no central heating. They had a pipe stove that ran on kerosene. It gave them all the warmth they needed in the cold winters.

"It surely is a cold day." Ali rubbed his palms together.

"Yes, it is. What made you come back so soon, Ali? I did not expect you back until spring."

"To tell you the truth, my friend, those infidels and blasphemers are going to send everyone to hell. I had to leave," Ali said frowning.

"What are you talking about?" Omar was confused.

"You wouldn't believe the things I saw there. Immoralities are spreading everywhere. The people there are living in sin. They drink all night in clubs, and their women, except the old ladies, are almost naked most of the time. Prostitutes are openly walking in the streets.

Tell you, man, they are pulling our young men and women who are studying there down to hell with them."

"Was that all you saw there?" Omar asked.

"It was enough for me to decide I must come back home," Ali added.

"I am really surprised at what you are saying. All your letters to me during your stay were filled with admiration for the education system, the civilization of the people, and how they treated each other. You wrote about how the people stand in line to wait for their turn instead of forcing themselves in front of others to be served first, as we have it here. What happened to your love of the culture? You wrote about the opera house you visited and the plays in the theaters that you watched. You wrote about freedom of speech. What changed?" Omar questioned.

"I was deceived by their appearances and their fake, colorful way of life. I am telling you, they have hell waiting for them, and us the spaces of heaven, if we follow the ways of our faith," Ali said in an absent-minded state, as if he was repeating a slogan and needed to convince himself.

Ali spent most of that morning talking to Omar about his thoughts and feelings concerning his new-found faith. It was his old faith, but now he understood it better with more knowledge of what the Quran and the Sunnah require the faithful to live by.

Omar listened in silence and did not argue. He had always listened to his friend and argued with him many times, but that day Omar preferred to be silent. What he was hearing from his friend was something very strange indeed.

"It is time for me to go now. I will call you later. I want you to meet some of my friends. We came back together from London," Ali said as he walked toward the front door. "By the way," Ali remarked before he left, "do not talk to my sister in the street, Omar. You are my best friend. Let us stay so."

"I am sorry my friend. I meant no insult. Rana is my friend just as you are. I would greet her with the same respect."

Ali's look turned fierce. "But she is not the same. She is a woman," he said with a sneer. "She shall be treated as such."

Ali glared at Omar for a moment, and Omar finally nodded, not knowing what else to do.

"God be with you," Omar said, choking on the words, stunned, as he closed the door behind Ali.

What Ali had said, and the undertone of his threat, did not sit well at all with Omar. He wondered what had really happened to his friend in England. His feelings towards Rana grew by the minute. He felt a knot and a tug in his stomach as he faced the reality of what was going to happen. He knew the traditions and followed them as much as anyone in the Muslim community. He was very much aware of the social standards in the fabric of society that either placed a person on a pedestal or brought them down to nothing, mostly measured by how much money a person had or what tribe he belonged to.

A feeling of desperation crept up his chest. He went to his room, hoping the shadow behind Rana's curtains was there to ease his worry concerning her safety. He felt very sorry for her, and anger built towards Ali began to fester. He could not forgive him for treating Rana like that. There was no reason whatsoever for his friend to be mean. This newly acquired knowledge of faith that Ali talked about confused Omar. He determined to find out more.

By the evening, the rain had melted away the thin layer of snow. The whole neighborhood was getting ready for the sheikh to declare the Holy Month of Ramadan as soon as the clouds dispersed and revealed the new moon. Everyone in the neighborhood would be fasting. Omar and his family kept the tradition as required by his faith except for the Salem family. As Christians, the Salems were not obligated to fast during Ramadan as long as they did not eat in public and respected the fasting people's feelings.

All his life, Omar had waited for Ramadan to come. For him it was a special time. Families got together at the end of the day to break their fast when the sun set. Each day of the twenty-eight days of Ramadan was spent at one of his relatives' homes. They sat around the table each evening with different types of food. He loved the Mansaf dish made of cooked yogurt, lamb meat, and rice and sprinkled with fried almonds and pine seeds. His mother made it the best. Then the Katayef dessert, a pastry like pancake stuffed with crushed walnuts, sugar, and cinnamon and dipped in rose scented sugar syrup to top the food feast.

They sat and talked, laughed, and discussed politics. Omar used to listen and learn about the history of his people. The stories about the immigration, the war, the fighting of Zionists, and the continuous struggle for ways and means to liberate their Land of Palestine always piqued his interest. Palestine had been occupied by the Jews since 1948.

What Omar liked best, when he was a child, was the holidays after the fasting month was over. All the children wore new, colorful clothes. High rope swings were erected in an empty field, and children paid--sometimes with bread if they did not have money--to ride on the swings.

The ringing of the telephone cut his train of thought. "Yes, this is Omar."

"Peace upon you, my friend. This is Ali. Can you go with me tonight to the mosque for evening prayers?"

"Sure, I will meet you in thirty minutes," Omar said.

"My friends are going to be there, and after prayers we are having a meeting." Ali sounded enthused to introduce Omar to his friends.

"Where?" Omar asked.

"Do you remember Kassem Noor? He used to go to the same school, but he was a year ahead of us. There will be a very important speaker."

"Wasn't he the one that you used to call 'the bully'?" Omar asked.

"Yes, but that was a long time ago, Omar. We were kids then."

"I really do not like him, especially when I remember how he taunted you with a lizard he brought to school. I still remember how cruel he was when he pulled the lizard's limbs apart. He enjoyed it," Omar said with disgust.

"Oh, Omar, people change. You know that. Give the man a chance," Ali said.

∼

AT THE MOSQUE, OMAR MET ALI AND HIS NEW FRIENDS, KASSEM, Mustafa, and Zahi. They shook hands and sat among the rest of the men, listening to the sheikh preaching. At the end of his speech, he introduced Sheikh Abu Qutaybah, who was visiting the city. He had a doctorate in Islamic religion, and he was a teacher at Al Azhar University in Egypt. The sheikh was well versed in the Quran and the Sunnah (the Shari'a Law).

He said the prayers, and after he was done, he approached Ali and shook hands with all of them.

Kassem approached the sheikh and said, "Peace be upon you. My car is in the front, and we are ready to go to the meeting."

They drove to Kassem's house. He lived with his crippled father.

"Peace on you, Abu Kassem. Allah has blessed you with a son like Kassem."

"Thank you, Master Sheikh Abu Qutaybah, and welcome to my modest home. Make yourself at home," said the father. "Kassem, get the coffee."

The sheikh sat down in the modest living room. All the young men sat on the floor around him, ready to listen to the philosophy and teachings from this affluent master.

"In the name of Allah, the merciful. Our meeting here is to guide you and tell you that our faith now, more than ever, needs young men who are ready to give their lives for Allah. The infidels and the kuffar (blasphemers) have corrupted our people with their filthy movies, their television shows, and their way of life that leads to hell. The Almighty commanded us in our Quran to do Jihad by fighting non-believers in Allah and Mohammad. If you cannot fight directly, you have to think of Jihad in your mind and heart always. I am now giving you some verses to study and engrain in your heart forever."

Omar looked around, feeling uneasy. He did not like the direction this meeting was headed. The sheikh continued to say, "Surah Al Toba 9, verse 5 states, 'Wait until the war-prohibited months have passed, make traps, ambush, seize, and kill the polytheists wherever you find them. If they repent, begin to pray, and pay the Zakat (obligatory payment made under Islamic law) then leave them alone for Allah is forgiving and merciful'. In verse 29 it says, 'Make war against those who do not believe in Allah and the Last Day, or those who do not accept and do not follow what Allah and His messenger forbid, or those who do not acknowledge the Religion of Truth from among the people of the Book (Jews and Christians), until they feel subdued, humiliated, and pay the Jizya (tax levied on non-Muslim subjects), with submission.'"

Omar kept his expression blank, becoming aware that any disagreement on his part might be met with aggression, but it astounded him to know this came from the Quran.

"In the same Surah, verse 14 we read, 'Fight them (those who broke their oath), for Allah will make them suffer by your hands, and disgrace them, and He will make you the victors over them. This will fill the hearts of the believers with satisfaction.'" The sheikh paused, watching the reaction of his words on the faces of the young men. He continued, "In Surah Al Anfal 8, verse 12, we read, 'God tells the angels: make the believers steadfast in their faith. I will fill the hearts of non-believers who blasphemed with terror, therefore, smite them over the necks and strike off all their fingertips.' We further read in the same Surah, verse 60, 'Prepare and provide all you can of power and war horses to strike terror in the hearts of your and Allah's enemies, and those who you do not know, but Allah knows them, for you shall be rewarded, and you shall be repaid what you spent. You shall not be unjustly treated.'"

The excitement in the room grew with fanatic zeal. Omar turned his head slightly to observe Ali, hoping his friend might show some sign of unease, but Ali looked every bit as enthralled as the rest of the assembled members, with an excited attitude to immediately apply what he was listening to.

The sheikh continued his impassioned speech. "In Surah Mohammad 47, verse 4, it says, 'Therefore, smite with your swords the necks of blasphemers whom you might meet, tighten the ropes when you thoroughly subdue them and take them captive. When the war is over, you can release the prisoner or demand a ransom. If Allah willed, he would have taken victory over them but that you may fight them, and those who were killed Allah will not forget their deeds.' In Surah Al Maidah 5, verse 33, it also reads, 'Death is the punishment for those who fight Allah and his Messenger, or crucifixion, or cutting their hands and legs from opposite sides, and be exiled from earth for they have shame in this world and a great torture in the end.'"

Abu Qutaybah continued, "Are any of you writing the Surah references down?"

Kassem said, "Yes, master, I am, and I will make copies for each and every one here to take with them so we can all memorize these verses."

"There are many other verses that command us to go for Jihad against idol worshipers, Jews, and Christians. Make sure to understand the following verse very well. Surah Al Maidah 5, verse 51, says, 'O Believers, take not the Jews and the Christians for friends and protectors. They are but friends and protectors for each other, and he amongst you who turns to them for friendship becomes one of them, verily, Allah guides not a people unjust.'" He paused for a moment, letting that last verse sink in.

All Omar felt was a sinking sensation in his stomach. This couldn't be right.

"You have to remember that the words of the Quran, instructions, and commands are fit for all times and places. We must comply when we can, and Allah willing, we will fight and defeat the infidels regardless of their technology and might. They lack morals and ethics, which we enjoy through the teachings of our prophet; we lack only the strong will of men. Those blasphemers helped the Zionists to steal our land. Once we really start fighting and put aside these humiliating negotiations with them, we will never stop until Allah gives us the promised final victory. We are 1.5 billion swords from Indonesia to Morocco. We can afford to fight and lose millions of brave men, if necessary, who are willing to make the ultimate sacrifice for the noble cause of Islam. They will be martyrs and go directly to heaven where the pleasures are infinite. But now we are going to take care of those leaders who were installed and protected by the infidels to suppress their own people and the true spirit of Islam."

Take care of the leaders? Omar did not like the sound of that. It came dangerously close to treason.

"We will take care of the Zionists sooner or later. Nothing on earth, even the Devil, can stop us from fulfilling the will of Allah. The United States, the big Satan, and Europe with all their power will kneel down as they did at the time of the Caliph's rule, and we will not stop until we spread the word of Allah in all the four corners of the earth. This might take some time, but the result is more than guaranteed because Allah is on our side. He is the Almighty! To Him, all men should submit. Let the infidels fight us, put us in jail, torture us, even kill us. We know what our reward is in heaven. Let them do what they can. They will lose, we will win, and Allahu Akbar and ours is the victory."

The young men seated around Omar cheered. Omar watched as the young men's faces lit up in exhilaration.

"Sheikh Abu Qutaybah, we swear by the Quran, we will follow your teachings." Ali jumped and knelt in front of the sheikh, taking his hand and kissing it in submission.

"Also, my brothers, remember you need to keep our meetings secret. As you well know, the Islamic Brotherhood is not tolerated here. Be careful, my children. May Allah bless you." He then added, "We will meet on Friday at the mosque after the evening prayers. I hope to meet all of you there. Time to leave, Abu Kassem. Bless you and thank you for allowing the meeting to be held in your home. Peace be on you all."

Peace? This sheikh bid them peace when his sermon covered nothing but intolerance and war?

Omar sat in silence as Kassem drove him, Ali, and the sheikh home. Omar and Ali stepped out of the car and waved goodbye, watching as Kassem drove away with the sheikh.

Finally, he turned to Ali and said, "I do not understand you anymore, Ali. You were full of admiration for the Western way of life. What happened? Come, come my friend. Tell me exactly what happened. I know you, Ali. You love the modern way of life, and you were never like this. You cannot hide anything from me," Omar insisted.

Ali stared at him with an anger that made the hair on the back of Omar's neck stand at attention. Then Ali's face broke into an impassive mask that chilled Omar even more.

"Well, it is getting late now. I will see you tomorrow. We will talk then," Ali said with a frown.

Omar sighed in frustration but let Ali change the subject. He couldn't force him to speak about it if Ali didn't want to. "I am going to pass by Michael's house. Do you want to come with me?" Omar asked.

"No, I will not associate myself with him. He does not belong to us," Ali said.

"He is our friend, Ali, what is the matter with you?" Omar asked in surprise.

"He used to be until I discovered the truth. It is in our teachings not to befriend or take help from among the idolaters."

Omar, extremely agitated, said, "Since when are the people of the Book idolaters? It is also in our teachings to respect the people of the Book. People are free to choose, and remember you said so. He was born into a Christian family. He had no choice."

Ali pondered on that for a moment and said, "We have to talk to him. He now has another choice. He needs to be saved. What do you think, Omar?"

Omar felt frustrated all over again. "Even the sheikh just mentioned to us the verse in Al Maida 5 about friendship with the people of the Book."

"I like Michael as a person," Ali said. "He was always there for me when I was bullied by the other kids. I know he is a good person, but he doesn't follow the true faith. A word of precaution that you may guard yourself from them. So, you see, my dear brother, Omar, we need to follow our Quran and be faithful."

"Ali, you are playing with fire now."

"It is our duty as good Muslims to try to convert people to the true faith."

"Well, you may try. Goodnight for now."

As Omar lay in his bed that night, a voice from his past surfaced, the deep voice of his teacher, whom he hated very much, came to haunt him that night. The teacher had told the class that everyone was going to hell, especially those who were non-believers. He took the rod and beat anyone who did not recite the assigned Quran verses properly. He told them that sinful people, and those who did not pray, would not only be punished on earth, but also in their grave. The bald serpent would come to them in the tomb after they died to torture them. This gave Omar nightmares every night. Fear of death filled his heart for a long time. He could not sleep or eat, and he became sick. It was not until he grew up, and Sheikh Muntaser had said this (hadith), this saying of the Prophet might not be true, which Omar immediately believed and enabled him to overcome his fears. In his head, he heard his teacher again telling the story of the Prophet Mohammad.

CHAPTER FIFTEEN

LAURAINE AND SHEIKH OTHMAN: NEGOTIATIONS

1194

The short tables were covered with all kinds of cooked food and fruits. Sheikh Othman and his brother were just sitting down on the floor cushions when Lauraine entered the quarters and remained standing, waiting for permission to sit down.

"Sit down and eat. We will talk when we are done." He appeared to slip into deep thought and began eating.

Lauraine was starving by then. However, the smell of food made her feel nauseated. She sat down and started nibbling on the rice, thinking she would feel better after she ate.

"What is your name?" Sheikh Othman asked casually.

"Lauraine Salem Catin." Lauraine watched the reaction on his face.

As sudden recognition dawned. Lauraine noted emotions of anger, confusion, and agony cross his expression. He paused. Sheikh Othman's jaw muscles tensed as he ground his teeth.

"Salem? I know your name. Lord John Salem is your father, and George Kane is your grandfather."

She nodded her head in silence, knowing this realization was enough. She didn't need to tell him how serious of an offense this kidnapping had become. However, she felt he had to know that she was not their only victim. With anger brewing in her heart, she switched to their dialect, and said, "Did your men tell you what happened to my husband?"

"They said they left the man for dead," Khaled replied, utterly surprised at her talking in their tongue.

"Like when you were left for dead, Sheikh Othman?" Lauraine raised her voice and eloquently continued. "What are you going to do with me? Wasn't it enough for your bandits to raid my grandfather's village of Bassa, kill many, rampage, and steal?" Lauraine tried to control the tone of her voice to keep it respectful but it was not without great difficulty.

At this point, Sheikh Othman suddenly stood and came towards Lauraine. She also rose to her feet as he approached. He took her face in one hand and looked intensely at her.

"By Allah! I do know you. You are that nosy, impish child with the head of curly fire." Othman was now fully enraged with his men and started yelling at his guards.

"Khaled, she is the granddaughter of George Kane. I remember her as a child when we used to negotiate trade deals," Othman continued yelling. "The stupid men, they only bring me trouble!"

"Then we will take her with us to Damascus and sell her there," Khaled suggested nonchalantly.

"Really? Are you going to be a fool too?" Othman continued. "Woman, we have not raided anyone for a year now. We did not kill or steal from your grandfather. I assume that the cruel clan of Hashim ben Zifa did that. I also remember that we were attacked in the Golan Heights by these thieves, and my men slaughtered them."

Lauraine returned to her seat as Othman's rage began to subside. He slowly chewed on his food while pensively trying to figure what his next step would be.

"Allow me to speak, Sheikh Othman. You are an honorable man. It seems that you did not break your promise to my grandfather. I have a solution by which everyone will be satisfied."

"I am listening. It also seems to me that you have a good head on your shoulders," Othman said with a smile on his lips. "This is the first time I have ever permitted a captive to talk, and I have certainly never listened to what a captive has to say."

"If you release me and send me back home, I will arrange for whatever amount of money you might get from selling me. You can send with me your most trusted man and give me Maryam, too, for I need her help, and my grandfather will never know that the bandits who kidnapped me and left my husband for dead were your men. He will be very pleased and grateful that you are taking care of me."

"Hmmm. Though I owe my life to your grandfather, I am not sure this is wise," Othman voiced his thoughts.

"Sheikh Othman, I need to tell you something in private, if you allow me."

Othman clearly enjoyed Lauraine's defiant and brave spirit, and she took advantage of this, knowing he had probably never seen or heard a woman speak so boldly before. Certainly not in his culture.

"You may approach me," he said.

Lauraine bent down and whispered in his ear, "I am with child. Traveling is very dangerous for me and the baby." She pulled back and waited for his reaction which she was sure would be explosive.

To his credit, Othman held in his anger, but she saw the tightening of his jaw and the clenching of his fists. That his people had kidnapped a nobly born married woman who was pregnant had only caused him more trouble.

He shifted in his seat. "You turned out to be a very beautiful woman, brave and smart. Maryam, take the woman and go to your quarters."

"But you did not tell me what you think of my suggestion," Lauraine objected.

"Go," Othman said with finality.

"Come, my Lady." Maryam took her hand and led her away.

"Anyway, I am still tired. I need to rest," Lauraine murmured, but her heart was heavy with disappointment and fear. She worried her husband was dead but did her best to hold on to hope.

~

LAURAINE'S IMPATIENCE FOR HER SITUATION GREW WITH EACH PASSING day, and she became very restless.

"Maryam," Lauraine called, "it has been a week since we were called to the tent. Anything new? Last night, I saw a shadow outside the tent, stealthily creeping around. I thought someone might try to enter the tent."

"My Lady, do not worry. It must be one of the guards. No one dares enter a tent without permission. Men were beheaded because of that."

Lauraine tried to feel comforted by these words, but she noticed Maryam appeared very uncomfortable and knew there might be trouble coming their way.

The clan had one hundred fifty men, women, and children, and her presence was seen by some to be a threat.

While Lauraine sat in her tent one morning, a young girl of around six years of age came shyly to the entrance.

"Come in, little girl. Can I help you?" Lauraine asked.

"May I touch your hair?" The little girl was amazed at the color of Lauraine's hair. The little girl was adorable with straight black hair, big blue eyes, and copper skin.

Lauraine welcomed her with open arms. "Come sit on my lap." The little girl climbed on her lap and put her tiny fingers in Lauraine's hair.

She looked in Lauraine's eyes and said, "You are pretty. Why do they want to take you away?"

"What is your name?"

"Hala. My father is Jaber ben Nijem. He is our sheikh's friend." Hala looked proud that her father was someone important in the clan.

"Who is going to take me away?" Lauraine coaxed.

"I heard the guard outside your tent talking to another man. He said he will take you tomorrow night." The girl stretched her arms and hugged Lauraine.

"Did you hear where they are going to take me?" Lauraine said.

"The other man said to the souq." Hala looked at Lauraine with her beautiful blue eyes. "I do not want them to take you away."

"Hala, listen carefully, please do not tell anyone about what you heard. This is a secret between you and me. Promise me to keep it to yourself. It might harm you and your family if you say anything. Come, let us go to your mother." Lauraine held the little girl's hand.

"I promise I won't tell anyone. Also, I do not have a mother, but I have a secret my mother made me promise to keep before she died last year," Hala said.

"I am sorry, little one, about your mother. You can tell me the secret, and I can help you keep it from the others. I promise not to say a word." Lauraine encouraged the girl to talk.

"She told me she was going to be with Jesus, and she was a Christian. She gave me this golden cross." Hala pulled it out from around her neck. "She said I must keep it on, hidden under my clothes all the time, and no one must see it." Hala's tears filled her eyes. "I miss her very much. She also said when I need anything and she is not there, Maryam shall help me."

"And so shall I. Now we both have a secret to keep. Let us go and eat lunch." Lauraine carried the little girl in her arms and headed to where the women gathered to eat.

After they finished eating, the little girl came to Lauraine and said, "Will you come with me to visit my mother? She is just beyond the stone fence in the forbidden land. I must not go there alone, but sometimes I sneak out and go talk to her." Hala was animated, full of hope that Lauraine would take her to her mother's grave.

"All right, take me to her."

The little girl held Lauraine's hand and walked towards a stone fence marking the encampment some distance away from the camp. But before they reached it, Lauraine heard someone yelling at her.

"My Lady, where are you going? No women are allowed to go near the stone fence. Come back. The sheikh wants us to go to his tent now. I was searching for you all over the camp." Maryam breathed heavily from running.

"And you, little girl, you should be punished for dragging Lauraine with you. I know where you are going. We will do that some other time." She picked up Hala and turned around. It was early afternoon. "Go now and play with the other kids."

Lauraine then followed Maryam to the sheikh's tent and waited.

"Young woman, we have decided to let you go as you suggested. Sheikh Jaber ben Nijem will accompany you. You can give the money to him." Sheikh Othman stood. "You are a brave woman worthy of being the granddaughter of George Kane. He should be proud of you. I owe him my life, and now I am paying back my debt."

"Thank you for your favor, Sheikh Othman, my family will not forget this kindness. I beg you to give me a sword for this journey," Lauraine requested firmly.

"Are you insulting Sheikh Jaber by not trusting him to protect you?"

"Forgive me, but I am well trained and can help protect us if need be," Lauraine said, dropping her eyes to the floor in a show of humility and respect.

Sheik Othman roared with laughter. "All right, but you have to prove it. Prepare yourself to show us before dinner. If you win, the challenger will be your slave."

"I am challenging your best swordsman. I could not save myself from the kidnapping because I was busy trying to help my horse. Thinking that we are safe because of the truce with Saladin, we lowered our guard and were taken by surprise. This time, they were your men who ambushed us."

"Very well. The challenge is accepted. I am pleased to tell you that your husband is not dead. He is injured and was taken to your city," Khaled said, not looking very pleased.

Lauraine's heart leaped with relief, but she wondered if he thought this situation was getting out of hand. After all, Roland was another witness to this crime.

Lauraine was still very happy to hear this piece of news. Peace flooded her like a wave. She was eager to prepare for her sparring match and now had more motivation to return home.

"With your permission, I will take my leave. I need to get ready for the sparring." She turned to go, when suddenly she saw a long object flying in the air above her head. She raised her arm quickly, jumped in the air, and grabbed the handle of a sword in its sheath. She stared at Othman who appeared astonished at her skill.

"By the way, I would like to take Maryam with me with your permission." Lauraine gave Sheikh Othman her most beguiling smile.

"To compensate for my men's actions, I am allowing you to buy Maryam and take her with you," Othman said shrewdly. "This match will be a great entertainment for everyone in this camp." Othman laughed loudly. "We do not have many entertaining events. If you win, you can keep my best swordsman as a slave." He chuckled and turned to his brother Khaled.

Lauraine noticed Khaled's stern look as he gazed on in consternation. She worried he found her threatening as most women with intelligence and talent were viewed.

The sheikh must have noticed the same thing. "Be careful brother. This one is not for us. Keep control over your emotions."

"I know brother, I know. I couldn't help but admire the woman. Not many of her gender are as strong. Besides, she is beautiful."

Lauraine didn't like Khaled's scrutiny.

MARYAM HELPED LAURAINE DRESS IN BREECHES, PULLING HER HAIR IN A tight band atop her head. She heard Maryam murmur under her breath but could not understand.

"You can say your prayers aloud, Maryam."

"My prayers are usually between me and my God." Maryam had to be careful with whom she shared her faith. Lauraine understood all too well.

"Maryam, you do not have to hide your faith from me. I know your secret. We are not going to talk about this now. We will have plenty of time. However, keep asking the Lord for our safe return home." Lauraine, now filled with hope, collected her courage and was ready for the challenge.

The clan gathered in a circle waiting for the competition between Lauraine and the man she had challenged. It was well known that women did not touch any weapons. For a woman to carry a sword, she had to be either a foreigner or have special permission granted in certain war time cases to help defend the clan.

Lauraine was given a round shield to protect herself. She held a sword in her hand and bravely stepped into the middle of the circle. She took an attacking stance when, to her surprise and apprehension, the challenger walked into the circle and revealed himself as none other than the head of the bandits. He was the one who had led the attack on her and her husband. He was the one who had beaten Roland and left him on the ground unconscious, yelling at his men and threatening them with punishment if they did not do as he commanded. Lauraine's anger raged, the feelings of insult and frustration building to a frenzy within her. She ran forward and attacked him with all her force, taking him by surprise. She did not wait for the rituals of the competition but rather kept on the offensive.

He was strong, light in movement, and well trained. However, she was young, fast, and her skills demonstrated her mastery. Her fencing lessons came in handy since she had no intention of killing him no matter how badly she wanted to.

Lauraine kept moving around to find a winning strike. The clash of swords continued, back and forth, when suddenly the bandit made a swift turn to relieve Lauraine from her sword, a mistake for which he paid dearly. She was prepared for him, attacking back using the same tactic and, smiling, she twisted her body so fast and charged so hard that his sword went flying from his hand, at which time she jumped in the air and grabbed the sword by the handle yelling, "Give up?"

He knelt down on his knees and said, "Here is my neck, my Lady, do with it as you wish, you won. I was conceited to think you would be easy to defeat."

Anger suddenly left her, and Lauraine bent to hold his hand, a sign of forgiveness and charity. In a loud voice meant for everyone to hear, she said, "Stand up. I need no slaves. This man's humiliation is payment for my kidnapping, and he could serve me as one of my guards, but I would like to take Zaid instead of this man. With permission, Sheikh Othman, I would like to have Zaid accompany me as payment for not controlling his men which then led to this mess," Lauraine demanded.

Khaled was beside himself with rage. He looked at Lauraine with hatred, and Lauraine saw it. She knew he was not going to leave her alone, and she had to leave immediately.

"Get ready. We will be leaving tomorrow," Lauraine whispered to Maryam.

Sheikh Othman approached Lauraine, clapping his hands and laughing. "You have my permission to take Zaid instead, and you will always be welcomed among us. I offer our clan's help when you need it. May Allah be with you." He turned and the crowd cheered.

The entertainment was over. Lauraine left the scene of the fight, listening to the gossip concerning her skill, bravery, and beauty.

Lauraine noticed the little girl take advantage of everyone's distraction. Hala trod up the hill towards her mother's grave. Lauraine felt a bit heartsick knowing she would have to leave Hala behind, but she saw no way of taking the child with her. She knew the sheikh would not allow it.

CHAPTER SIXTEEN

LAURA AND OMAR: HONOR KILLING

1964

*E*arly in the morning, anguished screams rang through the neighborhood, shocking Laura from her fitful sleep and the strange dreams of Lauraine fighting a battle for freedom. Laura jumped from her bed, threw on some clothes, and joined her mother and siblings in the living room. They were also concerned about the wailing occurring just down the street.

"These are the mournful sounds I made when your father passed away," Juliette said. "Something terrible has happened."

"Quickly, Mother." Laura grabbed her hand and pulled her outside. "We must find out what has happened and see if we can help."

Juliette pulled back suddenly. Laura stopped in surprise and turned to face her mother's ashen face.

"What is it?"

"Laura, this is coming from Rana's house."

"Oh my God, something horrible must have happened." Laura and her mother ran toward Rana's house where the neighbors could be seen gathering near the entrance. They joined the group and tried to ascertain what the commotion was about. Police soon filled the neighborhood.

Laura knew she needed to let the police handle things, but she didn't care. Her best friend might be in trouble. With dread building, she forcefully pushed her way through the crowd, running past the policeman and through the open door only to face the shock of her life.

She saw Rana on the floor in an unnatural position, swimming in a pool of blood, dead, with her head severed more than halfway from her neck.

Rana's mother stood there wailing as she stared at her daughter. Rana's father looked frozen in shock.

Laura wobbled on her feet for a moment and then ran back out, making it to some nearby bushes and throwing up. The pain in her heart was unbearable. Her mother approached and rubbed her back.

"Dear, your skin has lost all its color," Juliette said. "Tell me what has happened."

"Mama, Rana is dead. Her head was almost cut off." Trembling, she wailed and lamented the loss of her friend.

"Oh my God, oh my God! Who did this? Who could have done such a thing? Was there an intruder? Has the culprit been found?"

Laura shook her head, tears streaming down her face. "I don't know...I didn't...think...to ask. I saw Rana on the floor. That is all. Her parents look as if their whole world has crumbled."

"Come, my dear, let us go home. There is nothing we can do at the moment, and we will only be in the way." Juliette put her arms around her daughter, and together they headed back to their home. The moment they came to the door of their house, Omar came out from behind the wall.

"Do you know what has happened?" Omar asked. "I heard there were policemen at Rana's house?"

Laura's heart ached for him, knowing that Rana had desperately wanted to marry Omar. In a voice heavy with worry, Omar asked again what had happened. Laura could not utter a word. All she could do was sob.

"If you have sense, you would go home immediately," Juliette admonished anxiously.

"Why? Please, I do not know what happened! I just saw the police and the crowd in the street. What happened at Rana's house? You have to tell me!" Omar stood there begging for some answers.

"Omar, all we know is Rana is dead," Juliette told him.

After a moment of utter shock, Omar shook his head to clear his thoughts.

"Dead? How did this happen?" Omar whispered and waited for more.

"Laura is in shock right now. She saw something she never should have seen. I cannot stand here and talk." Juliette took her daughter home.

Another tragedy in her life. It had only been a couple of months since Laura had lost her father, her pillar, and now she was hit with the loss of her best friend. Would the misery never cease?

OMAR TURNED TO LEAVE AND HURRIEDLY APPROACHED RANA'S HOUSE. Suddenly, he saw Ali being led out of Rana's house. Ali was in shackles.

Omar rushed towards his friend, but a policeman held him back. Still he yelled, "Ali! What has happened?"

The moment Ali's eyes locked on Omar, his face morphed with rage. "I am going to kill you, too!"

With a demented look in his eyes, Ali accused Omar of the vilest things, including dishonoring Rana. Omar had no idea what he was talking about. He couldn't even begin to imagine how Ali had come to this conclusion. The policeman put Ali's head down and pushed him inside their car.

Ali's reaction stopped Omar in his tracks. He was stunned. The ambulance sirens filled the air.

Something more must have happened, thought Omar, as he rushed into the house behind the paramedics. When he saw the horrifying sight of Rana on the floor nearly decapitated, a tortured roar escaped his lips. Rana's parents didn't even seem to notice him as they stared at their girl and wept over her body.

He ran back to the street and did not stop. Ali's threats rang in his ears and followed him as he ran. Ali had done this. He had murdered Rana, but why? And how could he do something like this? Why would he accuse Omar of such vile things?

THE SKY WAS FILLED WITH THE ECHOES OF THE MORNING CALL FOR prayers. All the minarets of the city came alive at three in the morning, and Omar was still holding his Holy Quran, unable to sleep.

All through the night he had read page after page, volumes of verse interpretations. Books piled up on his desk while other reference books laid down on the floor all around him. He spent hours trying to understand what the verses said and the reason for them being there. He wanted to make sense out of Ali's rage. Ali had said that Omar had defiled his sister. If Ali had killed his sister due to this horrible, baseless assumption then Omar could only think that Ali had performed an honor killing. Yet how could Ali have come to such a conclusion, and how could he believe it was within his right to kill his sister?

As the call for prayers started, he stopped and held his head between his hands, tears running down his cheeks. Shock and sorrow filled his whole being. He felt as if his heart was squeezed tight, and he could not breathe. He felt that all he believed throughout his entire life was crumbling right before his eyes.

He remained unmoving, listening to the Muazen whose voice came through the loudspeakers, two blocks down the road. As the call for prayers stopped, he stood up without even changing his clothes. He threw himself down on the bed and closed his eyes, trying to go to sleep. Even though he was exhausted, grief kept its hard grip, squeezing tight. He kept tossing and turning until dawn crept in, with red streaks spread all over the sky. The command from Allah kept playing in his thoughts.

Surah Al Maidah, 5, verse 101: "O, ye who believe do not ask questions about matters that may hurt or cause you trouble. But if you ask about them when the Quran is being revealed, they will be made plain to you. Allah is all forgiving and most forbearing."

Do not ask, do not ask continued to repeat over and over in his head, but how could he not ask, and how would he understand if he did not ask? For the first time in his life, he felt he could not overcome the helplessness, and fear crawled into his chest. Omar did not leave his room for a few days. He kept reading the books, sleeping only at dawn.

"OMAR, WAKE UP MY CHILD, WAKE UP." OMAR'S MOTHER, SALMAH, HAD come into the room with a cup of tea in her hand.

Omar waved a dismissive hand and tried to go back to sleep. "I am tired, Mother. I need to sleep." Omar covered his head with a pillow.

"You need to wake up. Your father is not feeling well. He is beside himself with worry, and he wants to talk to you right now." Salma sat on the side of the bed and placed her gentle hand on his forehead.

He loved this tender gesture from his mother every time she came to wake him up. Her hand was always cool and loving. Could these gentle hands, giving him comfort, belong to what the books had described as a woman? The question came rushing to his mind. The hadith of the Prophet said women were "najas", dirty, and they were like the black dog and the donkey, the lowest category of God's creation. They spoiled men's prayers if they passed in front of them. The verse came loud and clear in his mind as he referenced the Scholar Muslim, part 9, page 338.

"Muslim narrated in his true book quoting the Prophet saying, 'If you are praying, your prayers will be defiled if a donkey, or a woman, or a black dog passes in front of you.'"

In Islam, taking a shower or a bath was not enough to be considered clean. A man had to wash before prayers with certain rituals, but if a woman touched them after washing, she was like feces that spoiled the (Wudo) or the washing of the men, and they had to wash again.

Omar remembered another verse to be found in Surah Al Maidah 5, verse 6 which said, *"O you who have believed, when you rise to [perform] prayer, wash your faces and your forearms to the elbows, and wipe over your heads and wash your feet to the ankles. And if you are in a state of janabah (after sex), then purify yourselves. If you are ill or on a journey, or one of you comes from the toilet, or you have touched women and do not find water, then seek clean earth (sand) and wipe over your faces and hands with it. Allah does not intend to make difficulty for you, but He intends to purify you and complete His favor upon you that you may be grateful."*

Disgust filled him. He could not believe that his mother was dirty. He lifted his mother's hand gently and kissed it, then he leaned his cheek into her palm and savored the tenderness of his mother's touch.

"Alright, Mother, I will be ready in a bit," Omar said.

"May Allah keep you, my son, and give you strength." His mother kissed him again on the forehead and left the room.

The thought of ignorance being bliss rushed to his mind as he suddenly realized how innocent his mother was to the teachings of their religion, as he had rarely seen her read in the Holy Quran. He had watched her pray since he was a child, and her prayers were marked in the book that laid on her nightstand. That was what she always read, no more no less.

Omar left his room to go see his father.

"Come here, my son." His father, Basem, gave him a weary smile, but it did not reach the man's eyes. Omar new the events that had transpired with Ali and Rana had taken their toll on the entire household.

"Good morning, Father. You need to talk to me?" Omar questioned.

"Your mother is now preparing your suitcase. Here is a ticket and reservations made for you to visit your Uncle Majdi in Egypt. The airplane will leave this afternoon."

Omar stared at him in shock. "Why? Why would you send me away?"

"I heard Ali is getting out of jail, and the rumors are all over town stating that Ali is going to kill you because you dishonored Rana. It is said she was going to have your baby."

"What?" Omar was flabbergasted. "That is not true, Father. I did not do anything wrong. I never touched her. He thinks I am responsible for what, I do not know. My relationship with Rana was pure and neighborly. I did have feelings for her, but I never acted on them, and she is Ali's sister. I never would have done such a thing."

"Omar, we all know you wished to marry her."

"True. I wanted to have her for my wife, Father. I feel guilty for putting you in a situation where her parents refused us, and it is true I felt strongly for her." A tear rolled down as he lowered his head so that his father would not see his pain.

"Walid, the neighbor, said that Rana told her mother she was with child by you, and that she would never marry anyone else," his father said sadly.

"So that is how the rumor was started. She must have lied to her mother to put pressure on her family, hoping they would accept my offer for her hand in marriage, not even imagining that a member of her family would hurt her like that."

"I am sure of that, my son, but Ali thinks otherwise. Until the coroner report comes out, you are in grave danger, and we are not going to take the risk of something happening to you. He has connections and knows many unsavory people whom he could hire to kill you. Leave, my son, and do not disobey me."

Omar took his father's hand and kissed it in resignation. His sorrow overwhelmed him. The light of his life went out.

Omar obeyed.

CHAPTER SEVENTEEN

LAURAINE: CAPTIVE

1194

*D*awn crept in with red skies as Lauraine and her companions raced their horses south towards Acre. Unbeknownst to Lauraine, bandits of Hashim ben Zifa were watching, as they had been told by their spies, which were planted in Sheikh Othman's camp, what had happened and when to expect Lauraine. The spies warned them that they were not facing the usual enemy. They explained to them how the woman defeated the clan's best swordsman.

"We will take our chances and follow them until they stop to rest in the evening. Then we will raid their camp and kidnap the woman. Khaled better make good about the money," said the leader of the bandits. They kept following from a distance.

LAURAINE WAS CONCERNED ABOUT THE BABY AND COULD NOT RISK

riding all day and night. Before sunset, and as they were crossing the mountain, they found a cave large enough for them to use as a shelter.

Jaber and Zaid went inside and checked the cave to see if there were any predators. It was safe. Lauraine dismounted, picked up a blanket from the horse, and stretched it on the floor. She placed the satchel that Sheikh Othman gave her on the ground. Feeling exhausted, she shut her eyes and went to sleep.

LAURAINE WAS JOLTED FROM HER SLEEP AS HANDS GRABBED HER AND covered her mouth. To her shock, she saw one of the men accompanying her, Jaber, was holding her prisoner.

"You will bring more money than what you plan to pay Sheikh Othman. The price for you will double because you are going to have a baby," Jaber sneered. He pulled her up to her feet and said, "Zaid is tied to a tree, and if you give me any trouble I will kill him. Now, you do as I say, and no harm will come to anyone. There are men coming, and now that I have given them a signal, they will be here to take you away. They were following us in the distance since we started riding."

Lauraine looked at Maryam who was on the ground thrashing about, trying to untie herself. Her mouth was stuffed with a rag, and her arms and legs were tied with a rope.

"I will do as you say. Do not hurt her. I need her to help me wherever I go."

Lauraine thought fast, trying to figure out what to do next. She needed to reach her sword hanging from the saddle of her horse outside the cave.

"Jaber, please have mercy on me. I need to go outside to relieve myself." Lauraine pretended to beg.

"No. This cave is very large. Go to the end. There is a turn to another part of the cave. Do what you need to do in there," Jaber said.

"It is too dark over there. I can't see my way," Lauraine pleaded.

"Here, take this." Jaber gave her a makeshift torch from a branch covered with rags. It was lit from the pit in front of the cave.

Lauraine took the torch, went inside, and tried to find another exit. If she couldn't leave the cave as she had planned, she had to search for an alternative escape. She bent down to go under a low arched roof and moved forward in a narrow tunnel. Intrigued with the cave's layout, she turned to her right. Inside was the most beautiful scene she had ever witnessed. The coral-colored stalagmites covered the low ground of the cave surrounding a pond. The small body of water collected drips from the stalactites hanging from the ceiling.

Beautiful rainbow colors covered the cavern. A few feet to the left revealed steps carved into the ground. She went down the steps and followed a track twisting to the right again and leading into a small room. After she had done her business, she stood and looked around. Her eyes caught something extraordinary. She realized that the cave was a hiding place for all manner of stolen goods such as gold, silver, weapons, and shields. They were piled up against the stone wall. She grabbed a dagger and hid it in her tunic. She ran toward the front of the cave. She immediately understood why this treasure was there. The thieves, who were killed by the men of Sheikh Othman, were the owners of this pile of loot, and now they were all dead.

She was sure by now that Jaber did not know about this hiding place. With trepidation in her heart that Jaber might discover it, she came slowly towards him and said, "Maryam is with you tied up. Please let me go outside. I need a change of clothes."

"All right. I'll allow it, but know I have my knife on her neck," Jaber said as he squatted down near Maryam.

As she walked outside, she saw Zaid tied up to the tree. She did her best to slowly walk to her horses, keeping her eye on the entrance to the cave to make sure Jaber couldn't see what she was doing. After pretending to look for clothes and seeing that Jaber had not breached the entrance to the cave, she quickly moved to Zaid behind the cover of the horses. Within seconds she cut the ropes with the dagger.

"Prepare the horses. I will keep Jaber distracted. If he sees what we are up to, he will kill Maryam."

"Not if I kill him first," Zaid said through gritted teeth.

Lauraine rushed back to her horse, pulled the sword from the saddle, unsheathed it, and put it behind her in her riding habit waistband as she returned to the cave.

Upon entering the cave and seeing Maryam struggling with Jaber she felt relieved. Maryam had done a good job of distracting the betrayer.

"Sheikh Jaber, please release Maryam. I am sure she needs to go too. You have a daughter, Hala. She admires you with all her heart. She told me how brave her father is. She is a beautiful girl."

"She is not my daughter. Her mother was raped before I bought her. I wanted a boy child, knowing that she was pregnant. I kept her but she had a girl instead."

Foolish man, Lauraine thought. *Hala would have been your saving grace.*

"I will allow her to take care of her business as long as you stay in the cave."

He began to release Maryam, not knowing that Lauraine had the sword. As he cut the ropes, Maryam jumped to her feet, at which moment the earth shook and rumbled again and again, throwing Jaber to the ground.

"Oh, this is good! I do not have to kill you or stain my hands with your dirty blood!" Lauraine yelled as she took Maryam's hand and ran for the horses that were untied and ready to go.

"It is an earthquake, Maryam! This will take care of Jaber." Lauraine saw Jaber stumbling towards the entrance of the cave. "Maryam, quick. Zaid is waiting."

As Lauraine and Maryam mounted the horses and galloped off, Jaber saw Zaid also getting away. He grabbed his dagger and threw it at him with all his power. The dagger flew in the air and hit the back of Zaid just as Zaid was mounting his horse. Suddenly, sand and two huge boulders from the top of the cave fell on Jaber, hitting him on the head. Blood ran down his face, and he fell unconscious, bleeding to death. Lauraine heard the sound of rocks falling but didn't look back.

The horses galloped fast, crossing the mountain and descending down to the valley. Lauraine heard another horse following them but did not look back. She was afraid that Jaber had not perished and would catch them again.

"The trusted friend of Sheikh Othman!" Lauraine yelled to Maryam. They rode as if the Devil himself was at their heels. A twinge of guilt tugged at her heart as she remembered Hala who was now an orphan. She wished she hadn't been forced to separate Hala and Maryam. She promised herself to get the little girl later when they were safe.

After a while, Lauraine looked back to see who was following them. She saw Zaid slumped over his horse. Without Zaid's guidance, the horse had fallen further behind them, running aimlessly.

Maryam saw it too. "My Lady, slow down. Zaid looks injured." Maryam screamed.

"We cannot slow down. We have to keep going. Jaber told me that he had men following us. He gave them a signal before the earthquake happened. He was about to negotiate selling us to them." Lauraine screamed her words above the wind.

"We need to make sure he is okay."

"I am sure Zaid is fine and can catch up with us. He is far better off than we will be if we are caught."

She hated to be so brutal in her logic, but the men following them would leave Zaid untouched. He wasn't their target. Lauraine and Maryam would be at the mercy of those men if they were caught. She kept riding, scanning the terrain, making sure her horse had a firm footing as they descended a hill.

Lauraine did not realize that Maryam had slowed down behind her to wait for Zaid until it was too late and she found herself alone. She stopped her frantic pace and looked behind her when, suddenly, bandits surrounded her horse.

No! How were they able to catch up to me like this?

Lauraine was captive again.

MARYAM WATCHED FROM AFAR AS THE BANDITS KIDNAPPED LAURAINE, disappearing past the horizon. Her heart dropped, knowing she could do nothing for the lady. She caught the horse bridle which Zaid rode and directed his horse after that. It took some time, but she was able to lead them to the gates of Acre.

Maryam approached the gate and asked to see Lord Salem.

"State your business. Lord Salem does not hold audience with just anyone," the guard said.

"It is about Lady Lauraine."

His expression changed, and he immediately took her and the injured Zaid to speak with Lord Salem. Miriam wasted no time in telling him what had transpired. As Lord Salem rallied his men, she prayed for Lady Lauraine's safe return.

THE BANDITS TOOK LAURAINE NORTH TO DAMASCUS. THE ARDUOUS two-week trip seemed never ending to Lauraine until they finally reached the city. They joined their clan and presented Lauraine, disheveled, hungry, and exhausted to their Sheikh Hashim ben Zifa. They planned to sell Lauraine to the highest bidder in the Damascus market.

She begged Sheikh Hashim to let her go and told him she would provide him with gold. She told him it was hard for her to travel on horseback because of her pregnancy and she was malnourished as a result.

Sheikh ben Zifa laughed at her and said, "We know what you have done in Sheikh Othman's camp. A woman like you is a treasure. We will sell you to the highest bidder. I promise you will rest, eat, and look as beautiful as the woman you are. The auction will be mouthwatering." Sheikh ben Zifa roared as he clapped his thigh with his hand.

Lauraine held her tongue though her blood boiled. She was not property and had never been treated as such, but she knew how common this treatment was among the sheikhs. Women had no voice.

The sheikh provided a sturdy, traditional camel seat (hodage) for Lauraine to travel on. Their caravan grew in numbers along the way. Some of the people who joined the caravan were afraid of ben Zifa, only joining because he asked them. Some were relatives and pledged allegiance to him. Women with their children rode the camels in the hodage seats which slowed the traveling pace.

A few weeks passed, and Lauraine could not yet cry. Tears did not come to her eyes. Her anger built every day. She was watched by the sheikh's guards at every moment, and she was spied on by women when she needed her privacy. The feeling of being trapped like a rabbit in a snare strengthened her resolve to escape if she found the opportunity, but once they entered a flat meadow land with nowhere to hide, her hope for escape grew dim.

"I will bide my time. I will escape when we reach the city." At that thought, she allowed herself to sleep. She needed to muster her strength, her cunning, and her wit.

Let them get complacent, she thought. *In the end, I will escape.*

She lost track of time as the weeks went by. Her belly started to show.

CHAPTER EIGHTEEN

OMAR: ENLIGHTENMENT

1965

Since his arrival in Cairo, Egypt, Omar found himself doing nothing of significance while living with his uncle. He submitted a transfer request to the University of Cairo, but even though his grades were an excellent referral for him, time was needed to process his registration and acceptance in the coming fall. He found so much free time on his hands, he decided to study the Quran and other books.

Confusion and sorrow made Omar restless, sleepless, and unable to think. He was at a loss as to whom he should ask regarding what he had been reading in the Quran. He feared being reproached, reprimanded or labeled as "kuffar" as questioning anything in the Quran was generally looked down upon. He was trying to find where the Holy Book spoke of honor killings, such as what Ali had done to his sister. Honor killings were allowed without trial, or even giving the accused the chance to defend themselves.

He started reading The Quran from the beginning once again.

This time he was making a point of truly studying and researching the teachings, especially if the teachings made no sense to him or seemed wrong. He had all the time in the world so he also began to study the books of the official interpreter Scholars: Al Bukhari, Iben Katheer, Al Qurtobi, Al Tabari, Sahih Muslim, and Al Jalalein. He knew he could rely on these interpretations from these scholars because when the interpretations were written, no future interpretations or changes were permitted. Muslims had relied on these interpretations for a thousand years thus far and changes were strictly forbidden. These books would endure for all time.

To his shock, he read from the history books that Uthman Ibn Affan, the third Caliph, was informed that conflict was rampant among Muslims because of the different dialect readings having various meanings. He was asked by Hudhayfah ibn al Yaman to save the Muslim Nation before they differed about the Quran. The personal writer of the Prophet Mohammad, Zaid ibn Thabit, the expert, was called upon to collect and write a unified manuscript from people who had memorized the verses, from different parchments, and scholars, after which all the original manuscripts of the Quran were burned.

He realized that no one would be able to confirm what the original verses said since all the original manuscripts were burned, and it was said that many of the men who had memorized these verses had perished in wars.

Some verses that looked easy to understand had a totally different meaning when he studied them in depth. Each scholar's interpretation of the Quran caused confusion as to the true meaning behind the writings. Most of the scholars, he realized, did not agree on one interpretation.

He thought of honor killings. In the Quran Surah Al Nour 24, verse 2, it said, "Punishment for an unmarried man and an unmarried woman who had sex was to be whipped a hundred times." It did not say to behead her as Ali had practically done to Rana. Although, he wondered if any woman could have survived a hundred lashings. The quick death Rana had received seemed far better than a hundred lashes and endless pain and suffering, but at the end of the day, he didn't agree with either punishment. He didn't agree with honor killings, period.

It was also said that a married woman who committed adultery was to be stoned, not decapitated. It still seemed like a horrible, painful death. Most of the time men escaped punishment. As Omar read the hadith about stoning, he saw that it referred to Aisha, one of the wives of the Prophet, whose teachings were taken as holy. In it she stated that the "Stoning and Adult Breastfeeding Surahs" were written on parchments, kept under her bed, and then a goat came and ate them. Omar noticed that the words were absent from the Quran but acted upon in the Surahs instructions and were still valid.

Omar felt dizzy as he questioned the stoning of the adulterous married woman. He questioned many other things that filled the books of history and chronicles of people who had supposedly lived with the Prophet. Omar did ask a few questions of the imams and sheikhs he met, nothing that would be met with chastisement, only to receive the answer, "Believe and do not question."

He read a quote in the section called "Human Rights" that stated, "Honor killings are acts of vengeance, usually death, committed against female family members, who are held to have brought dishonor upon them."

The mere perception that a woman had behaved in a way that "dis-honored" her family was sufficient to trigger an attack on her life. A woman who was raped, even if she could prove that she was a victim of sexual violence, could be killed by her husband, father, son, brother, or cousin. Were these considered human rights? As far as he could tell, even when the woman was not the one at fault, she still had no rights.

Rana's violent death tore him to the core. She hadn't deserved such treatment. To be murdered by her own brother. He could not under-stand why she lied to her mother. They could have found a way to be together without the lies, and he had never touched her even when they were alone.

He remembered how his feelings had grown towards Rana over

the years, and his heart ached that she was no longer with him. He continued to study, searching for answers that might make sense.

To Omar's ultimate surprise, he read in the Quran an address to Christians, *"O People of the Scripture, do not exaggerate in your religion or say about Allah nothing except the truth. The Messiah, Jesus, the son of Mary, was but a messenger of Allah, His word that was bestowed on Mary, and of His spirit. Therefore, believe in Allah and His messengers, and do not say three, so refrain because Allah is One* (Surah Al Nisa 4, verse 171)."

Omar banged his head with his fist, checking to see if he was awake, reading about the trinity in front of him. He was amazed that this was in his book. He kept reading Surah Al Imran, verse 55, which said, *"And God said, Oh Isa, (Jesus) I shall make you die, and shall lift you up to me, purifying you from those who disbelieve, making those who follow you above all those who are unbelievers until the Resurrection day, and to me, you* (meaning the people) *shall come, and I will judge between you about matters of adversity in which you differ on Resurrection Day."* What? Christians were above all unbelievers according to this verse? Where did this understanding come from when everyone was taught that Christians had to pay the Jizya taxes, with submission and humiliation?

Omar read that the Shari'a Law was created from both the Quran verses and the hadith, the spoken words of the Prophet by which they became (Sunnah) for people to obey and follow. The scholars also took from the hadith and the holy book, meanings and interpretation called Fiqh, or the essence of knowledge of the religion, used by imams when people were confused about how to react to certain events.

Receiving that counsel of, "Do not ask, just believe", in addition to reading the urgings in the Quran to kill blasphemers and anyone who did not believe in what the Prophet said, not to mention intolerance for other religions, made Omar realize that it was up to parents to bring moderation to raising a child in the Muslim faith, or to make the children become radicals and seek jihad and martyrdom to gain the prize of "horiat" or virgins in heaven.

Thus, the seeds of terrorism were planted in the hearts of young ones, thinking that they did Allah a favor by killing infidels and themselves. Omar was grateful that his parents had not raised him to be radical. He began to consider Ali's parents and how they had raised their children to believe. He knew they had not preached radicalism and wondered how they had dealt with Ali killing their only precious daughter.

One matter that Omar found repulsive was the teaching of incest. It hit him hard when he read the interpretation that a man can marry his own daughter if she was conceived by adultery:

Al Qurtobi, Surah Al Furqan 25, verse 54

"And it is He who created man out of water and then made him kindred of blood and marriage. And your Lord was ever Able."

These are two topics. 1. God created man out of water 2. How they become kindred by blood and lineage.

The interpretation of the first: "He who created humans from water and made them kindred by marriage and relations with blood lineage, is a reference to the origin of man that says anything living was created from water."

The interpretation of the second: "Kindred and lineage are two meanings common to two human beings. Iben Al Arabi (scholar) said, 'Direct kindred refers to the mixing of the water between males and females (sex) by Law. If as a result a child was born out of wedlock unlawfully or outside of marriage, the creation is an absolute creation and is not a true kindred,' therefore, this does not fall under the Surah Al Nisa, verse 23, that says, 'You are forbidden to marry your mothers and your daughters,' and, therefore, according to the scholar Al Qurtobi, the prohibition of marrying his daughter from adultery does not apply because she is not considered his daughter by law. So, if it is not kindred by Law, committing adultery with the daughter of the mother he impregnated is not prohibited, and what is prohibited legally, is permitted when it is unlawful."

Omar read a very important book written as a biography of the Prophet. The name of the book was *Al Sirat* by Ibn Hisham, and the story was about the Prophet's marriage to Aisha, who was referenced in the doctrine of Islam later on.

The Scholar Muslim page 1422: *Aisha said, "When we came to Medina and stayed with the tribe of Beni Hareth ben Kharja, I became sick, and my hair fell out. Later, as I was playing on the swings with my friends, Um Rumman came and called to me. I did not know what she wanted. She took my hand. I was panting with shortness of breath. She made me rest a little. She took some water and wiped my face and head, and we entered the house where women were gathered and said, 'In blessings, and plenty of good to come'. They dressed me and placed me on his lap. Nothing horrified me more than the Prophet."*

Omar continued studying and found that Muslim1422 also recorded Aisha saying, *"The Prophet married me at the age of six, and when they gave me to him, I was nine years old. The Prophet was fifty-four years old."*

Omar heard the story of Aisha's marriage at six years old but took it as false while growing up. He was stunned to read it in the scholars' books.

How could this be true? Omar pondered.

His revulsion grew when he read that girls before puberty could get married, get divorced and be given in marriage again three months later. They had to wait three months to make sure they were not pregnant. He read the interpretation from the Scholar Iben Kathir:

"...and those who do not have their period yet" from the Quran Surah Al Talaq (Divorce) 65, verse 4, which states, *"If you divorce women who have lost hope to have their period by menopause, and you were not sure, and those who did not reach puberty and do not have a period, then their stay before marrying again is three months. Pregnant women should wait until they deliver their babies, and those who mind, Allah will make it easy on them."*

Omar could not believe what he was reading. *Can Allah really allow a child of four, five, or six years old to be married and divorced and remarried again?* Omar wondered, but there it was in the books of scholars, which all Muslims live by.

After reading all the hostile, hate-filled verses against other people, not to mention the laws concerning marriage for children, Omar was drained. Regardless of the peaceful verses proclaimed in the Quran, what he had studied was more than he could handle.

~

ONE DAY, OMAR WAS WALKING IN THE ZOO GARDEN TRYING TO THINK about all he had read in the Quran and wrestling with the conflict he felt within his heart. He knew deep down that he couldn't adhere to the teachings of Islam that contradicted his conscience. He sat down at a table and watched beautiful swans swimming peacefully in a pond nearby. He marveled at God's creation and thought, *Dear God, show Yourself to me. Show me who You are. I am lost.* Omar began to pray fervently.

A couple of young men were sitting at the table next to him, drinking tea as they discussed the Bible. Many times over the years, Omar had heard his friend Michael mentioning Easter, what it meant, and how Christians believed that Jesus was the Savior of all who believed in him. Curious, and desiring to learn more, Omar gently approached the table. He introduced himself and asked, "How can I get a Bible?"

"Here, take this one, friend. I am Peter," the man offered his hand.

"Thank you, Peter." Omar returned the handshake, "My name is Omar, I am a Muslim from Jordan, but I want to read the Christian Holy Book." Omar was afraid they might change their mind and take the book away from him. He knew that they could get in serious trouble with the police for proselytizing to a Muslim.

"Omar, meet my friend, Nader. Would you like to join us? We are discussing the Bible and would be happy to share it with you," Peter said.

Omar sat down, wondering how to approach the subject of the Christian faith. "Thank you, yes, I do have some questions. Can you please tell me, in simple words, what Christianity is all about?"

"I am honored to share this message of hope with you, Omar. I will give you a brief explanation and you can feel free to ask questions as we talk." Nader began, "Christians believe in one God. Adam was the first man that God breathed his spirit into. Eve was the helpmate that God created out of Adams' rib, which represents that they were valued equally in God's eyes. Adam named her Eve because she was the mother of all living things, so in the sight of God, all men and women are valued equally to this day."

Omar was already intrigued by this idea that God viewed women as equal to men. He thought of his mother, her kindness and gentleness. It felt right to him that she would be valued as much as his father. He pondered the drastic difference between Christianity and Islam in just this one concept. He was eager to hear more.

"Adam and his wife, Eve, lived in the Garden of Eden that God had prepared for them as his children. They had a close relationship with God, their father. They walked and talked with him. God gave them everything they needed but commanded them not to eat the fruit of the forbidden tree, for if they did, they would surely die," explained Nader.

Omar thought back to the teachings he had heard about the necessity of being afraid of Allah, not seeing him as a loving father like the God of the Bible seemed to be.

Peter added, "Lucifer was an angel of light who fell from God's grace. He tempted Eve to eat from the forbidden tree. She ate and gave the fruit to Adam to eat also. Through this act of disobedience, spiritual death entered the world, which caused humanity to be separated from God. The Bible teaches 'the wages of sin is death, but the gift of God is eternal life in Christ Jesus, our Lord'. This is found in Romans 6:23."

Omar was surprised that Eve was not stoned or beheaded for her disgraceful act. That kind of punishment would have certainly been her fate had Allah been the one to command them not to eat of the fruit of the forbidden tree.

"When you read the Holy Bible, you will understand more of what we believe in. We hold the Old Testament sacred as the basis of believing in God and the coming of the Messiah, who is Jesus," explained Nader. "Jesus, who would reconcile all humanity to God and atone for the consequences of Adam's disobedience once and for all, came and fulfilled all the prophecies about himself. The New Testament is about the life and ministry of Jesus and instruction of how we are to live our life."

Peter added, "Before Jesus came, in order to temporarily atone for the sin of Adam, which was passed on to his descendants, God accepted animal sacrifice which had to be repeated every year for many generations. A Holy God must be just and merciful. Sin cannot go without punishment if God is just. Yet God loved mankind so much that he knew the only sacrifice that would truly atone for Adam's sin would be his own. Life is in the blood, but the blood of animals was never going to be sufficient to conquer spiritual death permanently. So God came in the flesh, in the person of Jesus, in the line of David, a descendant of Abraham, born to a virgin, as prophesied. The human nature of Jesus was pure and sinless. He became the perfect sacrifice, reconciling all humanity to God by dying on the cross for the forgiveness of all sin. In doing this, Jesus fulfilled the promise God made to Adam that *'He would crush the head of the serpent'.* This can be found in Genesis 3:15."

Omar was intrigued by the idea that the God of the Bible would love his creation enough to die for it in order to be reconciled to it. He was taught that Allah expected people to sacrifice themselves to earn his approval and entrance into paradise. Omar also noticed that the Quran did not discuss forgiveness of sin, only sacrifice to Allah and vengeance for acts perpetrated against believers.

Nader said, "Omar, before we knew to ask, we were forgiven. This is the grace and mercy of God."

Peter continued, "Jesus came to establish the Kingdom of God on earth, in the lives of his believers and to save mankind, his message was, and still is, love. We learn from the Bible, *'Love is patient, love is kind. It does not envy, it does not boast, it is not proud. It does not dishonor others, it is not self-seeking, it is not easily angered, it keeps no record of wrongs. Love does not delight in evil but rejoices with the truth. It always protects, always trusts, always hopes, always perseveres.'* That is in 1 Corinthians 13:4-7. Jesus said that to believe in him is to believe in God and that he is the only way to heaven. God is Love. In John 14:6, Jesus said, *'I am the way, the truth and life. No one comes to the Father except through me.'* In John 8:12, the Bible says that Jesus took the time to teach the people, saying, *'I am the light of the world. Whoever follows me will never walk in darkness but will have the light of life.'* Also, in John 3:15 the Bible says, *'that everyone who believes in Him (Jesus) may have eternal life.'* He came to die on the cross and redeem all humanity. He lived, died and, being God, he rose from the dead and ascended to Heaven in front of many witnesses."

Omar was so touched by the idea that God is love and that love was more than a romantic feeling. For God to be love meant that He was the ultimate example of love. This teaching was so refreshing and filled with hope. Omar longed to be loved by his maker, a heavenly father that showed his love through sacrifice. Omar thought about his earthly father and how he also showed love through sacrifice to his family. Omar wondered if his father would be open to the message of the Bible.

"Living out the Ten Commandments that God gave to Abraham as the Law to follow is how God wants us to relate to him and to others," Nader explained. "In order to please God, we have to forgive other people that hurt us as well as our enemies. Jesus also forgave those who crucified him, giving us an example to follow. In Luke 23:34, He said, *'Father, forgive them, for they do not know what they are doing.'"* Nader continued, "Forgiveness does not mean that there is no consequence to the offender. It simply means that we recognize that since we are forgiven by God, we must forgive others because He expects it of us. In Romans 12:19, it says, *'Do not take revenge, my dear friends, but leave room for God's wrath, for it is written: It is mine to avenge; I will repay.'"*

"The vengeance of God is nothing to be trifled with," Peter added. "When God sees his children suffering, he will act in his perfect timing. The vengeance of man will never be equal to the vengeance of a Holy God. We could never be fair in punishment, so we are expected to give what we have been given, that is, forgiveness."

Omar was surprised about this teaching, but he liked the idea that God would take care of any wrong perpetrated against his children. A shift of thinking began in his mind regarding paying evil for evil. One concept still wasn't clear to him, and he wanted to get some clarification, so he asked, "Can you please explain how God is three, yet one?

This idea is difficult for me to understand. I always thought that Christians believed in three Gods."

Nader gave an understanding look. "Yes, this concept can be difficult to understand. It is called the Trinity. Let me explain. God the Father is a person and is God. Jesus, the Son, is a person, and is our Savior, and the Holy Spirit is a person of spirit and is our comforter and guide. These three persons are separate, distinct individuals but one in purpose, leading us toward happiness and eternal life. Thus, we believe in One God who is God the father. You are one person. You are a spirit, you have a soul: your mind, will, and emotions, and you live in a body. Yet, you are one. Consider an egg. The outer shell is an egg, the yoke is an egg, and the white is an egg. Three in one," Nader explained. "There is a Quran verse that says 'to you Isa is God's Word Bestowed on Mariam and of His Spirit' mentioned in Surah Al Nisa 4, verse 171. This is referring to the Trinity."

The Holy Spirit was working in Omar. For many hours, Omar sat wondering and marveling at what he heard. He asked many questions that bothered him in the way Jesus and his Mother, the Virgin Mary, were written about in the Quran. He received all the answers he needed, and his heart was open to the Truth.

Peter continued his teaching. "It is important to tell you that I know of one terrible historical error found in the Quran which is that Maryam bint (or daughter) Imran is mentioned as the mother of Jesus, whom the Quran calls Isa. The fact is that Maryam bint Imran was the sister of Moses, who lived fifteen hundred years before the time of Jesus. Mary, the mother of Jesus was the daughter of Joachim, not Imran."

Omar was disturbed that even though the Quran was written hundreds of years after the Bible that it would clearly contain wrong information. Slowly, Omar realized that the Bible was indeed the inspired word of God. Omar knew that the Quran verses were recorded by the agreement of two scholars, rather than by direct inspiration from God. Perhaps that was why some of the stories sounded like the ones in the Bible, but they were incorrectly retold in the Quran.

Omar thought of the teachings of Jesus in Matthew 10:14 that said, *"If anyone will not welcome you or listen to your words, leave the home or town and shake the dust off of your feet."* He compared it to what he had read in his scriptures. In the Quran, the punishment for a Muslim who refused to accept the Prophet's message was beheading. For a Christian, they were forced to pay a hefty tax if they wanted to remain Christian. Omar was convinced that the God of the Bible was not the same Allah of the Quran. They could not be. The God of the Bible was a personal God, desiring relationships with his creations. Allah was not this way, but rather, an angry, hateful deity, expecting his followers to never question him.

The three young men spent hours talking. Omar had so many questions that Peter and Nader were able to answer.

"Thank you. I am sorry I took so many hours of your time. I will study the Holy Book. I appreciate all the answers to my questions. I've never been able to ask anyone about matters of faith for fear of punishment."

"We are honored to share this Truth with you, Omar. Questions are welcome in Christianity. God does not require blind faith. Now you know that all you need to do to enter into the Kingdom of God is to be born again by surrendering your life to Jesus, repent, and be baptized. Believe in him, his life, death, and resurrection and the Holy Spirit will then dwell in you as Jesus promised. Through this act of surrender, you will be adopted into the family of God as his child. Baptism represents dying to your old self and rising again as a new creation. Baptism is an outward expression of a change that happens inside of you, an outward declaration of your new faith. Do not be afraid, Omar. God does not give us a spirit of fear, but of power, love, and a sound mind. Jesus said that he would send the Holy Spirit after he ascended to Heaven and that through the Holy Spirit Jesus would always be with us. It is the Holy Spirit that teaches and guides us. He is also known as the Comforter and Teacher. In this way, God is in us, changing us to be better than we are, transforming our mind so we grow and mature in faith, and as He promised, we are never alone," said Nader.

168

They exchanged contact information, and Omar promised to call them. "Thank you again, Peter and Nader. I have much to consider after this conversation."

Finally, Omar felt a new hope. One that he had never felt before. He was able to have peace, and he slept that night with thoughts flashing like pictures in his mind, memories that would never be forgotten.

CHAPTER NINETEEN

LAURAINE: THE PALACE

1194

The souq was busy with various merchants selling their goods. Customers came from far and wide to buy all kinds of merchandise from food, to clothing, to furniture, to carpets imported from the far east and from all over the world. In the middle of the souq, there was a large elevated wooden platform where slaves were displayed for purchase ten at a time. Sometimes, performers would use the stage to entertain the crowds between slave auctions.

Lauraine was taken by the women to a Turkish bath where she was scrubbed and massaged to prepare her for sale. They used oil to shine her hair and hydrate her skin so that the sun would reflect on her locks, making her more attractive and appearing in pristine condition. She was left to rest for a while after her beauty treatment.

LAURAINE WAS LED OUT OF THE BATHHOUSE WITH HER HANDS TIED TO prevent her escape. As she stepped down the stairs behind her captors, a tall man with a turban standing nearby recognized her. Lauraine dazzled him.

While campaigning with Saladin at the battle of Acre, he had witnessed her surveying the battle from the tower. He remembered her when he visited the Village of Bassa to trade with her grandfather. She had stolen his heart, but he knew he could never even talk to her, so he created as much distance between them as he possibly could, hoping to eventually forget her. Saladin had lost the battle by then and returned to his home. Now that she was suddenly before him, his feelings for her surged within his heart. Time and distance had not altered his feelings for her. He approached the women.

"To whom does this woman belong?" he asked.

"Sheikh Hashim ben Zifa," they answered in unison.

"Take me to him now. I am Mazen ben Sultan. You women, run to him now, and tell him I am attending his tent," he ordered.

The women ran to their camp and approached their sheikh, telling him what had happened. He jumped out of his tent to receive Mazen. He bowed so low that he nearly hit the ground.

"I am your servant. Ask and I shall obey," he said.

"This woman will not enter the auction. Here are one hundred gold pieces. I am taking her now," Mazen said. He wasn't afraid of being denied considering his position as the head of the eunuchs in the Sultan's palace in Damascus.

"Thank you, Master, I accept your offer. She is going to have a baby. You might be generous enough to increase the price?" Hashim cunningly looked at the Master Eunuch. Mazen threw another hundred pieces of silver down on the table, and gently took Lauraine by the elbow. He gave her a warm smile to ease her fears, seeing the trepidation in her eyes. Without a doubt, if she had the opportunity, she would run. He could not let that happen. He had to protect her and return her to her home. They had quite a distance to travel since the sultan's palace was in the Citadel of Damascus.

Mazen and his men watched over Lauraine so that she would not escape before he had a chance to talk to her in private. Threatened by the death penalty, the men were to take care of and protect her from any harm.

The Citadel was recently remodeled, with a new tower added by Saladin. Beautiful carpets, wall canvases, and paintings were hung all over the citadel. The harem quarters where spacious and colorful. All kinds of comforts were provided. Ornamented water fountains were scattered around the yard. Gardens emitting lovely scents of jasmine, plumeria, roses, and many other plants were groomed and well taken care of. However, there were abandoned quarters that were fully furnished and ready for occupation. Mazen took Lauraine there to hide her from others in the palace.

Mazen called for the head woman of the harem.

"Jamilah, I want you to come with me to the far end of the Citadel. Follow me."

She demurely followed behind him.

"This is not a slave. This is Lady Lauraine Salem Catin. She was kidnapped and traded for money. Do me a favor and take care of her. She is not to be exposed to any prince or man of any prestige. She is with child. You can see for yourself why I am saying this. I need to negotiate her price later with her family."

Jamilah nodded and they returned to Lauraine. She lifted the veil that Mazen had placed over Lauraine's head and was dazzled by her beauty.

"I see now why you want her hidden. Do not worry, Master Mazen. I will personally protect her. I will see that she has a safe delivery for her baby. I promise."

"Where was your husband when you were taken?" Mazen frowned.

"We were together. He had just returned from Europe, and we were going back home from Haifa. We were ambushed. He was attacked and fell to the ground unconscious when the men grabbed me and put me on a horse, taking me to Sheikh Othman ben Hammad." She thought for a moment before saying, "He was kind to me and let me go because he owed his life to my grandfather. The rival clan of ben Zifa bandits followed me and captured me, and here I am."

Lauraine appeared anxious, and Mazen knew she missed her family. His heart broke as tears betrayed her raw emotions.

"Do not worry. I will find a way to return you to your husband."

HOPE CREPT INTO LAURAINE'S HEART, BUT SHE WAS SKEPTICAL OF THIS man's intentions. She didn't understand why he treated her so kindly. As they entered a private living room, Mazen beckoned Lauraine to sit down in front of him.

"Lady Lauraine, I know who you are, and I know your grandfather, George Kane. You are very lucky I spotted you before anyone else. I want to trade you for a ransom from your father. However, you need to trust what I am saying to you. Here in the harem is like any place where competition is great for the Sultan's regard. Even though Jamila and I keep tight control over the harem, and it is a very safe place, there are many women who are still angry due to their enslavement, or they are envious of those women who gain prestigious positions in the Sultan's favors. Follow what Jamilah tells you, and you will not encounter anyone here, and we will make certain that you have a safe delivery," Mazen said in a low voice, staring into her eyes.

"Then I am your prisoner," Lauraine accused angrily.

"No, you are my guest, and I am trying to hide you and keep you safe until your baby is born. You see, the Sultan has fifteen princes, brothers, and their children. Many stay in the citadel with their entourage. I cannot risk you being exposed to any of them. Most men lust after women and try to reach them by any means, even trickery. You are free to enjoy the gardens which are usually abandoned in this part of the building, although, there are some workers who tend to them. Do not roam around without Jamilah. I will visit you every now and then to see if you need anything," Mazen said.

"Why are you allowed to enter the women's quarters?" Lauraine asked.

"I am a eunuch."

Lauraine gasped putting her hand on her mouth.

"There is no danger from me or from the other eunuchs who serve the harem. That is why we are eunuchs," said Mazen, with obvious pain in his eyes. "I saw you at the battle of Acre. You were standing in the tower watching the battle, and the sun was shining on your hair." He gingerly reached out to touch her hair. "You were striking, like fire. You were the reason I lost the fight," he said, smiling. "Please do not try to run away. It is very dangerous. Lady Lauraine, I am telling you, I will escort you home myself when the time comes. It is not safe to leave now. You must be patient. Please do not be afraid, either. I promise to protect you."

"Thank you. You will not regret it, and I promise I will not run away or give you any trouble. I need to be safe, not only for me, but also for my baby."

ONE BEAUTIFUL DAY, LAURAINE DECIDED TO TAKE A QUIET WALK IN THE garden maze where she would be unseen. As she neared the middle of the maze, she heard the giggling of a woman and the subdued laughter of a man. She suddenly felt nervous about being in such close proximity to the couple, and she did not want them to see her. She hastily hid in the bushes before noticing the thorns that pricked her arms. She was sure the couple would be passing by her on their way out of the maze, so she hid quietly and tried not to move to avoid more pricks from the thorns.

"I want you to help me, my sweet lady, Sarah. If you do, I promise you will become a first concubine for the prince."

Lauraine was curious.

"What do you want me to do?" the woman asked.

"Here, take this locket. Inside, there is a very poisonous powder. You have to find a way to put it in Mazen's tea. I have to get rid of him. He has become too powerful. His influence is unparalleled, and he stands as an obstacle in the way of my advancement."

Lauraine put her hand over her mouth to suppress the gasp that nearly escaped her lips.

"But you see, I have very little contact with the man. He sees to our needs through the head harem woman."

"Befriend the woman and bribe her with money and jewelry. It will make you her favorite. Ask her to invite you to her quarters and there you will meet him. You are smart and clever, even I fell into your beguiling trap."

Lauraine heard the smack of a passionate kiss. She could not see their faces from her hiding place. She heard them leave after their romantic encounter, and she quickly returned to her rooms. Her mind was spinning with concern for Mazen. Lauraine had to wait for Jamilah to come for her daily rounds.

Intrigues and conspiracies were not new to the inhabitants of the citadel, but it was always shocking when real action took place. Lauraine paced her room, wringing her hands, not knowing how to reach Jamilah without exposing herself. Suddenly, Mazen came to check on her.

"I can't live like this, with no communication with anyone. What if an emergency happens! I am unable to reach Jamilah or you. As a matter of fact..." Lauraine was breathlessly ranting and obviously worried.

"Stop, stop, slow down. What happened?" Mazen held the frightened Lauraine in his arms to calm her down.

"They want to kill you! They want to put poison in your tea!" Lauraine blurted.

"Who wants to kill me, Lauraine?" Mazen frowned.

"I do not know his name. I was walking in the maze when I heard a man and a woman talking. I hid inside the bushes. That is when I heard them planning to kill you. The man mentioned you by name. He told the woman to befriend Jamilah, and through her she would be able to meet you and put the poison in your tea. He said you are standing in his way for promotion." Lauraine wrung her hands with worry.

"All right, you can calm down. I know who the man is," Mazen said.

"He promised she would be first mistress of the prince. They did not say which prince. Her name is Sarah."

Just then Jamilah entered the room and came to a stop when she saw Mazen holding Lauraine in an embrace.

Mazen turned to her with a look of relief on his face. "You've come just in time. Jamilah, if Sarah starts to become familiar with you and tries to befriend you more than usual, please inform me immediately." Mazen explained the situation and said, "Listen very well. Sara will try to bribe you, so you must go along with her charade. She is in for the surprise of her life." Mazen's voice shook with fury.

THREE WEEKS LATER, MAZEN ASKED JAMILAH TO BRING SARA TO THE Diwan (the Royal Court) in the main palace where women were paraded for the princes to choose from. The music and dancing stopped. The young women were escorted into the middle of the spacious hall. They wore beautifully colored silk gowns that were decorated with intricate golden thread embroideries, covering little of their flesh.

As the women paraded in front of the men, Mazen whispered in the ear of a prince who sat on a cushion with shining satin turquoise color, threaded with gold strings.

Jamilah came to join them. The prince beckoned for Sara to approach him.

"What a beautiful locket you have on your neck. May I see it?" Sarah, taken aback, was not expecting this. She reached for the chain, removed the locket, and gave it to the prince.

"Sarah, come. Mazen bring the tea. We are going to enjoy ourselves for a little while," he said as he pulled Sarah to sit on his lap.

Sarah, not knowing what was happening, suddenly realized with horror what Mazen was doing. The prince called for his guard Sharif.

"Sharif, take this locket, open it, put the contents in a cup of tea, and give it to Sarah," the prince ordered with a smirk on his face.

Sharif's face went pale. Mazen then knew Sharif must have been in on the conspiracy. Sharif looked at Sarah accusingly and did not utter a word, no doubt believing she had somehow ruined everything. He opened the locket, poured the contents in a cup of tea, and handed it to Sarah whose eyes were filled with fear.

Mazen almost felt sorry for her, but examples had to be set for such treachery. He waited for Sharif to give himself away or plead for Sarah, but the coward did nothing. Sarah appeared resigned to her fate, knowing what was going to happen. As she took the cup, she pleaded with her eyes to Sharif, who stood with a stone-cold expression. Sarah did not even ask for mercy or pardon. Realizing Sharif was not going to help her, brokenhearted, she drank the tea quickly and instantly fell to the ground. The people stared at her lifeless body in wide-eyed silence.

"Sharif, you are going to be the head of my guards. Stand there in the middle of the Diwan and swear your allegiance to me right here in front of all these witnesses."

"I swear, Master. I am your slave to do with as you see fit." Sharif knelt in the center of the room with his head bent low. In a split second, his head was rolling on the carpet, and blood splattered everywhere as Mazen sheathed his sword.

The Diwan was shut down for the day.

THE MONTHS PASSED QUICKLY AND LAURAINE'S BELLY GREW. SHE SPENT her time embroidering and learning from Jamilah how to cook different kinds of foods. Jamilah always picked the time to teach her when they were alone. Reading was Lauraine's joy. She read many books. There was a library that shelved so many materials, which no one in the harem touched.

One day, she looked for Jamilah, but she was not there. She decided to go out in the yard to walk around the garden. She picked fresh jasmine flowers and placed them in a bowl, then she sat on a bench and started to make a necklace.

Mazen approached her and sat beside her on the bench. It had become a daily habit for Mazen to never leave Lauraine alone for more than a few hours. She was grateful for his attentiveness, and fortunately for her, she was never bothered or harassed by anyone in the harem. She had done a good job of not drawing attention to herself.

"Are you content and comfortable, my Lady? You must be due any time now."

"Yes, and at times like this when Jamilah is not here, I get worried. You see, this is my first baby."

"It will be all right, Lauraine. When your baby comes, Jamilah will be ready to help you."

WHEN LAURAINE STARTED THE BIRTHING PANGS, A MIDWIFE WAS brought to her room with an assistant. The birthing was not as diffi-cult as she had expected. Lauraine had a girl and named her Johana. It was winter, December of 1193.

"Jamilah, can you please send a message to Mazen. I want to talk to him." Lauraine had become very restless as the months passed.

"He is in mourning for the death of Saladin. He is now trying to keep his position with the new emir," Jamilah said. "Mazen has good relationships with all of Saladin's sons. He had a unique position with Saladin in that he was not only the head of eunuchs, he was a fighting companion to Saladin in the battles. You have to understand that the new emir inherits not only the rule but also the harem." Jamilah said, trying to hide her worry. "I will send a message."

"Thank you, Jamilah. I will never forget your kindness." Lauraine's eyes filled with tears.

Spring brought bloom to the gardens of the palace where Lauraine lived with her baby. Johana was a copy of her mother.

Mazen could not hide his love for the child. He loved to hold Johana in his arms. Since he could not have children himself, he treated the palace children as his own, but this Johana was special. She was the daughter of the woman he loved in silence. All the tenderness and kindness he had were displayed as he picked up the baby and cradled her in his arms. If he could not show his love for Lauraine, he could revel in his adoration for the red-head Johana even though he was not her father. It would have to be enough.

After putting her baby in the crib, Lauraine decided to check on her part of the garden. She worked the soil and planted her favorite flowers. She knew she was in captivity and was never allowed to leave the citadel or go outside the palace. She needed to trust Mazen to help her go home, but the enormous amount of time that had already passed left her feeling restless. She missed Roland and was devastated to think he had missed even a moment of their daughter's life.

CHAPTER TWENTY

LAURA: CIVIL UNREST

1970

*V*ery unstable times loomed heavily.

Even though Laura and her brothers were loved and well provided for in their childhood, feelings of loneliness and alienation had taken residence within her heart. The abandonment of her father's side of the family after his death weighed upon her. To make matters worse, as Laura struggled to provide for her family, that awful sense of not belonging continually haunted her. Laura had never felt like she belonged. Her identity was not tied to a nation like her peers, who harbored strong feelings of patriotism to this country. Peers who were ready to give all they had, including their very lives to defend the country.

The knowledge that she was different because she was the child of immigrants, a member of the Christian minority, and the underlying discrimination from the locals, kept Laura on her guard. She had a hyper-sense of self-control with her mannerisms and how she treated and related to other people of different faiths. Even though Rana had been a Muslim, Laura was now even more concerned about her behavior and how it might be interpreted by other Muslims, especially after Ali had taken it upon himself to perform an honor killing, something Laura found completely abhorrent. She struggled with figuring out how to proceed, or live, or behave amongst such oppressive beliefs. She had never thought of Rana as different from herself, but now she had to recognize that there were things about Rana's religion she would never understand, and as a Christian and an immigrant she had to be careful. Isolated, with no deep connections, she somehow felt that other people did not have the feelings she had, and the deep desire to belong did not matter to others as it did to her.

Since her graduation and the death of her father, none of Laura's extended family had offered to help them. Laura felt the weight of responsibility on her shoulders. She knew she was the only one who could provide for her mother and siblings. With a huge challenge before her, she promised herself not to fail and vowed to show the men in her family that she would take care of her mother, brothers, and sisters, even if they wouldn't.

After finishing her diploma as a secretary, Laura worked and worked hard. She was promoted from one job to another. She was a fast learner and proved to be quite resourceful. Over time, she earned better money and gained a lot of life experience. She met people and built friendships that helped her through the years following the death of her father. Laura even found time to join a scout's club and be an active member. She slowly made friendships that lasted for the rest of her life.

Her brothers grew up and finished high school. Good grades qualified Michael to enter an engineering college with free tuition in Syria, which alleviated some of the financial burden for his education. Mark studied business administration and political science in Cairo, Egypt. Laura, thus far, had fulfilled her promise to her mother and brothers to assist them in their higher education, and she was just twenty-three years old.

Michael never failed her. He was always there when she needed him. Laura would never forget his kindness and big heart. Mark was very supportive as well. Laura felt so blessed to have wonderful brothers. They made Laura feel very loved and appreciated. Her sister, Nana, became her consoler and best friend over the years.

It had been twenty years since the "Truce" of 1948 between the Arabs and Israel. In 1967, the Arab world lost more land to Israel. Jordan had lost control of the West Bank, Syria lost the Golan Heights, and Egypt lost the Sinai Desert to the Zionists. Yet since childhood, it was implanted in her core that Palestine, the country of her birth, would be free again from the hands of the Zionists. Her family had lost, home, land, and identity, and like all immigrants in Jordan were encouraged in schools, on television, and in every newspaper and media never to give up the fight. Be a patriot and work to achieve the goal of freeing Palestine from Israeli occupation. Many responded and joined organizations claiming that they were planning the liberation of Palestine. Laura considered her options since she wanted liberation and a return to her homeland, but she wished to know how the group might peacefully accomplish this goal.

However, the situation seemed to be deteriorating without a peaceful solution in sight. The Arab countries once again failed the Palestinians. Leaders in the Palestinian communities started to establish the organizations in the form of small groups called the "Fedayeen", best known as the Palestinian Liberation Organization (PLO) headed by Yasser Arafat and other leaders in other countries.

"Years have already passed, and no one, no one, is helping us or going to support us to restore our land or even help us return to our land. We've tried politics, we've tried negotiations, and nothing is helping. The struggle must continue," said one speaker for the Palestinian Liberation Organization. He urged the members to upgrade the conflict into actual fighting.

Laura became disheartened by the direction the organization wished to take. She wanted to fight, but not with violence. She felt there had to be a peaceful resolution to the conflict.

Young men, who lived in what was referred to, still, as refugee camps, met in secret everywhere. The PLO smuggled weapons and started to harass the Israelis, crossing the River Jordan, bombing and fighting a guerilla warfare, then returning to their base in Amman, Jordan. Resentment built up as no support was received from anyone due to the fact that their escapades brought only disaster to the security of the surrounding countries.

Two years earlier, and in 1968, skirmishes on the border of Jordan with Israel in the village of Karameh took place, and this time with the support of the Jordanian army, the PLO won a weak triumph against Israel but the inability to regain momentum to widen the conflict and regain their lands did not last. The resentment culminated in establishing a kind of resistance inside Amman, the capital of Jordan, and an undercurrent of unrest and instability built up.

The streets in Amman became like a venue of occupying young men carrying arms and making checkpoints as if they ran the country, creating a state inside a state. PLO leaders thought they could force an all-time war to restore Palestine. The political tensions in Jordan worsened, and the rebels grew in numbers. Army checkpoints spread to keep the people safe, and the rebels gained strength in the areas they controlled, placing their own checkpoints. All the time, the King and the government were well aware of the chaos and were getting ready to contain the situation.

Assassination attempts were carried out on the life of the King of Jordan. They only succeeded in assassinating the Prime Minister. This ignited the wrath of the monarch.

It was amidst this social and political conflict that Laura continued to provide for her family, despite the dangers surrounding them. It was about six in the evening when Laura finished her work and left the office for the day. The moment she set foot in the street all hell erupted with bullets flying from every direction. Laura stood in the middle of the street with nowhere to hide. Fear filled her heart.

"Come here, lady, come here!" a young man called to her from a nearby store, and she ran inside.

"Thank you," Laura said, panting heavily. She gasped in horror as she saw a man outside fall to the ground. He'd been riddled with bullets. She felt both grateful and sick inside. It was a miracle she was not hit.

"Is this going to be the norm from now on? Crazy people shooting just for the sake of shooting?" Laura was filled with anger.

The young man closed and locked the door as Laura ranted.

"To fight for a just cause is an honorable thing, but to just disrupt people's lives like this is unbelievable. I was about to die for no reason! I was about to join a group of patriots for Palestine when I realized this kind of volunteering is dangerous and futile," Laura said. "My mother will now go crazy with worry. I have to get home as soon as possible. We do not have a phone at home anymore."

The man strode over and gave her a sad smile. "My name is Noah Fash, and I own this place. We are really suffering in our business, too. It's unlikely anyone will wish to shop amidst a shower of bullets."

"I'm so sorry! Where are my manners? My name is Laura Salem. Thank you so much for helping me, you saved my life!"

The skirmish stopped as suddenly as it had started. The streets became empty, and with no means of transportation, Laura walked home.

The people who hated war and instability lived in unsettling fear, never knowing what was going to happen to them or how it would affect their future.

It was towards the end of summer, on September 17, 1970, and just after her brothers left the country for college, that the Jordanian army surrounded the cities of Amman and Irbid and thus civil war erupted in full force. If Laura had thought it was bad before, she soon realized their situation was unbearable.

Bullets and rockets passed over the roof of the house where Laura lived with her mother and sister. Their neighborhood was caught between the middle hill where the army was stationed and the opposite side where the rebels were stationed--behind Laura's house. It was fortunate that Juliette had experienced many wars. She sensed the mounting turmoil ahead of time and recognized the need to be prepared. She filled the house with water and food supplies and many other things. Two days of non-stop horror filled the air.

"Mama, I am really tired from sitting on the floor. I am going to my room to stretch on my bed. It is further in the back and is not directly exposed to the hill," Laura said and lifted herself off the floor.

Suddenly, she heard the voice of her father shouting, *"SIT DOWN!"* She immediately changed her mind and sat down.

A moment later, an explosion lit the house, and a roar of ammunition filled the air. It kept going for about fifteen minutes and then it suddenly stopped.

"Mama they hit us, they hit us." Tears filled her eyes and she trembled uncontrollably. After everything was quiet, she dared to go and check on where the explosion had come from. Laura's legs could not carry her, and she collapsed on the floor as she saw her bedroom devastated. There were holes in the walls, and rocks and sand were spread all over the room. The bed, where she almost went to lay on, was covered with bullet shrapnel.

It was a miracle she hadn't left to go rest on her bed. Her father's voice saved her life. The Lord had protected her from harm yet again. It was clear her job was not yet finished. Her sister was still in school and had two more years to go before graduating, and her brothers had barely started their college education.

For twenty days, Laura, her mother, and her sister lived in the hallway leading to the bathroom which was the safest location in the house. They crawled on the floor to the kitchen when they needed to get food. Fear gripped Laura's heart, never knowing when the fighting would start or stop.

"Dad? Where are you? I need you to be here." Tears streamed down her cheeks.

"Who are you talking to, Laura?" Her mother turned to look at her.

"I am calling Dad."

Juliette kept quiet.

The radio announcer kept reading prayers, and every now and then a broadcast was released listing areas in which heavy fighting was taking place. Foreboding and worry filled her heart, thinking about the fate of so many people she knew. Many of her friends lived directly under fire in the locations mentioned in the news. A huge number of dead and injured from both sides filled the hospitals.

"Laura, Laura." She heard her name called loudly from the street. She ran to open the door and saw her friend Hani running down the slope towards her house.

Suddenly, Hani fell on the ground, yelling and screaming in pain. Laura bolted from the house and ran to him.

"Oh, my God, oh dear God. Please, please do not let him die," Laura prayed loudly.

"Mama, run. It is Hani. He is shot." Laura went and knelt down on the ground. No one was around to help her. "You fool! What are you doing here?" Laura yelled, hurting to see him in such agony.

Juliette rushed to them and helped Laura drag Hani's now limp body into the house. Juliette got her medical supplies. Laura sat on the ground, holding Hani's head on her lap. Hani's blood covered the floor.

He opened his eyes and looked at Laura. "I love you," Hani said and closed his eyes forever.

It was useless. Juliette took the blanket and covered the body.

"Not again, Mama, why does this keep happening? My heart is breaking."

In the ten years that had passed since she had met Roland, no one else had caught her heart. It seemed that Roland had lived there from the moment she had met him and never left. Laura did have male friends, and Hani Harb had been a great friend to her over the years. He had always been ready to help her when she needed him. She depended on him to contact people for the garden or house maintenance or go with her to certain departments that required a male presence. He had also arranged for parties at her house when a group of friends from the Christian Boys' and Girls' Scouts decided to have some entertainment.

Hani was in love with me? Laura thought as she held his head on her lap and sobbed.

She had always seen Hani as a brother or a friend but no more than that, and she wondered if he had somehow known this, which was why he had never confessed how he truly felt until now.

Sobbing, Laura gently set Hani's head on the floor and went outside to ask for help from the neighbors.

She noticed a truck slowly coming towards her. Laura stopped in the middle of the street, not even caring if the next bullet was for her. Her grief for the loss of Hani haunted her. The driver, Ghaleb Hussein, came down. Luckily, he was one of the neighbors, a civil defense employee, and a firefighter Laura had known for a long time. He was coming to check on her family and bring bread. Laura told him what had happened and asked for his help. With a sad expression and a heavy heart, he followed her inside the house.

As Ghaleb lifted the body and headed out the door, a group of armed young men surrounded the civil defense truck. Laura saw the men from the kitchen window yelling unintelligible words. She recognized the threatening danger for Ghaleb and ran outside while he carried the body on his shoulders. She went and held the hand of someone who seemed to be the leader and begged him not to harm him.

"Please, do not hurt Ghaleb. He is one of you. He just works as a firefighter. He lives next door, and he was coming to bring us bread," Laura begged. "He is helping us with a young man who was killed a few minutes ago. A sniper shot him from the other side of the hill."

The leader of the rebels said, "Is that you, Ghaleb? It has been years since I last saw you. Hurry up and go. It is not safe with your truck around."

"Thank you, Ameen, it is quite some time since we graduated from school. I remember all the enthusiasm about the cause and your wanting to always fight the enemy. The young man I carry is not your enemy. A tragedy that I am taking to his parents," Ghaleb said with anger.

They allowed Ghaleb and Laura to leave so they could take the body to where Hani's family lived. Laura left Hani's house with his mother's heart-wrenching wails trailing behind her. Ghaleb took her back home.

The incident left Laura drained, and for seven long days, Laura sat listening to the radio. The rebels lost and were driven out of the city towards the north. The war was over.

LAURA IMMEDIATELY BEGAN WORKING WITH AN ORGANIZATION THAT provided relief to the needy and poor at that time. Medical and relief services were needed the most. The day the shooting stopped, families living in different parts of the city started searching for each other to ensure they were alive and safe.

Laura came back from work the third day to find some of her friends visiting her house. Since no transportation was available, they had walked for miles across town to check on her family. They all grieved when they heard about Hani. Laura did not realize how much she had cared for him until the moment he was dying in her arms.

And life went on...

Hospitals, stadiums and many halls were filled with the sick and injured. Juliette found her calling, feeling she was needed. She felt alive again and volunteered in the Temporary French Hospital established in the stadium of the Sports City.

"I was assigned to Dr. Noel because I can speak English. An Army car will come pick me up and bring me home at the end of the day." Juliette was pleased with herself. "He was impressed by how I managed to take care of many injured kids in a very short time," Juliette told Laura.

At this point her mother was in her early fifties, and Laura felt happy that she had found more purpose in life.

"Hmm, impressed you say?" Laura chuckled, enjoying the smile that lit her mother's face. "You *are* still beautiful, Mama. I suppose that didn't hurt either." Laura could not help but playfully tease her mother.

"Yes, Dr. Noel was *really* friendly." Juliette chuckled. "I heard the government will start house-to-house searches for arms. Be prepared," Juliette told her daughter. She looked worried. Laura knew her mother did not trust anyone these days. Black September 1970 had marked another page in the history of the country.

People died, people lived, and each and every person, rich and poor, struggled for survival.

Although loneliness crept more and more into her life, Laura decided to join a local theatre group as she had always loved theatre. It was the most satisfying period of her life. She loved being the witch in *Rapunzel and the Witch*. The newspaper reports made her famous, praising her and wishing her the best. Acting was not a career she could dedicate her life to. It was just a hobby. In the years following, she gained success and popularity in the *Pied Piper of Hamelin*. She played the Frog, the Blue Fairy, and the Cricket in *Pinocchio*. The comedy of *Doctor in Spite of Himself* by Mollier gained fame and full house attendance. The same occurred with *Hansel and Gretel*.

She played the part of the old lady in *Behind the Horizon*, and theatre continued to fill her life. Acting was not considered a respectable career for a lady, but she could fulfill her dream of being an actress in the theatre for children. It was respectful and well appreciated as people found it desirable and wholesome entertainment for their children.

During this time, Laura continued to lock her heart, throwing the key away. She decided that love and romance were hurtful to the sanity of a human being after what she had experienced with Hani. Her dreams of being Lauraine and the heartbreak of kidnap and separation from Roland also played a part in her firm resolve to guard her heart and her sanity. Men had no room in her life.

Marriage proposals came her way throughout the years, and they were immediately met with refusals. She was not free.

That year, on December 31, 1970, she received some mail at her office. She separated the mail and found it all belonged to the business, except for one letter. She picked up the letter with her name handwritten on the envelope. There was no return address, and the stamps were from Germany. She hastily opened the letter.

My dearest Laura,

No matter how many years have passed, or how much I've tried to forget,

I finally took the courage to write, hoping you would reply and keep in touch. What we shared at your birthday party years ago has made me feel certain that you were wrong to deny me your love. I am truly sorry I was not there for you over the years, especially during this war. You decided our separation without giving me the chance to grasp some hope for a relationship. I never stopped thinking of you, however, and all I have to say is this:

> *From the entangled web of ethereal eternity,*
> *your tender face rose through immortality,*
> *enchanting, gripping in a never ending infinity.*
> *Green eyes ripped deep into my soul,*
> *pulling me from a place as dark as coal,*
> *giving my heart a path that makes me whole.*
> *My love is a chain of a long, silky string divine,*
> *stretched to wrap, to hook your heart with mine,*
> *yet the illusion of you disappears again in time,*
> *left behind the whisper, the sound of rhyme.*
> *Words engraved in my heart to forever remain.*
> *Goodbye my darling, 'till we meet again.*
> *"Until we do, my darling," I heard you often say,*
> *more than once the promise entrapped me to stay.*
> *But somehow destiny's grip always finds a way,*
> *to tug with never ending squeeze in the heart,*
> *to mark my days with the golden word "Apart",*
> *"Until we do" a promise from which never to depart.*
> *Love,*
> *Roland*

Laura steeled her resolve even though her heart broke. She did not answer the letter.

CHAPTER TWENTY-ONE

LAURAINE: ESCAPE

1195

*H*aron, the personal guard of the youngest prince, was passing through the long balcony that connected many different sections of the palace.

He suddenly saw a captivating apparition he had never seen before. She was a vision in her flowing white gown, embroidered with gold on the sleeves and all around the hem of the skirt.

She must be new here. What a beautiful woman. I wonder why Mazen did not bring this woman to the main palace for inspection, he thought to himself.

Gazing at the women in the harem was forbidden under the penalty of whipping and even execution. Only the eunuchs were allowed to be in close proximity to the harem. This kept the women safe. Unfortunately, it meant Haron was unable to spend time with any of the women he desired, and now he desired this woman in a way that made him lose his self-control.

He quietly watched her every day, careful to avoid being seen. He began studying the palace to determine how he could discreetly enter the garden below. He watched her with her baby, feeding and playing with her. Every day his lust increased and took him captive. He could not stop thinking about her, and he formulated a plan to act on his desire. He was making a fatal decision.

~

LATE ONE EVENING, LAURAINE HEARD JOHANA CRYING. AS LAURAINE walked to the baby's room, unexpectedly, a man appeared before her. Lauraine recognized him as one of the palace guards, but it unnerved her to find him coming out from behind the window curtains. She opened her mouth to scream, but he covered Lauraine's mouth with his hand and shoved her into a vacant bedroom.

"Don't make a sound, or I will kill you." He picked up Lauraine's scarf from a nearby chair and stuffed it in her mouth. He grabbed her arms from behind and bound them together. Lauraine kicked backward and hit him in the groin, but she couldn't muster enough force for it to be effective. He dragged her to the bed and pinned her down. He became enraged when he discovered she was not wearing the regular open skirts that the harem women usually wore. With one hand, he grabbed her silk pants and ripped them apart.

Suddenly, Lauraine stopped fighting. The man sneered, showing his crooked, tobacco stained teeth as Lauraine became quiet, feigning submission. The sound from the minarets calling for prayers filled the air. Lauraine prayed for deliverance when she heard footsteps enter the room. She lifted her head and looked over her shoulder. Relieved to see Mazen with a thunderous expression on his face. Had he not come at this moment, the guard would have surely succeeded in raping her.

~

MAZEN WAS SHOCKED TO SEE A MAN BENT OVER LAURAINE'S BODY.

Without thinking, he quickly pulled out his dagger and plunged it into the guard's back, pulling him off Lauraine.

"You bastard! Here is your final ticket to hell!" Mazen stabbed the man again as rage filled his heart. He left the man bleeding on the floor. When he removed the scarf from her mouth, she started sobbing uncontrollably. He untied her hands and held her in his arms, gently comforting her.

"It's okay, you are safe with me, Lauraine. Where is Jamilah? Why isn't she with you?"

Lauraine was too upset to speak so he continued to rock her back and forth as he stared at the dead man. He recognized him and realized the guard would be missed quickly as he was in frequent contact with the prince. Mazen's mind raced as he began to formulate a plan to get Lauraine out of the palace. Attempting to ransom her was now out of the question.

"Lauraine, get ready. We are going to leave the palace tonight. You are in danger here. Earlier, I received permission from the emir to leave the citadel to get provisions and supplies. I am not coming back. No one will know about my absence except Jamilah and the eunuch whom I am leaving in charge."

Lauraine nodded in agreement, her smile finally breaking through. She embraced Mazen with a tight hug.

"We will be ready. You will be a welcomed addition to my family."

Mazen left the room and called for Jamilah. She was baffled when she came into the room and saw the mayhem.

"Mazen, is he dead?" Jimilah asked full of fear.

"Yes, but do not worry. I will take care of the body. This man was a monster and deserved death. He can't even be called an animal. It would be an insult for them. I caught him attacking Lauraine. Clean up the room as if nothing happened," Mazen instructed. "Not many come to this part of the palace. There is more, my dear friend. I am leaving tonight with Lauraine and the child, and you do not know where I am. I gave orders to my friend, Yousef Gassam, to be in charge. He knows that I am going to get provisions which will take some time. He is a good man, and I trust him. Befriend him. He is also a eunuch that the emir trusts, especially when it comes to women. He is brave, well trained with the sword, and cares about the safety of the women." Mazen rapidly finished his instructions to Jamilah.

"Take me with you." Her eyes filled with tears as she begged Mazen. He wrapped his arm around Jamilah and held her tight.

"You know I can't. I know that you are a sensible, strong, and brave woman. All the women respect and mind you. What would you do in my place?"

"I would not take me." Jamilah sobbed as she voiced what they all knew. Her absence would draw too much attention.

"I promise I will find a way for you to join us." Lauraine hugged Jamilah. "I will never forget how much I owe you. Since you are not happy here, believe me, I will get you out," Lauraine assured Jamilah.

"I am becoming older, and as you have noticed, there are no old women in the harem. I trained a few good women to take over when the time comes and I am kicked out." Jamilah wiped her tears. "There are two ways this will end: to run away when I can and risk being caught, or become a beggar in the streets, which I will not allow," Jamilah said with a stubborn resolution.

"Don't do anything stupid, Jamilah. Do not do anything that might cause you harm. Just give us a short time to settle back home," Lauraine begged.

"Okay. No time to waste, let's clean up this mess." Jamilah got buckets of water and rags to clean the blood from the floor, while Mazen wrapped the body with bed sheets. He put the body on his shoulders and left.

Two hours later, Mazen returned and told Lauraine they were ready to leave. She said her goodbyes to Jamilah, who had packed two baskets of food for the travelers.

"Don't forget me." Jamilah kissed the baby.

CHAPTER TWENTY-TWO

LAURA: REUNION

1974

*L*aura sat at her desk, staring through the glass partition in her office as she watched a handsome man come into the bank towards the teller. She glanced at the glass-framed poem on her desk which she had received some time ago. She saw the teller direct the gentleman towards her office. He turned and her heart missed a beat. It was Roland.

He stood in the doorway of her office and tapped his chin in thought while Laura tried and failed to get her breathing under control.

"Let's see how many years have passed now?" Roland pondered aloud, smiling as he opened his arms to give Laura a hug.

Laura's eyes widened in surprise as she stood. He must have become used to the customs in Germany. In the Middle East, there were many social restrictions and traditions that were considered sacred. Hugging a woman would cause her reputation to be destroyed and could potentially cause her to be severely punished.

"Ten years, eight months, and..." Laura laughed as she came out from behind the desk and extended her hand instead, wishing she could give Roland a hug. She waited until Roland recognized the unspoken sign. He took her hand with his palms and gently caressed it.

"I forgot myself for a moment," Roland said with a chuckle.

"Please, have a seat. We close in about five minutes. Would you like a cup of coffee?" Laura asked as Roland read the placard on her desk.

"No, thanks. Personnel Assistant. Nice." He noticed the poem on her desk and picked the frame up. He gazed at Laura with deep longing.

Laura's heart leapt as Roland recognized his poem. "How did you know where I work?"

"Remember my cousin? Your friend, Dian," Roland answered, clearly feeling proud of his ability to find where she worked in such a large city.

She smiled and shook her head. "Where have you been all this time?"

"After I finished my school, I interned. The civil war convinced me that it was best to stay in Germany for a while."

"When did you come home?" Laura asked.

"Yesterday evening. It was too late to knock at your door!" Roland winked at her.

"Well, it's about time for me to end my work day. Care to accompany me outside?"

He eagerly nodded and watched as Laura cleaned up her desk. He followed her out as she shut her office, and they left as the bank closed its doors for the day.

"Can you join me for lunch?" Roland asked.

"Thank you, but my mother is waiting. You come with me. We will have lunch at home."

"All right, my car is this way." Roland led Laura to a Mercedes and opened the door for her.

"I drove this car all the way from Germany." Roland's wide smile gave away his smug feeling, while Laura stared at the exquisite vehicle in astonishment.

"That's quite the road trip. You must be exhausted," Laura said.

"No, I am fine. I stopped on the way and slept in good hotels." Roland eased her worry.

The drive to her home was short and pleasant as they conversed about little things. If Laura was honest, she felt nervous to scratch the surface and have any deeper conversations with him. She also wondered if any other past memories might surface in his presence. Soon, they pulled up to the house, and Laura rushed inside, calling to her mother.

"Mama, Roland came back. Look! I invited him over for lunch. I hope there is enough food."

Juliette greeted Roland with a warm hello and a smile. "I made chicken, meat, and rice, which I hope you will like. It's Laura's favorite dish."

Laura went to the kitchen and started preparing the table, and Nana came out to say hello.

"Nana, wow, a pretty young lady. When do you finish school?"

"Thank you. I finished some time ago, Roland." Nana laughed. "I am a civil engineer now. I graduated last May, and I applied for a job." Nana was proud of herself, and Laura felt she deserved to experience this sense of accomplishment. She was so grateful her sister had been able to graduate from college. They sat around the table catching up on each other's lives.

"Roland, it would seem you've never forgotten about our dear Laura," Nana teased.

Laura thought she might die of embarrassment, but Roland laughed good naturedly.

"Laura did amaze me from the day I met her." He gave Nana a mischievous look as he whispered loud enough for everyone at the table to hear. "Even though our encounter was short, to me it was unforgettable." Roland looked at Laura as if it had happened yesterday, hoping that she would acknowledge his hint, but she purposely ignored what he was getting at.

After they finished lunch, they sat on the porch, catching up on the years past and the civil war.

"Where are Mark and Michael now?" Roland asked.

"They are abroad, working and building their lives. They were offered very good job opportunities." Laura smiled. "Sometimes I worked three jobs to make it. Thanks to the Lord, He was always with me."

"I knew you could do it! The determination to focus solely on your family's welfare was really touching. It showed what a big heart you have, giving up things in order to make your family successful."

"You really think that, even though I had to give up...certain relationships?" Laura said, looking down at her hands.

Roland placed his hand over hers and squeezed it. "I understand," he said in a soft voice. "I can't deny that I've felt like I lost something precious by not having you in my life all these years, especially since I wasn't able to be here for you in your struggles. I hold a deep love and respect for you."

Laura smiled, swallowing down her emotions before they could become tears.

The day passed by very quickly as they spent the afternoon catching up. Roland knew he had to take his leave for the evening but wanted to ensure he would see Laura again.

"May I invite all of you for dinner tomorrow evening at Le Caesar restaurant?" Roland asked Juliette.

"Thank you. We would love to. What time do you expect to pick us up?" Juliette asked.

"How about eight o'clock?" Roland said.

As Roland left, Juliette placed a hand on her daughter's shoulder. "It's good to see you smile again, you know that? I haven't seen your eyes light up like this since the day you met Roland."

Laura blinked back tears. "He's a very special individual."

She gave Laura a wry smile. "I'd say he's far more than that."

"Mother, if I didn't know any better, I'd think you were trying to encourage this relationship."

"There's no hiding anything from you. Not that I was trying." Juliette laughed at Laura's expression. "For the first time in years, I'm going to sleep like a baby, knowing my Laura is finally going to be happy."

She patted her daughter on the cheek and headed for her room.

IT WAS A BEAUTIFUL SUMMER EVENING SIMILAR TO HER BIRTHDAY PARTY all those years ago. As the waiter brought their drinks, Roland raised his glass and toasted, "Happy Birthday, Laura." Roland took a small box out of his pocket and set it on the table in front of her.

"You remembered!" She opened the box and gaped at the small ruby pendant with a gold chain nestled inside. "How beautiful. My goodness, it matches my bracelet. Thank you very much." He clasped the necklace for Laura as she turned to her mother. "Mama, isn't this lovely?"

Juliette smiled as Nana said, "Happy Birthday, sis. You see? No one forgot your birthday. Here is mama's and my gift to you."

Nana gave her a small package which she immediately ripped open with the eagerness of a child. She gasped at the beauty of the earrings. They were long with delicate petaled flowers made also to match her bracelet.

They ate dinner and enjoyed the live music playing nearby. After dinner, Roland took Laura's hand and led her to the dance floor. He approached the leader of the band and requested a special tune.

CHAPTER TWENTY-THREE

LAURAINE: HOME

1196

*T*he horse's legs barely touched the ground as it raced against what Lauraine felt was time. Though they neared closer to her home and Roland, she couldn't help but feel that she was close to losing him, and she didn't know why. It was as if he would forever be out of reach. They avoided the main traveling roads and many small villages, as the riders spurred their steeds to go faster still.

Johana was securely wrapped against Lauraine's shoulders, chest, and belly. She slept with the rhythm of the running horses, content against the warmth of her mother's body.

They stopped periodically to rest for short periods and to take care of the baby's needs. They wore regular common clothes so that they would not attract attention. They did not speak much as each was preoccupied with their own thoughts about the events that had led up to their escape. Lauraine was excited and anxious to reach home.

It seemed to Lauraine that the road back home was actually shorter than it had been when traveling with the bandits. Since there were only two riders, they covered more distance at a rapid pace, thus they arrived at the inn located in the meadows at the edge of the Golan Plateau much sooner than she had anticipated.

The owner of the Inn gave them the best rooms he had when he saw the gold coin that Mazen put on the table.

He ordered fresh horses from the innkeeper and told the man that they were going to spend two days traveling north towards Lebanon. He hoped this lie would throw off anyone who might be pursuing them.

Lauraine was very exhausted and slept when her daughter did. The room was clean and spacious. The feeling of freedom filled her heart, and the expectation to see her husband again after all this time made her feel restless. She knelt and prayed.

To cross the plateau would take some travel time. The second part of their journey was slower paced. Johana was fussy and needed more frequent breaks. Lauraine comforted and cooed in her ear to calm her down, helping her endure the strenuous travel.

Early in the morning, they traced the trail which the bandits often used, it was clearly marked. Not much farther to go. If they started at dawn, they would arrive in Acre late the next day.

The stretch was uninhabited. When they reached the water springs at the halfway point, they stopped to rest and water the horses. The spring water flowed out of a rock like a small waterfall. Lauraine was eager to go down to the cove to bathe until she recognized the pile of rocks that covered the cave entrance from the earthquake. She made a note on her sketched map so she could return once they were safe. Mazen took care of Johana while Lauraine took her time freshening up.

They camped that night, ate from the provisions they saved from the inn, and slept. The next morning, they packed, and continued their journey. After a few hours they spotted the castle tower of Acre in the distance.

"We are home," Lauraine declared cheerfully.

The moment they entered the gate, she immediately went with Mazen to the main hall of the palace. Servants and pages were stunned to see Lauraine dashing inside with a man at her side and a baby in her arms.

She entered the hall and called out, "Father, where are you?"

Stunned, her father sat for a moment with his mouth wide open. "Lauraine, my dear daughter, my little girl! Thank God, you are alive." Lord Salem leapt from his seat into the open arms of his daughter, hugging her as if he would never let her go.

Everyone in the palace--servants, pages, and knights--ran towards the hall when they heard that Lauraine was back.

"What happened, Lauraine? We gave up hope of finding you alive. We even sent emissaries to Damascus where slaves are usually sold, but no one had seen you," Lord Salem told her.

"I will tell you the whole story later, father. This is Mazen ben Sultan who saved me, and this is Roland's daughter. Your grand-daughter, Johana," Lauraine explained.

Lord Salem's eyes filled with tears as he took the beautiful baby from Lauraine and embraced Johana. He was so relieved to have them home.

"Mazen? Is that really you? We heard that Saladin died," Lord Salem said.

"Yes, my Lord…"

"Sorry, I have to interrupt," Lauraine said. "I thank you all for the welcome, but I cannot spare another moment. Father, where is Roland? I was told he was alive. Please, tell me!" Lauraine said anxiously.

"Sit down, daughter. Roland is alive, but he was severely injured. The physicians from different parts of the world were brought here to help him recover. We still have hope. He is still fighting for his life."

"Please, Father, take care of Mazen and the baby," Lauraine said, dashing through the hallways towards the hospital.

"My Lady, wait a minute," a family friend followed her. "I will take you to him."

Lauraine followed him into a room filled with medicines where Roland lay resting.

"Roland, my love, hear me. Please, wake up!" Lauraine bent down, kissing her husband's face. Tears ran down her cheeks as she took his hand, turned it palm up, and rested her cheek on it.

"Lauraine?" he whispered weakly.

"Listen to me. I will never leave your side. You have to get stronger. You see, you are a father now. You need to get better so your baby, Johana, can play with you. You will be so close to her, and you will spoil her. Please, wake up, my love."

Roland could barely move as his eyelids fluttered open. Lauraine continued to stroke his forehead, gently telling him all about what had happened since they were separated.

"Your daughter is very smart, sweet, and pretty." Feeling exhausted, Lauraine put her head on his chest and closed her eyes, listening to his heart beat.

"Lauraine, my dear, come, let Roland rest for now." Her father came to stand next to her.

"I want him moved immediately to our room. The physician can come and see him there. I will take care of him myself until his strength comes back." Lauraine's tears continued.

"We will move him tomorrow morning. You need to rest. Your baby, the adorable child, is calling for you. You need to be strong to handle this burden, and with God's help, we will overcome this disaster," Lord Catin said as he entered Roland's room.

"Oh, I am so sorry, my Lord, please forgive me. I didn't mean to ignore you." Lauraine went to her father-in-law and embraced him. Lauraine was overwhelmed with emotion. She tried to control her sobbing. Her body convulsed with each wave of shock. After a few minutes, she began to regain her composure.

"Please come to my rooms, both of you. We have to talk." Lauraine led the way.

They sat around the room listening as Laura told her story. She told them that she knew she was pregnant when she was in the camp of Sheikh Othman. He knew who she was and punished his men for kidnapping her.

"Lauraine," Lord Catin said, "Zaid and Maryam came and told

their story. Zaid was wounded, and they both stayed until he was healed. Zaid had relatives in Egypt, and they decided to go there."

Lauraine let out a sigh of relief. "I am glad they are safe. Mazen recognized me when I was being led to the slave auction. He knew my grandfather. He saw me several times at the village when he used to come with messages from the Sultan. It was Othman's brother who conspired to sell me in Damascus. I owe Mazen our lives. He hid us in the citadel until we were able to escape."

Lauraine stopped talking for a little bit and said, "Mazen is not going back. I asked him to stay here with us as my personal guard. He is a eunuch, brave and smart. He was there at the time I gave birth to Johana. He loves her as his daughter."

Her father nodded and patted her hand. "We will treat him as an honored member of the family. Now get some rest, my dear. You need your strength."

Lauraine fell into an exhausted sleep. When she woke up the next morning, she heard the clamor of men carrying Roland on a gurney towards her room.

They placed Roland on a wide bed prepared for him. After the men left, Lauraine climbed on the bed next to her husband and sternly said, "You listen to me, Roland Catin, enough of this sleeping. You need to open your eyes." She got out of the bed and picked up Johana. She sat down on the edge, letting Johana crawl towards her dad and climb up on his chest.

"This is your Daddy, Johana. Da, Da." Johana cooed and tapped Roland's chest repeating after her mama, "Da, Da." Johana giggled.

A FEW WEEKS HAD PASSED SINCE THEY HAD RETURNED HOME. MAZEN came every day to play with Johana. He helped Lauraine and the nurse take care of Roland's needs.

One day, the physician came to check on Roland. Lauraine took Roland's hand and said, "Roland, now it is not the time to play with me. I do not like this silent game, and I want you to join me. Talk to me and play a game with Johana. Do you hear me?" Lauraine waited for some moments. Everyone in the room stood silent, waiting anxiously for the doctor to finish his examination. He stood, shaking his head.

"His heart is failing."

Roland barely opened his eyes as a thin, weak voice slipped through his lips. "Lauraine," he whispered.

Lauraine pushed the nurse aside and knelt beside the bed, taking Roland's hand again.

"Yes, my love, I am here. I am safe here with you. I have so much to tell you. First, grab this little hand." She put Johana's hand in his. "Your daughter, Johana!"

"Beautiful, Johana!" Roland murmured. Lauraine saw a teardrop forming in the corner of Roland's eye. He squeezed her hand and said in a shallow voice, "I love you, my lovely Lauraine."

"I love you too, Roland."

"Mazen, get some water please." Lauraine held a spoon of water to Roland's lips so he could sip it.

Roland whispered, "I am sorry I cannot hold on. I feel like I am slipping away. I will always be with you. Goodbye, my darling, till we meet again. I will find you. I promise." Roland closed his eyes and stopped breathing.

"Please, please, my darling, don't go. Not now! There is plenty to live for, and plenty to do," she cried. As she held him in her arms and his limbs fell loose, she looked at him sadly and said, "Goodbye my love, until we do, I will find you, too. I promise to take care of our child." She covered her face with her hands and sobbed.

Lords Catin and Salem were overcome with sorrow. Grief filled their hearts. Rage filled hers.

AFTER A MONTH OF MOURNING, HER FATHER TOLD HER HOW HE HAD found her satchel when they went to search for her. Lauraine's tears flowed down uncontrollably. The bracelet was still in the sack.

Lauraine visited Roland's grave in the afternoon and brought some beautiful flowers she grew in her garden. Her father was visiting his wife's grave, too, which was in the same plot reserved for the Salem family.

"Father, there is something I want to tell you." Lauraine told her father what she saw inside the cave.

"I was fearful that Jaber would follow me. I grabbed a dagger to defend myself but the earthquake that came suddenly was a blessing, and we ran outside. However, the rocks fell on Jaber and closed the opening of the cave. It left a big hole, large enough for someone to enter." She told him it hadn't appeared that anything had touched the place when she and Mazen had passed it.

LORDS SALEM AND CATIN RODE WITH A DOZEN TRUSTED MEN AS Lauraine led the way to the cave.

While they removed the rocks, she saw Jaber's remains caught between two boulders. The men took the bones and buried them nearby. The entrance to the cave was soon cleared. They left some guards outside the cave and went inside to check the place. They were dazzled by the sight and removed everything they found in the cave. They sent back two men to bring more horses and carts to carry the treasure. They were sworn to secrecy concerning the treasure. Their share of the loot made the dozen men rich for the rest of their lives, and they kept their loyalty to the family.

AS THE YEARS PASSED, LAURAINE ALWAYS FELT ROLAND'S PRESENCE IN her life. She knew he watched over them. Every time she or the baby were close to danger, he was there to warn her. One incident happened shortly after Roland died. Johana was playing in the room while Lauraine dozed off sitting on the couch.

She was startled out of her sleep when she heard Roland's voice say, "Lauraine, wake up, my love. The baby!"

Lauraine awoke to see Johana crawling towards the fireplace, reaching for the coal thong. She quickly picked her up, tickling her tummy with her face, and Johana giggled. Lauraine was always happy to see Roland's vision and hear his voice even if it was in her sleep.

One day, a ragged woman came to the Gate of Acre. She asked the guard to take a message for her.

"Master, please tell Lady Lauraine that Jamilah is outside."

Lauraine rushed to the gate and took the woman in her arms. Jamilah had not aged well. Life had been unkind to her after Lauraine had left.

"Yousef helped me. He told the emir to let me go as I am getting old. Have you ever known anyone who was happy to be kicked out of a job?" Jamilah laughed. "I had to look like a beggar so that no one would bother me."

They laughed and reminisced. Lauraine told Jamilah of her loss and all that had happened since she last saw her. Mazen and Jamilah committed themselves to serving Lauraine. They remained with Lauraine and took care of her and Johana.

Throughout the passing years, and while she progressively took over her husband's business and land management, Lauraine developed the habit of talking to Roland as if he was nearby. Any time she felt down, lonely, or sad, she would call him to come to talk to her.

Jamilah became concerned at one point and asked Lauraine questions but was rebuffed when Lauraine said, "Oh, do not worry about that!"

"Father, I want to go to Bassa and live with grandfather. I want Johana to have children to play with in the fields while she is growing up," Lauraine told him one afternoon.

"But Lauraine, it is safer for both of you if you remain here," Lord John said.

"There are no more raids, and I believe Sheikh Othman is keeping the area safe by residing in the meadows," Lauraine said. "Remember, after I was released, he attacked the clan that raided the village, and he made deals with their leaders. The clan of Hashim ben Zifa left the whole area and went to the meadows of Damascus. I will travel with Mazen, my trusted friend and good guard."

"I will come with you and stay for a while. Jeffrey can take care of things here."

Lauraine knew her father wanted to accompany her to make sure she was safe. He could also check on his tenants in the process.

"Bandits are unpredictable. If they do not raid the cities along the coast, they raid each other's camps. They believe it is in the core of their faith to have Jihad."

As Lauraine rode her horse with Johana in front of her, she looked towards her right and smiled at a vision of Roland riding his horse beside her. She was very happy to go to her grandfather's house where meadows with carob trees and wheat grew in abundance. Horses, cows, and sheep grazed the land and provided daily meat, wool, leather, and assets for trading to the villagers.

Lauraine kept busy at home and took care of the sick and injured farmers who lived in the village and around the area. Many came asking for her help and she never said no.

When she found some free time, she would ride her horse to the eastern meadow where a century old tree spread its branches. She would dismount, spread a blanket on the ground, sit, and wait for Roland to talk to her.

And so time passed.

Johana was tutored to become a knowledgeable young lady, just like her mother before her. She was gifted with music and arts. Fencing and horsemanship were Johana's favorite activities.

"Mama, who are you talking to in the garden when you are alone?" Johana asked one day.

"Well now, I talk to your father. Who else would it be?" Lauraine said.

"Oh!" Johana smiled and went back to her studies. Sometimes she wondered if her mother was in her right mind.

Lauraine worked on her embroidery, sitting near the window as her father came in with a guest. He was a very handsome man in his early forties.

"Lauraine, guess who is here?" her father said.

Lauraine stood when she saw Lord Adam Buckley. He had been Roland's friend and war partner. He was their best man at the wedding. Adam had gone to England after Roland's death. Sometimes she would receive letters from him telling her about his adventures in different cities of the world.

"I can't believe my eyes! Is that you, Adam? My goodness! Too many years have passed since I last saw you." Lauraine welcomed her old friend. "I hope you will stay and spend some time with us."

Adam smiled to himself. "I remember your lovey spirit, Lauraine. It's nice to see it hasn't diminished over the years."

"Before you two start talking politics," Lauraine interjected, "why is a handsome man like you not married yet? I remember you telling me about Anna Beauchamp in one of your letters. What came of her?"

"Well, it did not work out. That was many years back. She did not like traveling, and she did not want to leave her parents for adventure. She was not Lauraine."

Adam gave her a not-so-subtle look.

"So many things in life do not come out the way we want. I am glad to see you, Adam." Lauraine stood. "I'll leave you to your pipes and politics. I have a surprise for you, Adam. I am sure you will like it." She left the room.

"She didn't exactly catch my meaning, did she?"

Lord Salem smiled. "I'm sure she knew what you meant."

"Then I shall have to petition you. It may be the only way to win her heart. May I have your permission to court Lauraine?"

Lord Salem chuckled under his breath. "You have my permission with a strong prayer for good luck. Many men over the years have approached her, but she has refused them all. She told them that Roland is still with her."

Lord Salem sighed with sadness for the loneliness with which she lived out her days.

To Adam's surprise, Lauraine came back with a miniature of herself.

"Johana, I want to introduce you to Lord Adam Buckley, your father's best friend. He has been traveling abroad for many years. Adam, this is Johana, our daughter. She is ten years old," Lauraine said proudly.

"Hello, Lord Buckley, pleased to meet you. I am happy to see that mother is very excited you're here. She gave instructions to the kitchen to make your special food and dessert. Maybe now when mama goes walking in the garden she will not go alone, and she will have someone to talk to." She continued with enthusiasm. "Can you go riding with me? I love riding my horse."

Lord Buckley roared with laughter. "I love riding too! We can go riding before dinner with your mother's permission. What a beautiful girl you are, Johana."

Receiving her mother's approval, Johana ran to her room to get ready.

Lauraine felt a little embarrassed after what her daughter had said.

"How about riding with us, Lauraine? We can catch up," Adam suggested.

She agreed, and in no time, they had their horses saddled. As they raced across the meadow, they reached some tents erected at the edge of a forest. Curiosity as to who would be camping there led them to a group of people sitting around a large campfire.

"Hello there. The smell of your food is making our bellies growl." Lauraine climbed down off her horse and approached the ladies. They were gypsies, traveling to their clan's camp to the south.

Two men emerged from the tent and welcomed the riders to share their food. A young lady came running from the field and stood staring at Lauraine with her big blue eyes.

"Hello, my Lady. I kept the secret!" She smiled.

"Hala? Is that you? Oh, my dear girl, come here." Lauraine opened her arms and hugged the young lady, showering her with kisses.

"I am terribly sorry we left you behind. Jaber refused to bring you with us, and it was safer for you to stay with the clan."

"We found her years back, sleeping near her mother's grave," an elderly woman said.

"She spent two days alone, scared, hungry, and thirsty as her clan left the area without even noticing her absence. She is our daughter now. We take care of her. Come now. Join us and share our meal."

"This is the lady I told you about who defeated the best swordsman of the clan." Hala glowed with joy. She turned to Johana and said, "Who are you?"

"I am Johana, the lady is my mother, and we were racing the horses. I love riding," Johana said.

"Come with me to my tent." Johana looked at her mother hoping for permission. Lauraine was delighted that she immediately liked Hala with her gentle friendliness. Her mother nodded, and the girls went to the tent.

"Here, take this necklace and bracelet. They are made from seashells. I make these and sell them around as we travel," Hala said proudly.

"They are beautiful. Thank you, but I do not have anything to give you in return." Johana felt embarrassed.

"Do not worry about that. Your mother gave me the most important gift; her kindness and love when I needed them the most." Hala smiled.

The girls joined the rest of the group for the meal.

"Look, Mother, look at these beautiful shells. Hala gave them to me as a present."

Lord Buckley talked with the gypsy men, amazed at their way of life and the brief history of the clan.

"As we share bread now, I would like to offer you our assistance anytime you need help. We live in the village of Bassa down the road," Lord Buckly said with sincerity.

"Hala, do you want to come and live with us, with the permission of your family?" Lauraine offered.

"No. Thank you. These people are my family now. I love them, and I know they will take care of me. I am sure they will let me visit you if we come to this area for trading. But I want you to know, Lady Lauraine, you are in my heart as long as I live."

As they said their goodbyes, Lauraine embraced Hala and told her she would never forget her.

It was Johana's eighteenth birthday when Lauraine entered her daughter's room and said, "Johana, happy birthday, my love. I have a special gift for you. Your father gave me this bracelet on my eighteenth birthday, and I am passing it on to you. He had it made for me, and it is very special. You must promise never to sell it, even if you are poor. Pass it on to your first daughter. She must promise to pass it on to her first daughter, and so on."

"Thank you, Mother, but what if I do not have a daughter?" Johana asked.

"Then it should be kept hidden until the first daughter of a descendant is born," Lauraine mused.

"I promise to keep it safe and pass it on to my daughter, Mama. It is beautiful. I will cherish it always."

Johana became a beautiful young lady. Skilled in the art of healing like her mother. She helped babies come into the world and cared for the children of the village at an early age.

One day, Lauraine went to the beach ahead of Johana. Lauraine always felt happiest when she was near the open sea. It was her sixty-eighth birthday and fifty years had passed since Roland had given her the bracelet.

She lifted her now wrinkled hand to adjust the scarf on her neck as she watched the sun go down behind the horizon. She turned her head to look around, sensing someone watched her. There, right in front of her, riding astride his great horse, was Roland.

"Happy Birthday, my love!" Roland said. Lauraine closed her eyes and opened them again. She saw Roland was still there.

"I am losing my mind. I have been seeing things. Of course you are not here," Lauraine said. "Too many years have passed, Roland, for you to keep playing your tricks on me." She smiled, remembering her beloved. She had never remarried.

Lord Buckley had become her companion but never her lover or husband. Her grandfather had died, and her father had soon followed. Loneliness had gripped her heart since then. The only consolation she had was Johana, who was now married with four beautiful children.

Roland climbed down from the horse and came to where she stood near the surf. She rushed towards him with all the yearning and longing that filled her heart. He lifted her up in the air as he always did, placing her on his horse.

He declared, "You are finally with me. I was patient for far too long." The horse galloped into the fog, and they soon disappeared together.

Johana came down to the beach and found that her mother had peacefully passed away. She rested on the sand with a smile on her beautiful face.

Lauraine was buried next to her husband.

CHAPTER TWENTY-FOUR

LAURI AND ROLAND: REAPPEARANCE

1240

*T*he Blue Danube tune filled the air. Roland and Laura gracefully glided around the room with the music and were lost again in time. As the tune continued to echo in the hall, Laura reveled in Roland's arms. It felt like they were floating in the air while he whispered in her ear about how much he missed and longed for her, she felt like her world was complete. The calming and ethereal music dimmed all the surroundings as they entered a land of dreams.

IT WAS JUNE, 1240 WHEN THE NEW SULTAN, MALIK AL SALIH NAJM ED-Din Ayyoub entered Cairo, Egypt and bought slaves (mamluks) for his army, ushering in the era referred to as the Mamluk dynasty. The Mamluks came into power as slaves who revolted, overthrew their leaders, and took over the armies of Egypt. The Mamluk Qalawun, who took power by rebellion and force, set his goals to capture and take the lands that remained under the Crusaders' control. His son, Khalil, came to power in the year 1290 and continued with his father's policy. He destroyed Acre. He then went after each of the remaining Crusaders' strongholds in Damascus, and in a short span of forty-five days, he took over Tyre, Sidon, Beirut, Jubail, Anafah, Al- Batrun, and Sarfand. Thus, in 1291, The Holy Land was cleared of the Crusaders, who never returned again.

LAURI KANE STOOD IN THE WALL CREVICE OF THE CITADEL TOWER IN Acre, watching the training of the young knights, a custom she had developed over the past three years. She stood with her German Shepherd dog, Wolf, admiring the scene in the battlement. Her beautiful green eyes were particularly interested in the young Roland Catin. Her wavy, copper curls flew around her face in the sea breeze. It was her eighteenth birthday, and as she pushed away the hair from her face, the sun's rays hit the golden bracelet she wore on her wrist, reflecting a bright shining light. The bracelet had been a gift she had received from her mother that day. She didn't understand the importance of the promise she had made to keep the bracelet safe and to pass it on to her future daughter, but she knew that there was a sacred covenant she was now a part of.

THE BRIGHT REFLECTION COMING FROM THE TOWER CAUGHT ROLAND'S eye, and he looked up to see the ethereal, angelic figure watching from above. He always glanced at the tower and saw her there, watching him every time he had training. He smiled to himself and his heart skipped a beat.

Lauri was not the only girl watching Roland. Envy and jealousy filled the heart of Irene as Roland looked towards Lauri.

He never ever notices me with her around. Whether I'm in the same room, in the hallways, or in the other castle tower, thought Irene as she stood in the tower, watching, with evil brewing in her heart. Every attempt at getting rid of Lauri had failed so far, but Irene was sure that no one suspected her of trying to harm Lauri. Irene schemed again to bring about the demise of her rival.

WOLF FOLLOWED LAURI LIKE HER SHADOW. WHEREVER SHE WENT, WOLF was there. Wolf had been a gift from Roland for her tenth birthday. The puppy had been five months old at the time. Over the years, Wolf grew to be a loyal pet, protective of its human master. On this particular day, Lauri left Wolf behind and walked through a tunnel that started at the citadel and stretched a short distance to the seashore. She was deep in thought about the decision her father had made to move to Lebanon, to avoid the battle that was closing in from the south.

The Mamluk army was coming and they had to flee. She didn't notice the shadow following her. She sat on the beach unaware of any danger. She dreamily picked up some soft sand and let it sift through her fingers. Her heart was heavy with sadness as she thought of leaving her home forever. She was in deep thought, wondering about the safety of the love of her life, Roland, who would have to go to battle soon.

Lauri's sadness swiftly shifted to anger as she thought about the conflict. *Why do people need to fight, to destroy, and kill other people? And for what?* She wondered. *Power will not bring anyone any happiness.*

She sat with her back to the entrance of the cave and did not notice the shadow behind the big rock near the entrance. She stood and watched the sea waves for a short while, as if she was saying goodbye, and then she started walking back. She entered the cave when she tripped on a net that had been spread on the ground. Before she could stand up, the net was pulled tight around her, lifting her up in a bundle where she swung from the ceiling of the cave.

Lauri did not see anyone around her as she peered through the netting. All that could be seen were huge rocks piled at the side of the cave entrance.

"Put me down, whoever you are! If you want money, I will help you get it. Please, do not leave me hanging here. No one comes this way." Lauri felt fear take hold of her.

Lauri did not hear a sound. She was left alone and knew that no screaming or yelling would help her. Hardly anyone knew about this place. She wished she hadn't strayed so far without telling anyone where she was going, but surely her father would look for her once she failed to show up for her own birthday party.

IRENE STOOD BEHIND THE FIRST CURVE OF THE TUNNEL AND SMILED. *My plans are perfect!* She thought. She could not help feeling ecstatic with her success. *Now no one will come to save Lauri, and Roland will be mine.*

"LAURI, WHERE ARE YOU?" ROLAND CALLED OUT, WORRY PIERCING HIM when he did not see her on the beach.

"Roland, up here!" Lauri yelled, relief washing over her at the sound of his voice.

Her screaming and yelling came from the cave's entrance. He rushed inside, worried that she had slipped and fallen.

"My goodness, how on earth did you end up there?" Roland studied the net's rigging, trying to discover where he might untie the rope. "The other end of the rope is down here tied to the big rock. Who did this, do you know?" Roland asked.

"Believe me, I have no idea who wants to hurt me. I did not think I had enemies," Lauri cried. "Please, help me down."

"I think the one who did this is not very far from here. I have a feeling this person is somewhere close by watching. They would want to make sure their plan worked," Roland stated while looking behind the rocks.

"How did you know where to find me?" Lauri asked.

"I saw you standing in the tower, my Lady. I followed you here because I know you love to sit on the beach."

"I am very glad you did. Thank you for saving my life, Roland."

IRENE HAD STAYED BACK INSIDE THE TUNNEL, WATCHING TO SEE IF anyone would come to save Lauri. She intended to leave her there, hanging from the ceiling until she died. When she saw Roland coming towards the entrance of the cave from the beach, fury overcame her, but she controlled her rage and came out slowly as if nothing had happened. She feigned surprise as she talked to Roland.

"Is my Lady with you, Roland? I know sometimes she seeks solitude at the seashore when she is troubled. I saw her enter the tunnel a while ago, but when she did not return, I decided to look for her," Irene said in a kind, seductive voice.

Roland untied the rope wrapped around the big rock and slowly brought Lauri to the ground. "Yes, I found her entangled in this net!"

"Are you well, my Lady?" Irene feigned shock at seeing Lauri caught in a net.

"IRENE? IS THAT YOU?" LAURI ASKED WITH SURPRISE WHEN SHE HEARD the familiar voice.

"My Lady, you are the luckiest woman on Earth. Right in the nick of time Roland comes to the rescue," Irene said with a vehemence that did not escape Lauri's attention.

"I guess I am, Irene." Lauri thought back to how many times she had escaped the grip of death in seemingly minor accidents. If it were not for Wolf, Lauri would have been dead long ago. She remembered one day when she had been watching the young men training from the tower battlement as she used to do almost every day. She had leaned forward to watch, when Wolf jumped and grabbed Lauri's arm with his mouth, gently pulling her back before she toppled over the loose bricks that fell to the ground below.

On another occasion, when she had been hunting in the forest, she barely escaped an arrow that flew closely over her head. She had not seen where it had come from. These incidents were not close together, but they had happened over the span of a few months. Enough for Lauri to begin to wonder if these were no accidents. Irene was always nearby when these incidents took place, and now Irene just happened to be in the cave at the exact moment Roland came to her rescue. At that moment, Lauri recognized her enemy. She kept her accusations to herself and tried to make small talk with Irene.

"I am very happy you were concerned about my wellbeing. Thank you, I am most grateful. You are a good friend, Irene."

"Yes, my Lady. I will always be there for you," Irene answered as Roland assisted Lauri from the tangles of the net.

"Thank you, Roland. I love you!" Lauri stepped out of the net and went into Roland's open arms. She whispered in his ear. "Roland, Irene did this. Be careful."

While Lauri and Roland were preoccupied, Irene sneaked back to the castle, sensing that she had been caught, she decided to run away. Before Irene left the castle, she stopped by Lauri's room on her way out.

"And you, stupid dog, here is a dessert for you. This will give your mistress a token of my agony." She threw a piece of poisoned meat towards Wolf.

"Irene!" Lauri called out.

When Irene did not answer Lauri's call, they realized that Irene had left. Lauri told Roland about her many near-death experiences and how Irene always seemed to be nearby when these events occurred.

"Irene tried to kill me on my birthday. I can't believe she did this. Where did she get the strength to haul me up like that?"

"She must have been planning it, fixing the net and that wheel, there, hidden behind the rocks, to pull the ropes through that ring up on the ceiling," Roland said, pointing to the rocks.

Roland and Lauri immediately ran after Irene.

THEY ENTERED THE HALL TO THE SIGHT OF THE KNIGHTS STANDING together, watching a noisy commotion nearby. Wolf stood in the middle of the hall, holding Irene's neck in his mouth. Irene looked about wildly, screaming for help, but no one dared go near Wolf for fear he might kill Irene. Wolf bore his fangs, taking a stance of attack in case anyone dared to come near.

Lauri ran to her dog to soothe him and tell Wolf that everything was all right. She commanded Wolf to release Irene's neck. Wolf obeyed, and Irene's head dropped to the floor with a thump, a look of panic and fear flitted across her face.

"Irene must have done something bad to you, my Lady. We all tried to make the dog release her, but the fangs were mightier than our words. We decided to stay back and wait until you returned."

Lauri stood over Irene and said, "Why did you set a trap for me? I know it was you, Irene. There was no one else who could have done such a treacherous thing."

Irene tried to deny the accusation, but Lauri accused her of the multiple attempts on her life.

Outraged, Irene screamed, "I hate you, Lauri! You ruin everything for me!" She burst into angry tears. "Roland was supposed to be mine, but you have stolen him!"

"Guards, take her to prison to await trial for these crimes," Roland ordered.

The guards removed Irene as she kicked and screamed the whole way. Clearly, Irene was not in her right mind.

ROLAND HELD LAURI IN HIS ARMS, TRYING TO ERASE THE ANGER AND fear that she felt. They walked together to the castle gardens where he hoped she would soon forget the incident.

"Your birthday party start soon, but I wanted to give you a gift before everyone else has your attention. Happy birthday, Lauri. I've never forgotten your special day. You have become the most beautiful young lady I've ever seen." Roland gave Lauri a small drawstring pouch which held her gift. "This is a ruby with a chain to adorn your beautiful neck," Roland said.

Lauri smiled as she admired the necklace, and her anger at Irene subsided while she embraced Roland. "This is beautiful, Roland. It matches the bracelet my mother gave me this morning." She held up her wrist for Roland to see.

"That is a beautiful bracelet," Roland said as he had a sudden flash of recognition that passed as quickly as it came.

Lauri began to think about the coming danger that would separate her and Roland. Sadness threatened to take over her special day. Lauri lifted her head from Roland's shoulder and said, "I wish these wars and battles would come to an end." Lauri's tears came tumbling down.

"Lauri, I promise you I will take care of you."

Lauri snuggled against his chest, listening to his heartbeat. "Roland, I have to tell you this. I think you know that the enemy is marching with endless soldiers, and Europe is not responding to our requests for help. As if they gave up on us. My father is sending us to Lebanon where he believes we will be out of danger. His uncle lives there in the village of Itulah, in Jizzine."

"When are you leaving?" Roland's heart squeezed at the thought.

"On Sunday, after dark," Lauri said.

"I will join you for protection." Roland frowned. He had not seen this coming.

"You can't. I heard your father telling mine that he needs you here to defend the city," Lauri said.

"I will have to talk to my father then." Roland lifted Lauri's chin and kissed her with passion. "You should go rest and prepare for your party. I will see you this evening, my darling." Roland escorted Lauri to her quarters and left to speak with his father.

"FATHER, I JUST LEARNED THAT LORD SIMON KANE IS TAKING HIS family north to Lebanon on Sunday. I want to go with them," Roland said.

"Do not worry. They are being provided enough guards. You are needed here. Perhaps you forgot that the Mamluks have already ransacked the southern cities coming towards us," Lord Albert Catin said, berating his son.

"That is exactly why I want to join Lord Kane. Acre, with its weak reinforcement, is bound to fall too. The repeated request for help from Europe, if any, is very slow to come," Roland protested. "At least I can be of use to Lord Kane."

"What? Are you a coward? Do you want to run away from the fight? You can be of use right here!" yelled Lord Albert Catin.

"No, Father. I am no coward, but I have common sense. I will stay here if you force me, but remember what I say to you now. Send our family with Lord Kane. We will not be able to defeat the Mamluks." Roland turned and left the room, feeling despondent.

The next day, Irene stood trial and was found guilty of attempted murder. Her execution was swift.

THE SMALL CARAVAN STARTED MOVING FROM ACRE TOWARDS THE northern border. Roland rode on his horse with his gear, watching the love of his life disappear in the night with her family. Trailing behind them was his family. He followed, protecting the back of the caravan until he made sure they were safe and out of danger. When the caravan reached the border, he returned to Acre. He had to stay. His heart ached at the thought of how long it would be before he could reunite with Lauri.

The Knights Templar were preparing to defend the city of Acre, while the Mamluk army of the Sultan Baybars of Egypt advanced through Palestine from the south. Cities fell as the Crusaders were weak and became complacent through the years. The marching armies continually conquered, defeating city after city. In the end, the Crusaders surrendered. In 1268, Baybars destroyed the Crusaders in Antioch.

King Louis IX prepared an army to attack Egypt, but he turned to Tunis where he died. Prince Edward of England took his march to the Holy Land. He arrived at Acre to help the remnant of the Kingdom of Jerusalem. In 1291 a group of pilgrims were killed on their way to Jerusalem, and as a result, a Syrian caravan was attacked by the Crusaders. Sultan Qalawun sent demands for reparations.

After the Crusaders ignored the demand for a huge amount of compensation Sultan Qalawun took this as an excuse to besiege Acre. He died during the siege and his son, Khalil, ended the existence of the Crusaders.

Persecuted Christians and Druze people found refuge in Mount Lebanon. They created autonomous communities throughout the mountains and people were geographically sheltered and protected during the Ottoman Empire rule of the area.

LAURI KANE REMAINED WITH HER FAMILY IN THE SMALL VILLAGE OF Itulah where her mother's family, a branch of the Kanes, had lived for generations. Every day, she would check the road as far as her eyes could see, praying and hoping that Roland would arrive.

Winter was harsh, and a white blanket of snow covered the mountains. The Cedar trees were majestic, old, and beautiful. One day, as the snow fell relentlessly, Lauri saw a speck in the distance moving towards the village. She strained her eyes to see clearly from behind the windowpane. It was very rare that anyone traveled in such weather, yet that speck became larger, trampling the snow that accumulated on the ground.

She rubbed her eyes several times then yelled, "It's Roland! It's Roland!" She ran down the stairs, grabbed a shawl, and rushed into the snowstorm to meet Roland as he clung to his horse for warmth. He saw her running towards him, and he quickly closed the gap between them, cold and exhausted as he was, seeing her gave him a surge of energy. He lifted her up as the snowflakes showered them. They hugged and kissed, trying to erase the pain of separation. They took the horse to the shed and ran to the house, laughing and talking while Wolf ran ahead of them, wagging his tail.

They sat for dinner, and Lauri served the food. The house was built with stone, and the roof had brick shingles to ward off the harsh winter weather. The hearth in the middle of the room spread its warmth as fire crackled and oil lanterns lit the house with a silver light.

"I lost father during this wicked war. I knew we were weak, and I told him Europe was very slow in responding to our cry for help. He would not listen." Roland appeared sad and disappointed.

"Roland, this is your home, you know that," Lord Kane hurried to reassure him.

"Thank you, Lord Kane. I just want to leave this land and go back to England for a while to sort out father's business affairs. However, my coming back depends on you, Lord Kane. I am asking Lauri's hand in marriage. I can provide for her from my inheritance, and I will take care of her forever," Roland hastened to promise.

"Lauri?" her father asked.

She blushed and nodded her approval.

Many years passed as Roland stayed with Lauri. He postponed his travels when he received word from the manager of his estates that things were going well.

They worked together to cultivate the land and transform a rocky terrain into fertile soil where they sowed grains, grapevines, olive trees, mulberry trees, and other plants. They perfected the process of making purple dye which became famous for its quality in Europe.

Lauri delivered her first baby girl, the beautiful redhead, Katy. Wolf made it his responsibility to never leave her side. As Katy grew up, Wolf was her living toy. She had two other brothers, and they grew up in Mount Lebanon, running wild in the fields. They lived in freedom and peace for a long time. The day came when Wolf was unable to run around. Finally, the dog came to Lauri and looked at her with tears that never came down. Wolf curled up at Lauri's feet and closed his eyes, never to wake up again. Lauri grieved.

One day, Roland came from the field after he received the mail.

"Lauri, I've decided to travel to Scotland and England to take care of our properties and settle some outstanding matters. Would you come with me?" Lauri became very excited at the prospect of traveling. She loved to see new lands.

As they were saying their goodbyes, Lauri said to her daughter, "Always remember, I love you very much. Take care of yourself and the family and keep the bracelet safe. Katy, I made hand copies of all the documents that we are taking with us. Keep them safe in case you need them."

"Do not worry, Mother, I will take care of everything here. I love you and hope you have a wonderful trip. I will pray for safe travels for you and father."

THE SHIP WITH ITS MAJESTIC MASTS SAILED FROM THE PORT OF BEIRUT on very calm seas and the convenient breeze of the Mediterranean. It was early June as Roland and Lauri walked the deck, hand in hand, watching the sun set in the western horizon. Roland wrapped his arms around Lauri.

The Mediterranean was mostly a safe sea to sail on, but suddenly it became treacherous. A storm began to brew, the skies grew dark and foreboding. The waves crested high as they crashed over the rails. The wind howled, turning a once calm sea into a furious swirl which already held the ship in its relentless grasp.

At this moment, Roland and Lauri tied a rope around themselves, securing them to the solid bunk beds. They held tightly to the wooden frame. Other passengers aboard the ship scurried around in a panic, looking for the hatches to take them down to their cabins below decks. Once in the dry relative safety of their cabins, the trembling passengers huddled together as the loud, grinding noise of stretching timber accosted their senses. The crew fought to lower the sails, and they were able to secure and clamp down the hatches before another huge wave pummeled the deck.

The tempest raged, continuing to pound the ship, broken pieces of the masts crashed with deafening thumps. No one in the cabins knew what was happening above with the untamed, ruthless, and vicious weather attack. The power of the wind twisted the waves into a funnel which went down towards the bottom of the sea. The funnel suddenly became a monstrous vortex in front of the ship's keel as a magnificent wave lifted the carved, nude lady on the hull. The ship was a miniscule object in the wind as she flew through the rain and crashed down right in the center of the whirlpool.

The sea swallowed the wreck and all. The tempest disappeared, and once again the seas were calm and peaceful.

EARLY THE NEXT DAY, PEOPLE RAN TO THE BEACH AS THE WAVES SILENTLY carried the wreckage and the remains to the shores of surrounding villages. It was the small Island of Elba where Roland was found unconscious but alive. It took all the efforts of the old retired physician to help Roland regain his health, and for over two long weeks Roland hovered between life and death.

AFTER A LONG RECOVERY, ROLAND STOOD ON THE SAND WITH THE FOAM washing his feet. He was sure that he was the only survivor of the wreck.

"Goodbye, my darling, till we meet again." He turned to go back. A whooshing whisper brushed his ears, making him stop and turn his head towards the sea.

"Until we do, my love," he heard Lauri say over the sound of the sea waves and the rush of a breeze. A tear rolled down his cheek as Roland went back to the cottage. He prepared to leave, heartbroken and filled with grief. Roland returned home to Itulah.

KATY WAS OVERWHELMED WITH SADNESS AT THE LOSS OF HER MOTHER and the immediate change in her father. His grief ate away at him.

"Roland! You have to stop grieving. You have to take care of what is coming."

It was her voice. He thought he must have lost his mind. He heard Lauri's voice several times but dismissed it as imagination, never answering back.

"War is coming. You have to prepare. Dangerous times for the grandchildren." The voice kept nagging.

The Mamluks armies trod from the south, erasing, killing, and destroying the land along the shore's cities and valleys, furthering their conquest to occupy all the northern parts of the lands. The resistance of the local people was tragically weak and unable to stop the march. However, some pockets of courageous local leaders were able to protect the small villages by talking to the Mamluks and making agreements to pay money or provide warriors to join them.

TWO YEARS HAD PASSED SINCE LAURI'S DEATH. ROLAND RODE HIS HORSE to the top of the hill, watching from a distance at the never-ending train of marching soldiers. The dozen men standing behind him were anxiously waiting for a message from the Mamluks to agree on a meeting with Roland.

"I am proud of you, Roland. You will save your people. And this time, I say to you goodbye, my dear, since I couldn't the last time we were together. Until we meet again." The voice that he heard so clearly faded away.

"Until we do, my love," he murmured under his breath.

A rider with a white flag left the lines and raced towards the men on the hill. Roland raised the white flag.

"Who is the leader?" the man asked.

"I am," said Roland. The soldier handed him the message.

"You are expected at the camp tomorrow at noon to meet with our Sultan Khalil." The soldier turned back.

Roland addressed his men and explained the Mamluks demands. "I will provide the monies to be paid to them," explained Roland. "The Mamluks are demanding twenty able-bodied men, but I will not force anyone of you to join them. It is up to each man in the village to decide for himself. Call a meeting right away to see if there are any volunteers." They rode down the hill towards the village.

Twenty young men between the ages of twenty and twenty-five years old stood ready to go with Roland, volunteering to risk their lives to defend their families. They said their goodbyes to their dear ones among the muffled wailings and cries of mothers, wives, sisters, and daughters. Thus, they saved their village from pillaging and destruction.

However, Roland's deep anger at putting the young men's lives in danger to join a cruel and merciless regiment kept eating at his heart. He decided to join the men as their leader with a plan in his mind. He once again said goodbye to his children and grandchildren, entrusting the business to his eldest daughter, Katy, and her husband.

"Ah, Sheikh Roland, the famous producer of the purple color dye. Your reputation is well known to so many in the region. Now you come to show your commitment. Good, where is the money?"

Roland took a bag full of gold and said, "Here is the gold you asked for, and here are the most able men who volunteered to join your army. However, I am demanding to be the leader of this regiment of men."

The Sultan was astonished at the request and said, "Do you think I am going to trust you, you infidel, to lead my men?" He spat the words out in a clear insult.

"They know me and trust me to take care of them. There is

nothing I want from this world anymore, and I give my life to protect my men and my people," Roland answered defiantly.

The Sultan stood up and yelled, "Guards, take this infidel and put him in the dungeons of Tyre Fortress until I come back. Take the men for training with Abdul's men."

A few months passed, and Roland was kept prisoner with very little to eat despite the coins he passed among the prison guards. A slave would come to bring him his meager food plate and drinks, and she would talk to Roland every now and then while the guard was happy to turn his back, expecting the shining piece soon to be in his hands.

"You infidel, come here. There is someone here to visit you." The guard who gained most of the coins from Roland yelled at him. "You have a few minutes."

Roland came to the iron bars closest to the guard. He was surprised to see a very old woman standing in front of him. His mother-in-law, Janet, was smiling at him, looking older than he remembered.

"My son, this guard was very helpful in allowing me to see you. I'm very sorry you are here. We looked for you everywhere when we received word of what happened. Here is some food I made for you. You look thin. Eat the food. You will be strong again."

"Thank you, Mother. How are the children?" Roland stared at her eyes and realized she was blinking her eyelids rapidly, communicating with him in a code that had long ago been established by their family, practiced and memorized for such emergencies.

"They are safe, my son. I am just grateful that you are alive." As she talked, he read the message that he was not alone and would soon be rescued. He was instructed to look carefully at the details of the designs on the cookies she had baked him. The plain cookies were given to the guard in return for his silence.

"Time is up. You must go now." The guard pulled the old woman away.

"Be nice to her, and you will be happy. She is coming to see me in a couple of days from now," Roland told the guard.

The guard looked at him sideways to see his meaning. Roland smiled at him, and the guard knew it meant more gold.

~

KATY WAITED FOR HER GRANDMOTHER OUTSIDE THE FORTRESS. SHE WAS happy to see her coming out and ran to meet her.

"He is fine, do not worry," the grandmother whispered. "It will be over soon. I promised the guard some gold next time I am here. He said he will wait here for us." She rode her horse with her granddaughter back to the village to arrange for Roland's escape.

~

ROLAND OPENED THE BAG OF FOOD AND PUT THE COOKIES ON THE floor to look at the design. There he read what he had to do the next night. He slowly cracked the cookies open and found gold pieces that would help him bribe the guards.

It was late in the evening the next day, when the Sultan returned to the fortress in Tyre after conquering the Northern lands on his way back to Egypt. The camp for the army was set outside the fortress. The slaves were frantic to get things ready for the Sultan, who neglected to send them word that he was arriving.

A banquet was made ready for the Sultan, his entourage, his assistants, and other high-ranking generals.

After everybody had finished eating, the entertainment began, and music and dancers filled the hall. One general whispered in the Sultan's ear, "What are you going to do with the infidel in the dungeon?"

The Sultan had already forgotten about Roland and he said, "Let him rot in there." He turned and continued to enjoy the festivities.

In the chaos of the Sultan's leaving the fortress, three soldiers stayed behind to attend to the needs of the slaves and prisoners there.

It was time to bring the meal to Roland in his dungeon, and the slave girl assigned to him was approached by one of the soldiers. He told her to bring him a jug of wine and a tankard. He put some herbs in it and told the slave to follow him with the food.

"Hello, friend!" bellowed the soldier as he approached the guard. "You missed all the merriment earlier, and I thought you might like this." He handed him a tankard of wine.

The guard was surprised but welcomed the drink as he was feeling thirsty. He gulped down half of the tankard, while the slave gave the food to Roland. Suddenly, the guard felt drowsy, and in a few moments, he fell asleep on a nearby bench. The soldier took the keys and opened the cell.

"Roland, put this soldier's uniform on quickly, Let's go!" the soldier urged.

"Jamile, is that you? Oh, my goodness, thank God you're alive! I heard some of my men didn't survive." Roland rushed to change his clothes. "Here are some gold pieces. Put them in the guard's pocket." He left the cell and was sure no one would recognize him in the soldier's uniform.

"And you, young lady," Roland turned to the slave girl, "here is some gold for your kindness. Run away right now. Thank you for all your help."

"Thank you, sir. I have been separated from my family for so long. I will leave tonight to return home." The slave girl took this opportunity to flee as she knew that if she stayed, she would have surely been punished for Roland's escape.

At the top of the stairs, the two other soldiers were impatiently waiting. They saw Roland and Jamile approaching. Roland did not say a word, so as not to draw attention to himself, but he recognized his men and gave them a grateful smile.

"Where are the rest?" Roland asked with apprehension.

"Dead. We are the only survivors." Roland felt disheartened that hadn't been given the chance to protect his men or resist the enemy in an effective way. He promised himself to avenge those who were killed.

The general who had reminded the Sultan of Roland's existence managed to recognize him as Roland ran to his horse. He was one of the army's most courageous warriors. However, he was born in the village of Itulah and knew the Kanes and the Catins. He volunteered to be in the army as a young man to fight the Crusaders because of his family's abject poverty. After joining the army of Qalawun, he recognized his folly, but he decided to continue in the service as it was his only source of income. He decided to look the other way and let Roland escape as a kindness, for he had heard that Roland's family was looking after his widowed mother in his absence.

The news of Roland's return with three of his men travelled like wildfire. The villagers gathered in the streets, some cheering, some clapping, and some crying as they realized that their other young men were not coming back.

Katy ran towards her father and clasped at his neck, kissing his face with joy at his safe return. His men left to see their families. Lord Simon and Janet Kane stood at the door, welcoming their son-in-law.

Six months had passed since Roland had returned home. He concentrated on his business, and one day four huge bags of the purple dye were ready for shipment at the port of Tyre. There was a relative calm from attacks and war, and he decided to take the merchandise himself.

He crossed the distance to the city of Tyre and went to the inn to reserve his room for a few nights. He ordered a jug of wine and food for dinner.

He paid the innkeeper in advance and left towards the wharf where ships had already docked. After leaving the inn, he started to feel that someone was following him. He tried to dismiss the feeling of danger and kept walking with his sword ready at his side.

The agent with whom he had previously made agreements for trading was sitting in a cafe smoking a hookah. "Ah, Roland, my friend," he called and stood up. "So, what do you have for me this time?" The old man with missing teeth welcomed Roland with open arms.

"I have all these bags ready to ship as you ordered. Do you have any new orders for the dye?"

"Yes, my friend, here is the new order to be shipped in two months to Italy and France," the old man said.

"Good, I will be here in two months." Roland and the old man called porters to unload the merchandise. It would be ready for shipment the next day.

The old man paid Roland with gold coins as usual. Roland felt very tired and ready to rest. He continued on his way to the inn. It was dark, and just before he arrived at the inn's court to put the horses in the stables, two men ambushed him. He unsheathed his sword and tried to defend himself, but two more men joined the others, stabbing him repeatedly. They took the money and left.

For a while, Roland couldn't move due to pain and blood loss, but when he opened his eyes, Lauri stood in front of him. She came forward and smiled her beautiful smile as she reached for his hand. He stood and held her in a tight embrace and soon they both faded away.

WHEN ROLAND DID NOT COME BACK AFTER TWO DAYS, HIS FATHER-IN-law went searching for him. He found his agent keeping Roland's body in a box at the local church cemetery. He took the body and buried him in Itulah.

CHAPTER TWENTY-FIVE

LAURA AND ROLAND: LOVE REKINDLED

1974

*W*hen the music stopped, Roland and Laura stood in the middle of the dance floor staring at each other.

"Did it happen again?" Roland asked.

Laura stood dumbfounded, unable to move. She whispered, "I guess it did. We better go back to our seats."

Roland asked Nana to dance with him, noticing Laura's preoccupied expression. She was gratful that he wished to give her the time to process what they had just shared. She remembered her vision in the seer's cave when she had been swirling in a whirlpool caused by an angry sea storm. She had seen two of her past lives in that seer's cave. She simply hadn't realized the vision's significance until now. Was there a way to stop these rebirths? She wanted to live just one last life with Roland and then be with him for eternity in the heavens.

They returned home a little after midnight. Laura allowed herself the luxury of staying up late since the next morning was her day off.

"We need to talk, Laura," Roland said after Juliette and Nana left them alone for the night.

"Yes, Roland, I know what you are going to say. Yes, it happened again, just like it did my eighteenth birthday. I do not understand how this is possible, but I realized after my eighteenth birthday that there is a secret, a powerful promise, held within the bracelet you gave me in our first life together. It is connected to what is happening now. I was afraid if I acknowledged the visions I saw, the past lives we shared together, you would believe me to be crazy," Laura said with a blush. "Truthfully, I have dreamt of our past lives together since I was seven years old."

"I had no idea! I am sorry you have carried this knowledge alone," Roland said. "I was trying to tell you what I had seen on your birthday. I should have pushed for us to talk about this sooner." Roland cracked up laughing and said, "To think that I thought you were going to call me crazy if I opened my mouth then!"

"Did that really happen to us?" Laura whispered as waves of disbelief rolled over her.

"Twice in time must be proof that it did. I found you for the third time, my love, and I will never let you go. I promise we will never be apart again." He knelt down on one knee and pulled a small box out of his pocket. Laura gasped at the sparkling mound of diamonds that sat nestled on a beautiful platinum ring. "Will you marry me?"

"Yes! I love you," Laura exclaimed.

Roland kissed Laura in the moonlight.

CHAPTER TWENTY-SIX

LAURA: A DREAM COME TRUE

1975-1983

A month after the wedding, Laura sat on the edge of the bed where Roland was reading the newspaper. She held a cup of coffee in her hand, sipping slowly as she thought about how to start this conversation. She put the cup on the bedside table, gently lowered his newspaper, smiled and said, "Roland, we are going to have a baby!"

"Yippee!" Roland jumped out of bed and pulled Laura into his arms, spinning her around and gently setting her down. "The best news ever!"

They celebrated the growth of their family and talked about their future. Life was perfect.

∾

DURING THE YEARS THAT FOLLOWED, ROLAND BECAME A VERY successful pharmacist. He operated his own pharmacy and was well liked by his customers. His good reputation spread throughout the city, and he was able to expand his business. Roland and Laura were blessed with a baby girl, and a year later, she gave birth to a baby boy.

During that time, a revolution occurred against the Shah of Iran, bringing the exiled Imam Khomeini back to the country. In the year 1979, the Shah and his wife, the Empress, went into exile to the United States and hid in the Bahamas for a while. Later on, the Shah got sick and passed away. The danger of him returning back to Iran was gone. The empress eventually moved to France.

Little did anyone know that the influence of Imam Khomeini's radical religious views would sweep the Middle Eastern countries like wildfire as turmoil and unrest prevailed.

Tensions in the social fabric mounted between the moderate followers of Islam and the radical believers. While it had once been rare to see a woman covered with a hijab in earlier years, a massive reversal from modern western appearance to the oppressive customs of a thousand years prior began to take shape. Muslim women everywhere began covering their hair. Some were even fully covered with mere slits for their eyes as they followed their sheikhs' interpretation of Shari'a Law.

Young men in the downtown areas of Amman, especially the unemployed and those with no education, walked the streets with little to no purpose, spending their time in the cafes drinking coffee and smoking the hookah pipe while harassing uncovered women who passed by.

"ROLAND, WHAT DO YOU THINK ABOUT GETTING AN IMMIGRATION VISA to the United States, just in case things get worse for Christians here? It is becoming more dangerous for us to live here," Laura said. "My boss, Mr. Thomas, can help us get one."

"We have a very good business here, and we have a nice house built the way you want. It will be difficult to give up our lifestyle. However, I am concerned about our daughters," Roland said.

"I have noticed a new phenomenon in the bank," Laura said. "A year ago, there was only one girl that had her hair covered. Today, it is only me and two others who do not cover their hair."

"The situation here is getting worse for Christians," Roland said.

"Yes, I agree. I have a heaviness in my heart. In the streets, young children are taught to spit on the cross, just as they do when I pass by because I do not cover my hair." Laura was angry. She tried to control the rage. "Things are not getting any better in society. Some women in sleeveless tops are being attacked here and there. I heard that a man threw acid on a woman yesterday because she was wearing a sleeveless top, and he wanted to shame her by burning the rest of her clothes off. The radical men are pushing for Shari'a Law to be applied on all women, regardless of their religion, and I fear they will get what they want. It is becoming very dangerous."

"I have been worried at some of the things I have heard, but I had hoped things would die down," said Roland.

"I believe this persecution will only get worse. It is tragic that some women are still being oppressed. We used to have more freedom. Not anymore," lamented Laura.

They were able to acquire a visa. Laura gave birth to their fourth child, a baby girl. With one son and three daughters, Roland and Laura made their plans to explore immigrating to the U.S.

"YOU ARE BREAKING MY HEART." JULIETTE KISSED HER DAUGHTER goodbye.

"Mama, as of right now, we are just going on vacation. We haven't made a firm decision to move. Plus, if we stay, the airport is nearby. You can come visit anytime you want," Laura said with a pang of guilt in her heart.

"I know you are not coming back. I know you," Juliette cried. She held her fourth grandchild, Ronda, in her arms, and sobbed.

On July 29, 1983, their airplane touched down in New York, the first step towards becoming citizens of the United States. Sandra was seven, Ronni was six, Mona three, and Ronda was forty-nine days old.

ROLAND AND LAURA UPROOTED THEIR FAMILY FOR GOOD. LAURA yearned to breathe free in a land that did not condemn her or oppress her for being a woman and a Christian. Starting over in a new country was not without difficulty. Roland was unable to establish his own business in the U.S. and found it necessary to travel back and forth to Jordan in order to earn money to support his family. They were very fortunate that his pharmacy was successful, and it made their life in the U.S. possible. Despite the struggles of adjusting to a new way of life, they were able to assimilate into the culture of their new country.

Laura refused to let the pangs of loneliness take over, especially when Roland was traveling. She made the best of her situation and time rolled on.

ROLAND WAS HAPPY TO SEE HIS WIFE AND, BY THEN, FIVE CHILDREN, healthy and happy too. Their youngest son, Sam, was born in the United States. Roland longed for the day that he would be able to stop traveling for work and enjoy time with his family. He loved being home with them and made every moment count.

Roland bought an RV, and they traveled all over the western part of the country. They visited California and Nevada, seeing the majestic mountains and ancient forests that covered the landscape. They traveled as far east as Wyoming but decided to head north when they saw desert lands which reminded them too much of the Middle East.

As they passed through Oregon they were fascinated with its beauty. The snowcapped mountains, the Columbia River Gorge, the bridges, the rivers and forests captured their hearts. Roland and Laura decided to settle there.

Juliette had come to visit and help Laura with her fifth and final child, Sam, in 1985. Juliette loved being with her daughter and grand-children. She traveled with them and was fascinated by the diverse geography and beauty of the land. Juliette especially enjoyed going to Reno and Las Vegas where she discovered that she enjoyed playing the games in the casinos. Seeing Juliette's fascination and childlike joy as they visited Disneyland made Laura feel less guilty for leaving her mother behind. Juliette would visit from time to time but not more than a few months as she felt compelled to be in Jordan where her other children lived. Once Sam was five, Juliette visited for the last time.

CHAPTER TWENTY-SEVEN

LAURA: TERROR

2001

*E*ventually, Roland was able to retire, and they moved to Orlando, Florida where they built a house on 2.5 acres of land that Roland had purchased some years prior. They loved the smell of orange blossoms that emanated from the orange groves on their property.

On the morning of September 11, 2001, Laura was watching the news, when a horrible scene came across the screen. A scream escaped her throat, and a moan of grief and anger filled her being.

To her astonishment, Laura watched as two jumbo jet passenger planes slammed into the World Trade Center towers within minutes of each other. She watched in horror as people located above the wreckage jumped to their deaths from the high-rise buildings.

Soon after, reports came in of a third airplane crash that hit the Pentagon building in Washington, DC, starting a violent fire. One of the World Trade Center towers collapsed, crumbling down like a house of cards, the structure tumbled one story after the other.

Passers-by covered with ashes and rubble ran in the streets not knowing where to go or where to hide. It was like the end of the world to those who were there. Yet another plane fell from the skies in a field in Pennsylvania. Soon after, the second World Trade Center tower collapsed.

As she cried out in agony at what she was seeing, her daughter, Ronda, who was visiting for the summer came into the living room to see what had disturbed her mother.

"Oh Mother, this is bad, this is really bad," Rhonda cried.

Laura hugged her daughter and said, "Al Qaeda did this! We moved you from an area where the populace was influenced by radicals who nurtured hate and fought those whom they called infidels. We brought you here for safety. They followed us here!" Laura moaned.

"Why would they do this? I don't understand!" Rhonda said.

"Rhonda, what you see before you is the culmination of religious militancy and hate that has existed for more than one thousand six hundred years. This hatred is directed towards everything that is different from what Islam teaches."

Laura remembered how people had changed in their behavior from being civil and tolerant of Christians to burning churches in Egypt and imposing their way of life on everyone through aggressive means.

"Every Friday when Muslims go to the mosques, the imams called for Jihad against the kuffar (the Christians and Jews). Every call to prayer from the minarets is a reminder of this call to Jihad," Laura explained to her daughter. "Terrorists in the name of Allah started burning churches and attacking Christians whenever they could after Khomeini took over Iran. However, we were lucky in Jordan because the King of Jordan, to his credit, controlled the country with an iron fist. Minor violence—like church windows being broken—was met with force. The Christians were somehow safe there but experienced harassment on a smaller scale, from which I personally suffered. They spit on my cross or called me names because I did not wear the hijab while walking outside, and this treatment escalated," Laura said while Ronda sat and listened.

Ronda was in college, old enough to understand what her mother was telling her and connecting all of the terror that happened on this tragic day to an ideology, the purpose of which was to make the whole world follow one religion, their own. She understood that not all Muslims were terrorists, but all the foreign terrorists were Muslims.

Ronda realized that domestic terrorists were also a threat, but domestic terror acts were rare, and they were executed by mentally-ill individuals who were not following a radical religious call. Yet these foreign terrorists acted frequently and worldwide. When they executed their acts of terror, it was in response to a call to Jihad with the hope of martyrdom and reward.

As they watched the news broadcast, the news anchors kept asking rhetorically, *"Why would they do this?"* Laura wanted to scream. "Anyone who wants to know the answer as to the source for such brutality, whether in the past or present, simply needs to look to the Quran and the hadith. It was in Al Bukhari No. 42, page 148 and 149. The Prophet declared that Allah gave him five privileges, *'I was victorious through a terror reputation of a one-month distance. Looting permission was granted only to me and no one before me. All lands were given for prayers, so pray. I was given the gift of intercession. A prophet came only to his people, I came for all people of the world.'"*

Laura continued to explain to Ronda why the terrorists did this. "Ronda, no one will ever see an old sheikh over the age of fifty put bombs around his waist and sacrifice himself to gain the gifts of paradise. Suicide bombers are all between the ages of thirteen and forty because they are easily manipulated to do these acts." Laura was anguished. "For some it is avarice and lust for power, and for others the control of young men, molding them and indoctrinating them with what they believe in, enticing them for Jihad with martyrdom and virgins (horiat) in paradise as their payment. Some young men, with the encouragement of zealots, chose the shortcut to paradise."

Ronda was so heartbroken, she clung to her mother for comfort.

ROLAND WAS TRAVELING BACK TO JORDAN FOR THE LAST TIME WHEN THE terrorist attack occurred. Laura missed him very much and worried about his travel back to the U.S. After the dust settled, the story was told over and over again. Nine young radicals wanted to fight for their Allah, gain martyrdom, and please their Prophet. They were convinced that they would go to paradise and receive unimaginable pleasures in heaven.

CHAPTER TWENTY-EIGHT

LAURA: REUNION

2009

It took sixteen years for Laura to go back to Jordan and visit her aging mother. A longing hit her heart when Laura felt she needed to travel to see her. Old age forced the bustling woman of youth to become bedridden, with deep pain in her old bones and dementia. Juliette was ninety-two years old.

Laura boarded the airplane excited to go see her mother, yet the feeling of apprehension tugged at her stomach. She shut her eyes to shake her fear of flying over the ocean. She couldn't help but remember her visions at the seer's cave so many years before, living her past lives together with her darling husband. The most terrifying event was the memory of the vortex that took her previous life at sea.

∾

"LAURA, HOW COME YOU ARE HERE, MY DARLING?" JULIETTE WAS surprised to see her daughter.

"Well, I missed you and wanted to hug you." Laura knelt down at the edge of the bed and gave her mother a long hug. Laura was also feeling the burden of the years. Long gray hair crowned her head, pushed back by a brown headband. Her mother hugged her back.

Laura sat on the porch on an old couch, remembering a special day, long ago, when she was eighteen. She smiled as she watched what remained of the beautiful garden that her father had once created. Few trees still stood, the lemon tree, the plum tree, and a huge pine tree that her sister Nana had planted the year they left the country. Rana came to her mind, and the feeling of loss for her friend came back along with the remembrance of good times.

"Oh Rana, how I wish you were here. I still miss you even though it was so long ago that I lost you," Laura whispered.

Since Rana had been buried in a Muslim cemetery, Laura did not know where to go or who to see to find Rana's burial site. To her, another grave was lost forever.

It was late in the evening when Laura and her sister sat watching their mother sleep. That was the only time when she was not in pain.

"Oh, Mother, please forgive me. I was selfish to uproot the children and leave you, but believe me, Mother, this was the right thing to do. All I want is to let you know that I am very happy," Laura whispered.

Laura turned to her sister and asked, "Why didn't the doctor give her anything for pain?"

"He said they do not give medication of that kind to people this age. However, you know our mother. She refuses to take any kind of medication anyway. At one point, after her gallbladder surgery, the doctor stopped all her medication. She was happy for a while and—" She was interrupted by three knocks at the door.

Laura said, "Who do you think would come at this hour?" She opened the door with a bit of misgiving.

"Nana, there is no one at the door. Do you have pranksters around?" Laura asked.

"No. This has never happened before." Nana went outside to the porch and looked around.

"Very strange. I heard the knocks, too, but no one is there," Nana said.

The nurse who took care of Juliette came out from her room and said, "I know who it is. I saw him yesterday near your mother's bed. It is your papa."

"What nonsense!" Nana was very upset.

They came back to Juliette's bed. Suddenly, Juliette stopped breathing. She quickly turned blue. Laura instantly began CPR to revive her mother, while her sister called the ambulance. Juliette started breathing again but was unconscious. She was rushed to the hospital.

Waiting for the doctor to come out from the emergency room, Laura's heart squeezed with sadness as the expectation for her mother to regain consciousness waned further away. The doctor came out after a while and announced that Juliette was in a critical condition with no hope of recovery. He allowed Laura to go in to see her. In a dreamlike vision she saw him, her father, waiting for her mother to come to him.

Emile said to his daughter with a smile, "She will be at peace, with no pain or worry." At that moment she saw her mother standing near her father, as beautiful as she was in her youth, looking over her crooked, old body. Juliette looked at her daughter and smiled. She took Emile by the hand, and they both faded away. Laura kept this vision to herself, a gift from her parents to ease her grief.

Juliette was buried in a cemetery in a desert location. Juliette's trepidation of this happening came true. She was always scared to die and be buried in an arid, desert land, but Nana swore not to let this happen. She planted green grass, an olive tree, and bushes around the elevated tomb.

This time, Laura made sure she knew the way to her mother's grave. Nana decided to put her father's name on the same tombstone. Now Emile would not be lost anymore.

As Laura bent to put flowers on the tomb, she raised her head to a sight she would never forget the rest of her life. Standing behind the statue of the Virgin Mary, her father and mother held hands and smiled at her.

"Okay, Dad, time for you to move on now. I know you will always watch from above. You have your love with you. Goodbye, Mama, and I will always miss you. Both of you will live in my heart forever. I love you." With a sad heart and tears welling in her eyes, she watched once more as her parents disappeared together.

Laura looked around, inspecting the names on the graves neighboring her mother's. She walked through the well-designed plots, and there she found engraved on marble, "Hani Harb 1945 - 1970". The man who had died too young and risked his life to come see if they needed help during the civil war. The residue of guilty feelings emerged for a few seconds.

"God bless you, Hani. I am sorry you died so young, my friend. I know you are resting in peace." Laura's tears rolled again as she bent down to put a flower on the grave.

LAURA DECIDED TO VISIT OMAR'S FAMILY BEFORE RETURNING TO Florida. The father had already passed away a year after Omar left for Egypt. Omar's mother lived with a niece who took care of her.

When Laura was ready to leave, Omar's mother said, "Omar is in America now. You should call him. He would love to hear from you." She gave her a card with his contact information.

Laura went back to her home in Orlando where the love of her life was waiting for her. The vision of her parents together made her heartache ease a little.

"HELLO, MAY I SPEAK WITH OMAR ABBAS. THIS IS LAURA SALEM CATIN," Laura said.

A yell in her ear made her jump. "Laura, oh my goodness! Laura, is that really you?"

Laura laughed heartily and said, "Yes, Omar, I would like to see you. I told my husband about you and my friend Rana. I have so many questions. I really miss you. How are you? What happened to you after you left the Country? Are you married?"

"Yes, and a proud father of three. It is a long story," Omar answered. "How did you get my number, and where are you calling from?"

"I visited your mother in Jordan. She is in good health, and she gave me your number. We live in Orlando, Florida," Laura said.

"We live in Clearwater, Florida! I have so much to tell you." He and Laura agreed to meet.

Laura and Roland drove to Clearwater, about three hours from where they lived in Orlando. An astonished and puzzled look on Laura's face made Omar laugh as he greeted them. Behind him came his wife.

"This is my wife, Sylvia."

"This is my husband, Roland." Laura introduced them.

Laura took a look at a painting that puzzled her. On the wall hung a beautiful painting of 'The Last Supper'. Yet, Omar was Muslim.

"Omar?" Laura looked at him for clarification.

"Surprised? Yes, I am now a devout Christian. The Lord Jesus was, is, and will always be my Lord, and through him, by the Grace of God, is my salvation. It is a long story. Come, let us sit down on the porch." They settled into comfortable seats as they enjoyed the calm gulf water view.

The painful memory of Rana rushed to his mind. Omar described the horror he felt when he saw his beloved stretched on the floor, swimming in a pool of her own blood. Laura could not control her tears.

Omar said, "I left Rana's house and kept running in the streets like a mad man. I went home and took all the books that my father had collected and sat all night and all the next day, reading every word and every sentence, trying to find where Allah gave permission to men to kill another human being, and I found plenty in the religion I grew up with. Even though stoning is not practiced, except in very militant countries, the use of other weapons is. That's what Ali did. My best friend turned into a religious militant, a monster who followed a group applying what Sheikh Abu Qutaybah was telling them to do. My father, upon hearing Ali's threats, sent me to live with his brother in Egypt."

Laura gave Omar the other side of the story. "Ali spent some time in jail, but with his father's contacts, he was able to get released due to temporary insanity, resulting in an honor killing. As you know, this is legal in the Middle East. I know that Ali became more deranged. He joined a terrorist group of men, a branch of Al Qaeda. He was shot trying to sneak into Israel from north of Syria with some other young men who wanted to become martyrs by giving their lives to free the occupied land," Laura said. "I can't understand why he became a radical terrorist."

Omar said, "Actually, that radicalism Ali practiced is what is taught to all Muslim children. For the majority, they dismiss the hostile teachings and choose to live a life of peace. However, any Muslim could be triggered to Jihad by a call of a popular imam, a feeling of indignation by social rejection, or strong feelings regarding political issues. This is how a terrorist is born anywhere, even those living in a western country. Remember, they have a reward of virgins in paradise if they martyr themselves for Allah's cause."

"That is horrible, Omar! Thank the Lord that you have left Islam behind," said Laura.

"It belongs in the dustbin of history," said Omar.

"By the way, the coroner's report proved that Rana was not pregnant. He killed her for nothing. I did not understand why she lied to her mother. She probably thought that saying she was pregnant would put her parents under pressure to accept you as her husband. All I know is that she loved you very much. The whole family left the country, never to return. They were somewhere in Europe as one neighbor told my sister."

For a few minutes, Omar sat silent with his head bent down. His sadness was difficult to bear at times, but he was overjoyed to share his experience about the love of Jesus and the miracles that had happened to him. Sylvia came in with coffee, and the heavy sadness was diffused.

"In Cairo, I met two young men who introduced me to Jesus and told me about God's love for me. They gave me a Bible, and I read it and understood it. I knelt down in a church near my uncle's house and prayed for Jesus to forgive me, to help me, and heal me. I promised I would dedicate my life to him and surrender to him as my Lord and Savior," Omar declared.

Laura and Roland sat silently, listening to Omar. They were grateful that God had moved so mightily in Omar's life.

"My uncle got word that I went with some friends to church. He was very upset. He said I would bring disaster to the family, and if I did not stop going to church, my life would be in danger. At first, I did not believe him because I didn't think anyone would care about what I believed in. Why trouble themselves with my beliefs? But it seemed many did." Omar hadn't thought about these events in years.

"One day, I was coming out of the church, and the police were waiting. They dragged me into a truck and took me to the station. The Officer was an evil man who beat me with a stick. He called me kuffar and shoved me in a cell. If you could have seen the cell, you would not have believed your eyes. Not even a cockroach could have lived in the filth that covered that place." Omar remembered the horror of rats and other bugs that crawled in the dark. He paused for a moment while his face contorted, trying to hold back tears. "Laura, I tell you if you have as much faith as a mustard seed, you can tell a mountain to move and it will. How true. A bright shining light filled the room and stayed lit. I did not see anyone, only light. All rats and bugs disappeared in the holes and crevices. I knelt on my knees, thanking the Lord for his protection. My uncle was able to get me a release after two days, telling them that I went to church just to look inside, being curious, and it would never happen again. He later kicked me out of the house, and I went to my friends. I knew what my life would be. I was baptized. One day, I met Sylvia, the daughter of an American missionary who worked as a teacher in a private school." Omar took Sylvia's hand and tenderly kissed it. "You see, the Lord led me to them, and they saved my life. I came to the United States, we got married, and my mother sent me some money from selling the store my father had owned. I decided to drop out of school and opened a grocery store instead. After all, that is what I know best. God's grace covered me and my wife and children. I have three boys. They finished college and are now in different states, successful and happy with their careers." Omar smiled proudly.

"What a story. Miracles do happen, and the Lord never leaves us," Roland said.

"Roland, do you know how to play backgammon?" Omar asked.

Roland laughed. "Who doesn't? Yet it has been a very long time since I played it last."

"Do not worry, it will come back to you."

Omar went to the living room, brought a small table, and opened the backgammon game with the dice.

"Dinner will be ready in a little while," Sylvia said.

"Do you need help?" Laura offered.

"No, thanks. I am fine," Sylvia assured her and went back to the kitchen.

"I want to go down to the beach. I want to spend a little bit of time on the sand before the sun sets," Laura said and left them to their game.

Laura stood alone on the beach. She watched as the fireball in the sky lost its zest, and slid down the horizon, leaving the sky red. The waves rolled and crashed along the sand, leaving white foam behind in their retreat back to the sea. Omar's experience with the Lord brought a smile to her face.

She remembered Roland's shout of joy as he called her on the telephone when he was alone in Jordan. He was practically yelling as he said, "Laura, the book of the Lord is alive! I was reading and suddenly I understood the message and felt the Holy Spirit, the Comforter that the Lord sent so that we shall not be orphans. I am very excited and can't believe it took me so long to read the Holy Book and understand it. Laura go read John 14:16-17. It says, '*And I will pray to the Father, and He will give you another Helper, that He may abide with you forever -*

the Spirit of truth, whom the world cannot receive, because it neither sees Him nor knows Him; but you know Him, for He dwells with you and will be in you.' And in John 14:26-28 it says, 'But the Helper, the Holy Spirit, whom the Father will send in My name, He will teach you all things, and bring to your remembrance all things that I said to you. Peace I leave with you, My peace I give to you; not as the world gives do I give to you. Let not your heart be troubled, neither let it be afraid. You have heard Me say to you, 'I am going away and coming back to you.' If you loved Me, you would rejoice because I said, 'I am going to the Father,' for My Father is greater than I.'"

His renewal of faith was very exciting to him, and he never stopped talking about the Lord to his children and anyone who would listen.

Laura's long white hair blew in the breeze, the gorgeous copper color gone with age. She shut her eyes for a moment, trying to digest what Omar had told them. She opened her eyes when something touched her bare foot. She quickly moved, thinking it was some fish, but noticed it was a big seashell. It was exactly like the seashell that had sat on the side table in their living room when she was about eleven years old. Her father had kept it from a young age. Laura picked it up and put it to her ear.

The hum of the deep sea coming from the seashell filled her with nostalgia for a time long, long, ago on a beach somewhere near a citadel wall with her knight approaching on his horse. The hum continued to tell the story of years past and years to come.

Laura and Roland returned home, discussing how the Lord works in mysterious ways.

CHAPTER TWENTY-NINE

LAURA: MEMORIES

2001 - 2019

The two motorcycle engines roared behind the car early in the morning on his way to work.

"Die you infidel," *the murderers yelled, fleeing the scene...*

Laura sat with tears rolling down her cheeks while she read an article about a Christian man who was gunned down while serving the poor in the Middle East. She was moved with sorrow. It seemed to Laura that regardless of where one went in certain parts of the world, hatred and bitterness filled some people, brainwashed by an ideology that endangered the existence of humanity.

After the 9/11 attacks, tensions between the Christians and Muslims grew and more terror attacks followed. Nothing surprised Laura anymore.

Thus, the Prophet Mohammad had once again changed lives, but this time throughout the entire world. In the US, Germany, France, and the United Kingdom, radicals became emboldened and active at the urging of imams, in various mosques, calling for Jihad. They bombed trains, cafes, and shot people in concert halls and shopping malls.

Because of all the terrorist activity, security for travel by air was increased significantly. In an effort to ensure passenger safety, all passengers were treated with suspicion, as if a new rule was implemented: *Anyone can be a terrorist, be it children or adults.*

Laura realized that the reason all people were treated with equal scrutiny at airports was to avoid the appearance of prejudice or bigotry. It angered her that political correctness was elevated above all other values.

Freedom of speech seemed to also be under attack, as any criticism of Islamic ideology became labeled as Islamophobia, in the pretext of protecting the innocent from persecution and discrimination. At the same time, the revival of an ideology of hate, death, and war by some radicals spewed over television and modern media, resulted in churches being burned in Egypt, Pakistan, and Afghanistan. Killing Christians unsettled millions of people who lost all sense of peace and safety, yet no political leader would acknowledge the ideology from which these hate crimes stemmed from.

Sorrow and grief gripped the nation, but the resiliency of the people prevailed. They vehemently decided to build again what was destroyed and fight the terrorists that were responsible.

To Laura, the most shocking part of the aftermath of 9/11 was the Western culture's apparent acceptance of the idea that Islam was a "peaceful" religion that had been hijacked by radicals. It seemed to Laura that the people of the West did not understand that the "radicalism" of Islam was actually what true Islam was meant to be.

She wished that there was some way to bring truth out. Others who seemed to want to reveal the truth of Islam emerged but were quickly silenced over time.

Out of fear of retaliation from non-Muslims, moderate Muslims succeeded in deceiving the West into believing that Islam was a religion of peace and the atrocities were done only by mentally sick individuals. Laura wondered if moderate Muslims really knew what the Quran taught. She also considered that if they did know what the

Quran taught, fear from being attacked by other Muslims would keep them quiet, never questioning the Quran teachings, silencing them into submission.

Laura and Roland had left the Middle East because of the radical Islamic ideology that had become so prevalent. Her fears that the same ideology was slowly creeping into the United States were materializing more and more with every passing day. It began with the increased numbers of women wearing the hijab, a symbol of the oppressive ideology that wished to suppress women's rights and strike fear in the hearts of non-Muslims.

ROLAND AND LAURA LIVED A QUIET, CONTENTED LIFE, TRAVELING TO SEE their children and grandchildren whenever they could in different states. Laura would sit and crochet blankets, tablecloths, scarves, sweaters, and many other things, while Roland would sit and read the Bible aloud so she could listen. They prayed together for everyone to be safe and healthy and successful. When he finished with the Bible reading, she would watch movies she had missed due to all the busy years she had spent raising her family.

It was Laura's seventy-second birthday in 2019. It was a very special day as all of her children and grandchildren came to celebrate.

Laura sat down on the porch and called her daughter saying, "Sandra, sit down. I have something to tell you." Using Sandra's endearment name she said, "Sousa, please promise me not to laugh."

"I promise, Mother. What is it? You are making me anxious!" Sandra said.

Laura raised her hand and said, "This bracelet was supposed to be given to you on your eighteenth birthday."

"Oh, you never took it off your wrist." Sandra's curiosity grew by the second.

Roland brought some soda and gave it to Laura and sat down. Laura told her story in detail, and Sandra listened with her mouth hanging open, unable to believe the idea of a past life where her mother and father had loved each other.

"Dad," Sandra said, "did this really happen to you?"

"Yes," Roland said as he held Laura's hand.

"Now, Sandra, I did not give you the bracelet on your eighteenth birthday because I did not want to burden you with its secret. Therefore, when my time comes and I go to be with Jesus, I want you to take the bracelet. Pass it on as a family heirloom to your eldest daughter, along with a note telling its history, to be proud of, and in turn pass it on to her descendants thereafter."

Roland was shocked. "What are you doing?"

"I am stopping the earthly rounds with all the pain, agony, and even joy. We have to move into the light when our time comes. Jesus is waiting for us." Laura's eyes filled with tears, but they did not spill on her cheeks.

LAURA'S LAST UNMARRIED DAUGHTER, RONDA, SAID HER VOWS IN A wonderful wedding event. Roland and Laura found themselves with no direct responsibility except to love and support their children and grandchildren.

One morning, Laura was sitting on the couch watching their aviary members picking on the birdfeed, and the glory of God displayed in the different colors of the birds, canary yellow, the love-bird blue, and especially the cardinal red. Roland loved these birds in particular and lamented their long absences.

"Roland, look! Your birds are back! What a beautiful day. Can we go to the beach today? The weather looks good," Laura said even though she felt tired. She wanted to be near the ocean. It called to her. At seventy-two, the burden of the years had started to affect her movement and energy.

"Why not? I will go and prepare our supplies. Can you prepare the sandwiches? All you need to do is pack them," Roland said.

"Sure, but I need to rest on the bed for a few minutes. I am just tired." Laura went to her bedroom.

Roland prepared the van, and he even had the food ready. When she didn't respond to his call, he found her still in bed, and he gently called her name again.

"Laura, do you want to go to the beach? Everything is ready. Wake up." Roland came to the side of her bed.

He looked at Laura and saw a smile on her face, suddenly looking young again, as if the years did not leave a mark on her.

"Laura. Wake up my dear. It is time." Roland shook her gently as he was aware that anyone waking her up suddenly would startle her.

Laura opened her eyes for a moment, smiled at him, and raised her palm to cover his cheek. "I am a little tired. Thank you, Roland, for giving me a good life, and for your kindness in my old age. It is like a balm to my soul. The beautiful bracelet will always be our link." Laura fell silent and stopped talking for a minute.

"I really wanted to go to the beach today." Laura felt panicked, worrying she wouldn't have the time to do or say what she wished.

Roland interrupted and said, "What's wrong? We have everything ready to go."

"My love, you need to take what I am going to say as God's will. I am very tired, and an angel is calling me to go with him. I am sorry, my love. I feel I have to say goodbye for now, my darling, till we meet again." Laura closed her eyes.

Shocked at this, Roland's tears drenched his cheeks. His memories took him back to the previous lives they had lived together. He held her hand to his cheek, kissed it, and this time he was the one to whisper, "Goodbye my darling, until we do!" He wrapped his arms around her and closed his eyes.

Laura heard his loving whisper as she peacefully passed on.

THE END

LAURA'S DIARY

*S*andra, Laura's eldest daughter, was sorting through her mother's documents when she came across part of Laura's diary.

Dear Diary, May 1963

Today my dad, Emile, told me the most amazing story about his mother, Regina Dabes Salem.

Regina was eighteen when she married Jacob Salem, an affluent merchant known mostly for being the wholesale distributor to the fish market in the city of Jaffa, Palestine.

She was smart and very much interested in medicine. She became the chiropractor of the town, and many people sought her help. She raised nine children, besides the three babies she lost at birth or shortly after.

Tragedy hit the family when her husband, Jacob, died in 1910. The youngest son was four years old at the time. Fortunately, Regina had wisely saved gold pieces that her husband would give her at the end of each day. Over the years, she accumulated a healthy sum, and she was able to provide for her family. After Jacobs' death, Regina raised her children and sent them to the Jesuits for their education.

In early 1916, another disaster hit the family. Regina's eldest son, twenty-eight-year-old Gabriel Salem, was appointed by the Muslim Ottoman government as the director of the Taxation Department. He was honest, well respected, and served many years. However, being a Christian with such an important position did not sit well with radical Muslim employees. Envy brewed.

One day, Gabriel found a newspaper clipping on his desk. The article reported that the British were planning to invade the Middle East. No sooner had he finished reading the clipping when law enforcement barged into his office and claimed that an employee had accused him of being a British agent and a traitor. The accusation was enough grounds for arrest. The newspaper clipping was the evidence to show proof of the charges of treason and secret communications with foreigners. He was immediately imprisoned without trial and deported to the Mezza prison in Damascus, Syria. Mezza had a reputation of being the worst prison on earth; a prison where the incoming never saw the light of day again. It was located about 130 miles from Gabriel's hometown of Jaffa, and sadly, in the Middle East, the accused were guilty until proven innocent.

When Gabriel did not return home that day, Regina was beside herself with worry. The next day, she went to the department where Gabriel worked and asked about him. She was told bluntly that her son was found to be a traitor, and he was arrested and taken by the police to the Mezza prison in Damascus.

At that time, Damascus was governed by a man named Ahmad Jamal Pasha who was known as "the Butcher". He had military training and was educated as a chemist. Nevertheless, he was merciless and did not tolerate anyone accused of being a traitor or who opposed the rule of the day. He gained his nickname by being responsible for the brutal bloodshed during his years as governor of Syria. He was responsible for the genocides of the Greeks, Assyrians, and the Armenians because they were Christians and affluent.

That was the person under whose mercy Regina's son, my uncle, had been placed.

Dejected and full of fear for her son, she gathered her family members together and told them what had happened to Gabriel. The family was distraught and did not know what to do.

Without telling anyone, Regina devised a plan to save her son. She knew that if she told her family what she planned they would stop her, so she told them that she was traveling to visit her relatives in Jerusalem. She joined a caravan headed for Damascus. Her donkey was her safety, as she wanted to appear to be a poor woman, otherwise, she would have had a camel with a hodage seat, but she did not want to draw attention to herself.

The caravan would stop at inns for rest, water, and food along the way. The two-week journey to Damascus was arduous, but Regina was eager to get there.

After her arrival in Damascus, she stayed in an inn close to the famous prison, and every day for a week she went walking around outside the walls of the prison to see if she might find someone to ask about her son. No one paid attention to her, and she could not find anyone with authority who could give her any information.

Regina went to the owner of the inn. *"Do you know where Jamal Pasha lives? I was told he was a humble man and lived in a regular house."*

"Yes, everyone knows. If you go down the road and walk straight for a mile you will see his house surrounded by a white stone wall. There is a guard at the gate."

Very early the next day, Regina dressed as a peasant and went to Jamal Pasha's house. She told the guard she was the clothing washer woman.

At that time, clothes were washed by hand in large trays of water and soap. People always hired expert women to do their washing, expecting all kinds of stains to be removed. He directed her to the kitchen. She knocked at the door.

"Do you need a washer for today?" Regina asked the woman who opened the door.

"Yes, yes. Thank God, you saved the day. My regular woman sent a message that she was sick and couldn't come. What is your name?" the woman asked.

"Regina Salem. I am from Jaffa."

"Come in, come in. My name is Samiha." The woman led Regina to the washing room near the kitchen.

It was six o'clock in the morning when Regina sat on the floor and began washing the clothes. Her tears started to flow down her cheeks as she worried about her son. Every time the woman came to check on her, she found her crying with no sound.

"Why are you crying?" Samiha asked.

"It is a long story, my Lady," Regina answered.

"When you are done, I would like to hear it." She left the washing room.

At noon when she finished the wash, Regina felt exhausted, and her fingers were wrinkled from the hot water and soap as her hands were not used to such work. She had her own washer women and a live-in maid to help her. She was a noble woman, but never hesitated to take a humbler role if the need arose.

"You do not look like a washer woman to me," Samiha said.

"I am not, my Lady," Regina said.

"Then why the charade?" Samiha asked.

"My Lady, I beg of you to listen to me. You are a mother, and I know you would never stop at anything to help your children, especially when they are innocent and in grave danger. My son, who was trusted and honest in his work as Director of the Taxation Department in Jaffa, was falsely accused of being a traitor by a coworker, who was envious of him. To be a traitor means the death penalty, and my son is not a traitor. The police arrested him without evidence or even a trial to defend himself. He was taken with other real criminals to Mezza prison. I have no one to help me appeal to the Pasha except you. To reach you, I had to become a washer woman." Regina smiled for the first time.

Samiha couldn't help but laugh at the ingenuity of Regina and her boldness. She liked her very much. She liked her courage and found her to be wise. She would do what this woman was doing and more for her three daughters if they were in danger.

"Listen," Samiha said, *"despite the ruthless reputation of my husband, he has some decency in him when approached properly. I will talk to him. I am*

inviting you tomorrow for lunch as my guest. You must not open your mouth in his presence. You must wait for what he would tell you to do."

She was sure that rescuing her son was possible. She prayed for God's help and favor with 'The Butcher'.

The next day she rushed to the Pasha's house.

"This is Regina, our lunch guest," Samiha announced as they entered the dining room.

The Pasha invited her to sit down in a friendly tone. They all sat down around the table, visiting and talking about the times, and after they finished eating and coffee was poured, the Pasha asked her what her request was.

"My son has been wrongfully detained, my Pasha. He is an innocent man. I humbly ask for your help," Regina said.

"Come tomorrow to my office at three in the afternoon. Bring this paper with you and show it to the guards to permit you to go in."

"Thank you. I will be on time, my Pasha." Regina thanked them for their hospitality and asked permission to leave.

The next day could not come fast enough for Regina. With the paper in hand, she was at the office fifteen minutes early. She sat waiting until she was called in.

"Your son is a traitor and a foreign agent. Get out! I do not want to see your face!" the Pasha yelled at her.

The guard led her out and closed the door without even listening to what she wanted to say. She sobbed and went directly to the Pasha's house, begging Samiha to help her.

"Stay away for two days and come back here. He needs to calm down. He is furious, and I could not calm him down. Give me some time. I do not know why I am helping you, but I like you," Samiha said.

"I will be here, my Lady." She left Pasha's house and went back to the inn, crying her heart out.

When she arrived at the house two days later, Samiha told Regina to immediately go to the office. Regina went. The guard gave her a letter from the Pasha. He did not allow her to see him.

She read the letter and ran down the stairs as if she was riding the wind. She went to the prison ward and gave him the letter. A guard took her to the stairs that led down to where the prisoners were kept under the ground.

"Wait here, woman!" The guard appeared extremely surprised at this order in his hands.

A month had already passed since Gabriel was put in prison. He put his life in God's hands and prayed every night for deliverance. He was supposed to be executed with the other traitors. When the guard called his name from the top of the stairs and told him to come up, he was shaking like a leaf in the wind. He could not believe his eyes when he saw his mother standing at the top of the stairs with the guard. Her face was wet with tears, and she signaled him with her hands that everything was finished. He thought that "finished" meant he was going to face execution, and by the time he reached the last step, fear gripped his heart, and he fell into his mother's open arms unconscious.

She hugged him and showered his face with kisses and tears, and the guard brought some water for him to drink. Sitting on the stone floor, Regina took the water and wiped her son's face. He opened his eyes. His face was bug bitten, and sores spread all over his body. He had entered as a healthy man of 180 pounds and exited the doors a man of 120 pounds, unable to walk without help. She had her donkey tied up to a wooden pole in the yard. Regina put Gabriel on the donkey and went to the inn.

Regina was horrified at her son's appearance but ecstatic for his release. She was able to save his life. Regina nursed her son back to health until he gained some strength to travel back home.

She went to the Pasha's house one afternoon to visit Samiha and thank her and say goodbye. She gave gifts of gold bracelets, rings and necklaces to Samiha's daughters, which she had purchased in Jerusalem on the way to Damascus.

Two months had passed since Regina had left home. When she and her son returned, no one could believe what she had done, considering the Pasha's cruel and ruthless reputation. However, he was eventually assassinated for all the brutality and wickedness he had committed in his life. It was unbelievable that Gabriel was still alive.

This heroic endeavor of Regina must be kept alive with the retelling of the story to my children and their children...

SANDRA TUCKED THE PAGES HER MOTHER HAD WRITTEN INTO HER OWN diary and shared the story with her children.

REFERENCES

A list of resources used when researching the history of the Middle East.

en.wikipedia.org/wiki/Main_Page

www.biblegateway.com/

www.al-islam.com/

Dar Al Furqan The Holy Qur'an. Translator, Abdullah Yusuf Ali, Roman Transliteration of the Holy Qur'an,
           Dar Al Furqan, 1934

ABOUT THE AUTHOR

Nuhad Banna has always had a strong passion for storytelling and writing. As a mother, it was a tool she used to calm her children when they were very young. She loves the arts, theater, and painting.

She lives in the United States with her husband and her five wonderful children. They spent many of their summer vacations traveling and exploring the beautiful country they live in.

Nuhad receives the utmost pleasure from the many God-given freedoms she enjoys in the United States as well as the opportunity to make her dreams come true.

Contact: dreamylass91@gmail.com

www.ingramcontent.com/pod-product-compliance
Lightning Source LLC
Chambersburg PA
CBHW021516240626
47154CB00002B/658